OUR
WAYWARD
FATE

ALSO BY GLORIA CHAO

American Panda

OUR WAYWARD FATE

Gloria Chao

SIMON PULSE

NEW YORK LONDON TORONTO SYDNEY NEW DELHI

ᗯᗯ

SIMON PULSE

An imprint of Simon & Schuster Children's Publishing Division

1230 Avenue of the Americas, New York, New York 10020

First Simon Pulse hardcover edition October 2019

Text copyright © 2019 by Gloria Chao

Jacket art copyright © 2019 by David Field/Caterpillar Media

Jacket photograph of girl copyright © 2019 by Stocksy/MaaHoo Studio

Jacket photograph of earring copyright © 2019 by Getty Images

Turtle image copyright © 2019 by bartamarabara/iStock

Cowgirl image copyright © 2019 by Bullet_Chained/iStock

Cow image copyright © 2019 by STRIPBALL/iStock

Paper clip image copyright © 2019 by SergeiKorolko/iStock

For information about special discounts for bulk purchases, please contact Simon & Schuster Special Sales at 1-866-506-1949 or business@simonandschuster.com.

The Simon & Schuster Speakers Bureau can bring authors to your live event.

For more information or to book an event contact the Simon & Schuster Speakers Bureau at 1-866-248-3049 or visit our website at www.simonspeakers.com.

Jacket designed by Sarah Creech

Interior designed by Tom Daly

The text of this book was set in EB Garamond.

Manufactured in the United States of America

2 4 6 8 10 9 7 5 3 1

Library of Congress Cataloging-in-Publication Data

Names: Chao, Gloria, 1986- author.

Title: Our wayward fate / by Gloria Chao.

Description: First Simon Pulse hardcover edition. | New York : Simon Pulse, 2019. | Audience: Ages 12 and up. | Audience: Grades 10-12. | Summary: Seventeen-year-old Ali is simultaneously swept up in a whirlwind romance and down a rabbit hole of family secrets when another Taiwanese family moves into tiny, predominantly-white, Plainhart, Indiana.

Identifiers: LCCN 2019028306 | ISBN 9781534427617 (hardcover) | ISBN 9781534427631 (eBook)

Subjects: CYAC: Taiwanese Americans—Fiction. | Family problems—Fiction. | Secrets—Fiction. | Dating (Social customs)—Fiction. | Arranged marriage—Fiction. | High schools—Fiction. | Schools—Fiction. | Indiana—Fiction.

Classification: LCC PZ7.1.C4825 Our 2019 | DDC [Fic]—dc23

LC record available at https://lccn.loc.gov/2019028306

For Anthony. Every word I write is for you and because of you.

And for anyone who feels alone. You are not, and I promise someone else has experienced something similar, whether it's struggling to fit in or not understanding why your mom thinks going to sleep with your hair wet is the worst thing you can do aside from becoming a professional writer. This book is for the Ali turtles in the world: keep your heads up and jiā fàn! (Sorry, that will make more sense after you read the book.)

AUTHOR'S NOTE ABOUT THE MANDARIN WORDS

In this book, Mandarin words are spelled using the pinyin system, with the lines above the vowels indicating the pitch contour of the voice:

A straight line (ā), the first tone, is high and level, monotone.

Second tone (á) rises in pitch.

Third tone (ǎ) dips, then rises.

Fourth tone (à) starts high and drops, producing a sharp sound.

For some of the Mandarin phrases, I chose to depict the tones as the words are pronounced in conversation in my family's accent. There may be some discrepancy with other accents and dialects.

Ali is Taiwanese American and learned Mandarin from her parents through conversation and context. There is no glossary, because it is my hope that readers can get a small taste of what it's like to be in Ali's head, learning a second language this way. Some words and phrases will have clear meanings; others will merely be attached to a broad emotion or idea.

CHAPTER 1

DRY TOAST

My mom believes in magic penises.

Because at the moment she was saying for the umpteenth time, "If you had been a boy, things would be different." The problem wasn't my genitals—it was my mother's outdated belief that boys were better. Plus, it wasn't *my* fault Dad's X sperm had been faster than the Y.

She waved the crumpled note in my face. It was only a sliver, a tiny corner of the whole with five measly words scrawled in my friend Brenda's loopy handwriting, but it was enough to cause all this.

"I'll ask one more time—what were you doing on the baseball field?"

Brenda was the one who'd rounded second base, and I was the one getting in trouble? It was so backward I wanted to laugh. But I didn't. I just stood there, my MO to the point where I often wondered if this next time would be the one to turn me into Buddha, bird poo on my head and everything.

"So disrespectful!" my mother huffed. What would she have done if I'd laughed? "If you had grown up in Taiwan, you wouldn't be so mù wú zūn zhǎng. And you would know what that phrase means."

Well, if you had grown up here, maybe your lifelong dream wouldn't have been to grow a penis inside you.

Again, instead of voicing my thoughts, I stood there. Stared. Just like I had done yesterday when Mrs. Finch had asked if I was related to P. F. Chang, just like I'd done a week ago when Ava had told me I should wear eyeliner to "fix" my eyes, just like, just like, just like always.

"Baseball is too expensive a sport, all that equipment," my mother uncharacteristically continued. "And it's dangerous, and it doesn't stand out on college applications. . . ."

Since she'd given me a rare peek inside her head, I returned the favor. "Don't worry, Mǔqīn, I've kept it to first base so far."

"First base, second base, it doesn't matter! No more baseball field, okay?"

My father walked in, not looking at either of us, not caring what was going on—aka his MO.

Since I knew his presence would hollow my mother into a shell, I escaped our duplex in silence, wishing, for once, that my mother would mutter "mù wú zūn zhǎng" again under her breath, just so that someone would be saying something. Neither of my parents said good-bye, and I was guilty of the same because apple, tree, and all that.

I spent the rest of my free first period walking to my high school, located in the center of town in the sad triangle of "happening" places: the elementary school/middle school/high school, a tiny mom-and-pop grocery store, and a deli/hardware store.

When I arrived in our peeling, pubescent-boy-scented hallways, my friends ran up to me, more excited than anyone in Plainhart, Indiana, ever should be.

"No running, girls!" Mr. Andrews, the social studies teacher, yelled at us. "Hey, Allie," he added, turning to me so he was walking backward. "You'll love class today. We're discussing North Korea, and I can't wait to hear what you have to say!" He followed that doozy with sad, finger-pointing-guns, which was inappropriate on so many levels. I managed a straight-lined, half-assed smile and didn't bother to remind him I was Chinese.

As soon as he turned his attention to his next victim, Ava, Kyle, and Brenda fully encircled me.

"God!" Kyle exclaimed. "Took you long enough to get here."

"Have you seen him yet?" asked blond, perfect, white-as-a-bāo Ava as she grabbed my arm, which meant that whatever it was, it was big enough to make her break my no-touching rule.

I shook her off. "Who?"

"Okay, she hasn't seen," Kyle said in the bossy tone she'd developed to survive being a girl with a mostly boys' name.

Since they were being so annoyingly cryptic and the only way to spill the gossip beans was to pretend I didn't care, I walked to my locker and started making myself a PB&J for lunch later. I actually hated peanut butter, but better eating that than hearing yet again how my congee looked like bleached vomit.

"Allie, pay attention! This is going to blow your mind!" Brenda said, which made me pause, because the excitement was so out of character for her.

I stared at White, Whitey, and Whiterson, holding my face steady even though I wanted to scream at them to freaking say it already.

But before they could, I saw him. I froze, a deer staring into the Asian headlight of the new student. It was almost as if there were a spotlight from God shining on him to tell me, *Ta-da! Finally, another person in this school who looks like you!*

I found myself taking in his clean-cut khakis, the guāi olive zip-up sweater, his tidy, close-cropped hair. His eyes met mine, but as the whispers around us grew, we both looked away.

Out of the corner of my eye I saw him disappear through the BC Calc classroom door, the same door I'd be slouching through in a moment.

Kyle grabbed my arm and shook it. "Allie, you two should totally become a thing—you go so well together!"

I wanted nothing more than to disappear, but to defuse the situation, I made a joke. "Why? Is it because"—I fake gasped—"we're both . . . nerds?" I gestured toward BC Calc.

Brenda started shaking her head, and I knew she was getting

ready to say the obvious—*No, because you're both Asian*—but luckily, Ava cut her off by squealing, "And he's hot!"

That got my attention. "Hot like sriracha or hot like Szechuan food?" They stared at me. Oops. Slip-up. I was off my game suddenly. "I mean, hot like Noah Centineo or hot like *Fight Club* Brad Pitt?"

"Noah Centineo," Brenda and Kyle said just as Ava said, "Brad Pitt."

We all turned to stare at the odd one out as dictated by high school rules. Ava shrugged. "I saw him smoking just now. That's more Brad than Noah."

He smokes? Part of me was turned on, and the other part was just like *Gross* and *What's wrong with him?*

"You all know what's number one on my dream-guy list," I said to the nosy trio. Two words: *not Chinese*. (Yes, I realized the new kid might be another East Asian ethnicity, but my friends didn't know the difference and I wanted to shut this down.)

Kyle cleared her throat. "I hate to say it, Allie, but maybe you should forget that list. I know Jimminy Bob sucks"—Jimminy Bob was our code name for everyone we hated, and we always knew from context which Jimminy it was, in this case my mother—"but you're allowed to date Chinese guys!" More like *only* allowed to date Chinese guys (hence my aversion—I took every opportunity to stick it to my mǔqīn), but my friends were privileged enough not to understand the difference.

Ava leaned toward me. "Think about it, Allie. You'd finally have a hot boyfriend, who's also smart—well, I mean, I assume he is.

And he'd probably understand you more than the rest of us do. That sounds like a dream guy to me."

As I went back to my half-built PB&J, I turned their words over in my head, but only for a second, because I refused to fulfill this Podunk town's stereotype. The only two Asians getting together—I could taste some bile just thinking about everyone saying, *Of course, of course, that makes sense; they belong together.* And besides, if my last interaction with another Asian had proved anything, it was that no one understood me, regardless of race.

I broke the end slice of bread into four pieces and rapid-chucked them at each girl, emphasizing a word per hit. "Not. Interested. At. All." Kyle got the extra hit, to the boob.

I made my way to BC Calc, and, of course, as soon as I entered, whispers of "meet-cute" and "so perfect" and "both Asian" filled the small, suffocating room. My fists clenched to keep from hurling chalkboard erasers at every last one of them. I tried to purposely ignore the giant not-yellow-but-also-not-white spotlight as I walked past, my head in the air, but then—I couldn't help it—I scanned his notebooks, textbooks, papers for his name, and finally, on the corner of the class schedule in front of him, there it was: Chase Yu.

Possibly Chinese, maybe Korean?

"Oooh, checking out the new Asian meat?" someone called to me from the back of the room.

Womp womp. Mission to blend in and be as dry as white toast: failed by my own doing for the first time in years.

I ignored them and slunk into my seat, hunching in the hopes

6

of shrinking the massive bull's-eye on my back. Who knows what Chase did in response, because I was already tuned the F out.

"Settle down, settle down," Mr. Robinson said as he entered, shuffling papers.

But he stopped in his tracks when he saw Chase, apparently also a deer in the Asian headlight. "Oh boy, now there's two of you?" he said, looking from Chase to me. "The rest of the class better watch out for you guys ruining the curve."

Surprise, surprise: Racist Robinson strikes again. Seriously, there wasn't much that could make me hate math, but Mr. Robinson was up there. I folded in on myself even more, keeping my head down as I waited for the naked-in-school dream-turned-reality to pass.

But Chase shot up out of his seat. "Well, by that logic you, Mr. Robinson, must love Dave Matthews, and you probably have a Chinese tattoo on your butt that you think says 'strength' but actually says 'butthole.'"

Hole-y crap. Chase wouldn't last two days here, not when he was being Taiwanese pineapple cake with red New Year's streamers— the opposite of white toast.

Robinson gaped at Chase, then shook off the shock and said with a laugh, "Aren't you Asians supposed to kowtow, especially to authority?" He waved a hand in my direction. "This one certainly does."

Chase looked at me, and even though my blood was hotter than Szechuan food, I gazed out the window. He grabbed his books and stalked out of the room, slamming the door behind him just as Mr. Robinson yelled, "Hey! You better be on your way to the counselor's office!"

A muffled "fuck you!" drifted past the closed door.

Who *was* this clean-cut bad boy?

I laid my head on my folded arms. I knew—*knew*—there had to be a better place than this, where shit like this didn't happen every day. I didn't even know what my inner voice sounded like anymore. (Maybe deep and a bit gruff from constant annoyance?)

When the bell rang, I trudged out of the room, and in the hallway, his back against a locker, was Chase.

Pleeease don't be waiting for me....

"Why didn't you say anything?" he asked as he fell in step with me. "Didn't it bother you?"

I shrugged. "Easier to let it go."

"Doesn't mean it's not worth trying. I couldn't *not* say something."

I shrugged again.

He shook his head at me in disbelief. "Bú xiàng huà," he muttered, so quietly I may not have heard, but I'd been holding my breath.

The Mandarin threw me. Like, threw me across the room and knocked the wind out. I hated that this was the first time I was hearing Mandarin in these desolate hallways, and even more, hated that it created a bond between us. And by hated, I mean I was 100 percent drawn to him. I could practically hear my mother laughing her head off at me. *I'm always right, Ali. This is why you need to be with a Chinese boy.*

8

"Hope you grow some balls someday, Allie," Chase said as he started to walk away.

My fingernails dug into my palms. I fucking *had* (proverbial) balls. I also had a brain, which was why I hadn't said anything. That was the way to get out of here unscathed . . . right? Regardless, I was sick of people accusing me of not having male genitalia. I preferred my vagina, thank you very much, not that anyone in my life cared to ask.

I don't know why—maybe it was because my blood was past boiling—but I called after him, "It's Ali, jackass." And for the first time, my name rolled off my tongue the way it was supposed to: *Āh-lěe*, after the mountain in Taiwan, my mother's favorite place in the world. I'd never said it that way before, with beauty. With meaning. With pride. It had always been Allie, the dry-toast way, at first because it was easier, and then for survival.

Chase turned back to me. "That's a start."

A smile lifted the corner of his lip. It made me want to smile too, but I shrugged instead. He chuckled with a shake of his head before jogging down the hallway.

"Hey, wait!" I yelled after him. "How'd you know my name?" When he didn't respond, I embarrassingly yelled, "Chase?"

Which, since I technically shouldn't have known his name yet either, was the opposite of dry toast.

CHAPTER 2

BROKEN EGG ROLLS

That evening, while my mother swished her spatula rhythmically against the wok, I hovered near her, setting the table with chopsticks, napkins, and lots o' bowls (we didn't own plates). I'd be eating alone later because I had kung fu soon, but I was waiting for my opening like a Putt-Putt ball trying to clear the windmill. As usual, my mother was oblivious to my inner unrest.

Chase's abracadabra appearance out of nowhere had torn through the school like that gonorrhea outbreak last year, and as much as I'd wanted to escape him, he had shown up in every single class of mine today. Everywhere he followed, so did the "yes, yes, they belong together" whispers. Why did he have to be the only other person taking a more-than-full load of honors and APs? God, Chase, you just *had* to give us a bad name. There was only room for one stereotypical Asian in these Podunk hallways, and I had nabbed the title against my will years ago.

When the sizzling from the stove lessened and my mother's movements quieted, I cleared my throat, a signal of how infrequently we talked.

"Hmm?" she said, her eyes never leaving the wok.

"You know how you always tell me that when I date—"

"Only Chinese boys," she said automatically, like it was a programmed response, which, well, at this point, it was.

"Why is that so important to you?"

She poured the now thoroughly stir-fried meat-and-veggie egg-roll filling into a large bowl. The silence stretched so long I wondered whether she'd heard my question.

But I stood my ground, both figuratively and literally.

"You know I want the best for you, right?" she finally said, still not looking at me and instead sitting down to wrap egg rolls. But she pushed the skin and filling toward me, and by inviting me to join her, I knew she was extending a hand and a little love.

I planted my pìgu at the dining room table a little too eagerly. "But what does that even mean, Mǎmá?" *How can you know what the best is when you don't know me?*

"I've had experience, Ali. Don't you remember? In Chinese culture, we revere the elderly for their wisdom. Just trust me."

There it was, that condescending tone with no explanation, just instructions and pithy Chinese sayings. I started to ask her to elaborate, but she hastened her folding and I knew the door I'd briefly opened was sealed as tight as her egg roll.

Not wanting to leave just yet, I carefully peeled a thin sheet of egg-roll skin off the stack, irrationally wondering if she would open up more if I impressed her with my wrapping skills. You know, reminded her we were mother and daughter, not strangers.

Her eyes were glued to her hands as she spoke. "Ali, have you thought more about taking the trip to China I suggested?"

This again. I'd been lulled into a false sense of security since she hadn't mentioned it in two weeks—actually, now that I thought about it, we hadn't *spoken* in two weeks except for the second-base debacle.

I proceeded carefully. "You said you want me to go there to find my roots, but you're from Taiwan."

"Yes, but before me, our family was from China."

"Doesn't it make more sense for me to visit Taiwan, though?"

She sighed. "Aiyah, Ali, you always have to make everything so difficult. I'm trying to do a nice thing."

"We don't have the money," I stated, a simple truth.

She didn't disagree with me. After a brief pause she started to say something, but at that very moment the front door opened and closed.

No "Honey, I'm home" for this household, in either language. My mother stiffened, her fingers flying as her jaw set in its clenched position (I often worried about her teeth and whether she had ground them down to the pulp yet).

My father passed through the kitchen because he had to, and

as usual he nodded at each of us with a forced smile.

How was your day? and *What did you have for lunch?* and *Will you please talk to Māmá?* all floated through my head and danced on my tongue before dissolving in the graveyard where the other hundred thousand questions were buried.

My mother didn't even look up. Was it improvement or regression that she hadn't bothered to glare at him? If experience showed anything, it was the latter. The worst step had been when they'd stopped fighting, when they'd chosen to ignore each other instead of trying.

My dad disappeared into the bedroom and my mother's shoulders relaxed again. Just like hers, my fingers tackled the egg roll with desperation, as if that were somehow the solution.

Filling—corner—corner—tuck and roll. Like riding a bike. I stacked my finished egg roll next to hers, and it looked almost identical, only a smidge looser. No longer was I the child making egg rolls that spilled meat and veggies out one or both ends or through an accidental hole made by a clumsy fingernail.

My hand froze, and for a moment I pretended it was years ago, before we had moved here, before my parents had become the ghosts they were today. I used to be so disappointed that, unlike my mother's perfectly jǐn and tidy egg rolls, mine were fat and luànqībāzāo, like a drunk, sloppy Santa on December 26. But my mother would always tell child Ali, *Patience. One day, if all goes as planned, you'll do better than me. In everything. Qīng chū yú lán.*

But it hadn't gone as planned. My father had been denied tenure at Boston University, and then he'd accepted a job against my mother's wishes at a tiny, "not prestigious" liberal arts school. To my mother, rankings were everything, to the point that she learned how to use the internet just to stay up to date with *U.S. News & World Report*'s college rankings. She chose to put all her trust in those numbered lists and didn't care that everyone else in town seemed to be impressed by my father's job at the "local gem," Frank College. For the record, I didn't care either, but it was because, as with everything, there was a sprinkle of racism on top: *Of course he's an intellectual—he's Asian, so smart.*

After my father moved us here to our own little microaggression hell, the Chu family fell apart faster than shaved ice in hot pot. At the time, I hadn't understood how something so small could have such a huge ripple, but then—hello cornfields and lower pay—I learned way too young that it's harder to be happy when you're ostracized and worried about the roof over your head.

When I aligned my second egg roll—this one as tight as hers—with the others, I noticed my mother had tears in her downcast eyes.

Was it because of my egg roll? Or because of what had just happened with my father?

Seeing a crack in her wall, I reached a hand out and placed it on hers, which was mid-wrap.

How it played out in my head: she grasps it back, tells me she loves me, then apologizes for being so distant the past eleven years.

Okay, maybe that was a bit too cheesy and unrealistic, but I definitely didn't expect it to play out as horribly as it did.

She startled and yanked her hand away, which then knocked over the stack of papers, books, and folders that perpetually lived on her "off-limits" side of the table, where she cut coupons and pored over our unending bills.

To hide my face and the possible tears that had pooled (I got some filling in my eye, I swear), I dove to the floor, scooping up the fallen debris.

"Mā, why do you have a picture of this park?" I asked, pausing on a clipped newspaper article. "'Zhè shì Zhōngguó de . . . ,'" I started to read, very slowly, but she snatched the paper out of my hands, ripping it in two and giving me a paper cut in the process.

"I'm surprised you know any Chinese characters," she said down her nose to me, "given that you barely paid attention and quit after only three years."

I was so bewildered I sat there frozen as she crumpled the torn pieces and shoved them into her pockets. But when she rushed for the rest of the scattered papers, my instincts kicked in and I fought with her, nabbing several things, but never having enough time to read the Mandarin characters cluttering the pages. I caught an errant *Chu* here and there, my eye homing in the way a child recognizes their name in a sea of letters because it's the only word they know. A few *liáng*s also stuck out because of repetition, but that told me a whole lot of nothing because I couldn't remember what it meant. Was it also a surname? I had never kicked myself so hard for not putting more effort into my homeschooled Chinese lessons.

Five paper cuts later, she disappeared into the bathroom (which was her only option, since my dad was in the bedroom). I tried to force myself to call out something—anything—but I merely goldfished a few seconds before retreating to my room, definitely not to cry or anything.

Affair? Clandestine plot to get us out of here? So, in short, it was either the worst news or the best.

And during that entire scuffle, my father hadn't surfaced once.

THE PARK

AS SEEN FROM AFAR

Liang Zhu Park was born a serene escape, but now, over a century later, it has evolved to serve a higher purpose. At first glance, the wayward pieces of paper resemble litter, out of place next to the manicured grass and decorative rocks.

Except the scraps at eye level aren't trash. Aren't random. They were hung deliberately, strings attaching each flyer to branches overhead. Within the black sea of simplified Chinese characters, patches of color congeal to form a face here, an arm there. Below the pictures, a description: Height. Weight. Animal. The town she calls home.

Each sheet is almost indistinguishable from the last—dolls cut from a folded piece of paper. Yet to those who pad along the cobblestones, hands behind their backs, heads in serious thought? Each picture, each person is just that—an individual. Different from its neighbor, clearly better or worse, ranked higher or lower based on various standards and traits.

What kinds of secrets does this garden hold? Perhaps the clutter creates pockets for information to hide. If a secret never sees the light of day, does it exist at all? Of course it does, but once tucked away in a corner of the park, a corner of the mind, it's easier to forget.

But the park never forgets.

CHAPTER 3

NERDS

I jabbed, beads of sweat flying off my fist in a satisfying spray. The punching bag was slick with perspiration, reminding me how hard I'd already worked.

Years ago, I had convinced my mother to let me take kung fu by agreeing to first try ballet, probably because it was the more appropriate, ladylike choice that would help me ensnare a winner husband one day. But after I had embarrassed her by punching and kicking my way through the *Nutcracker* (I was fighting sexism as literally as I could), my mother finally gave in—just kung fu.

Ali: 1. My mother: everything else.

With each punch I mentally fought to keep my mother and her

secrets out. I'd since confirmed that Liang was indeed a surname, but I couldn't recall any family friends or acquaintances with that last name. As for the photo, I had searched the internet for "parks in China, Liang, Chu" because I was really that desperate, and, well, no surprise at the millions of hits I got.

As soon as I successfully booted my mother out of my head, Chase flooded in. With each successive hook, uppercut, and side kick, my mind wandered to a place I normally didn't let it go. I couldn't stand the stereotypes this town projected onto my family and me, but what did it mean that a lot of them were true? Not just for me, but now also for Chase?

I didn't see him come in, but I felt it. There was a stillness in the room, the kind that happens with fresh meat in shark-filled waters. No doubt everyone was sizing the newbie up, taking in his age and build, worrying whether they would be kicked one rung lower.

A chuckle bubbled in my throat. When I had first arrived, the rest of the group had barely looked at me, thinking a girl couldn't be any competition. Ha. Nothing feels better than showing up a group of sexists with a metaphorical and literal kick in the ass. Now they still didn't pay attention to me, but it wasn't because I was worthless. The opposite: I was out of their league.

When his face appeared in my peripheral vision, my fist faltered and met the bag with a pathetic thud. Even though I had to drive twenty minutes to the next town for a kung fu class, and even though there had never been another Asian student before, of course it had to be him.

Chase gave the obligatory martial arts salute, left palm meeting right fist, as he entered the expansive practice hall. Clearly experienced, at least somewhat. On my first day, I hadn't known the rules, and my failure to salute the portraits on the wall had cost me a punishment of twenty push-ups. I did forty. Now, every time I entered, I took the time to acknowledge each kung fu grandmaster in my head: *Beardy, Mole Hair, Baldy, Shīfu*, the last of which was my teacher's teacher, and thus called "teacher" by the rest of us. Our grand-shīfu, if you will. But when I had suggested that name to the rest of the class, the raised eyebrows and sudden interest in extra push-ups spoke louder than words. I never made that mistake again.

I turned back to beating the crappity-crap-crap out of the punching bag, but Chase made a beeline for me. Again, I could just feel it. Something about being in this room heightened my senses.

I kicked the bag's proverbial nuts. "Stalking me?" I said when I sensed he was beside me. My skin crawled—had I somehow ended up in one of those sappy rom-coms I hated?

He rolled his eyes. "You're the one who already knew my name . . . though I guess I'm guilty of the same. Well, sort of. Turns out that wasn't actually your name."

Sometimes I wondered if our names defined who we were, like maybe I was destined to be confused about my identity because I was not-quite-Allie—I was this amorphous blob of a name that could apply to either gender and many races.

Instead of telling me how he knew my name, he grabbed a handheld pad and motioned for me to hit. "Show me what you got."

A smile curled on my lips, more sinister than intended. Or

maybe not. Maybe it was exactly as sinister as I wanted.

I wound back, then slammed my right fist into the pad, using my hip turn to power it. He barely flinched. Pissed, I stepped to the side, then roundhoused the pad square in the center.

This time he took a step back, but instead of being upset or spurred into competition or whatever I thought I was going to get out of him, he said, "Damn, that was quite a kick. Finally mad at yourself for not saying something in calc this morning?"

Even though the situation wasn't funny in the least, I laughed. As much as my mother wished she could tell you my laugh sounded like chimes and syrup, I actually sounded like a witch with a wart on her nose. Okay, maybe not that bad, but it was certainly a bit of a cackle, made harsher by my windedness. Chase stared at me like he was flummoxed by my weirdness. (Good.)

Our instructor, Marcin, entered, and I automatically saluted, partly because it was the rule, but also because I respected him deeply for going against the norm and becoming one of the few (only?) Polish kung fu masters in the world.

During warm-ups, I kept my eyes on Marcin, the weapons wall, the tumbling mats stacked in the corner—anything but Chase. But after we finished our last set of sit-ups, it was hard *not* to watch him. Because, much to my dismay, he was a ninja. A graceful, infuriating ninja. His butterfly kicks soared and his extensions were endless, his lines all crisp and straight. I worried he'd think I was beneath him (his jumps raised him two heads higher than me), but he was staring at me with a weird-ass sort of amazement on his face. Which only pushed me harder, because it made me worry he had lower standards for girls. I stretched every muscle, put power behind each move, and strove for perfection. The energy between us crackled, and I wondered if the others could feel it.

We broke into pairs to practice a Chángquán matching routine. Because we had an odd number and I was the only girl, I usually fought with Marcin. I preferred it that way—I wanted to go up against the best.

But I didn't need "Asian genes," as Racist Robinson would say, to figure out who I'd be sparring with today.

Gawwd. At least we were fighting, not pairing up to take care of an egg or something. I usually went full-out with Marcin . . . and that didn't have to change, right? I was sure Chase wouldn't want my pity.

I attacked: fast fists, explosive kicks. Chase sprang into action, blocking, swiping, and ducking, matching me blow for blow. It made me speed up more. A familiar breeze from my swinging limbs enveloped me, the same one that always made me feel powerful, untouchable—the very reason I was so in love with this art form, this room, my canvas Feiyue shoes that gripped the floor perfectly.

"Whoa, whoa, easy, Allie!" Marcin said, grabbing my cocked fist. "You're acting like he killed your puppy."

No, my mom was the one who gave Cupid away because she thought he was distracting me too much from school.

Out of breath, I panted, "Sorry, M., you know I like—"

"It rough, I know." He turned red—his face never flushed from physical exertion, only embarrassment. He dropped my hand. "I mean, you like to go at it hard." Then he just backed away. He knew as well as everyone else here that his save attempts became worse—yes, believe it—at tries three, four, and five. He'd once had a fifth attempt involving me in a threesome with a monkey (referring to the monkey style of kung fu, of course, but he never specified).

Chase stared after Marcin the way everyone did following their first Phil Dunphy moment with him. Then he shifted his gaze to me. "I can get on board with rough and hard."

I scoffed. "You couldn't handle it."

"I'm not the one panting right now."

"Maybe I'm panting because I've resorted to just faking it. Can it be called a 'matching form' if I'm doing all the work?" Pineapple cake never tasted so good.

He laughed. "You win."

He smiled at me, and finally I smiled back. No better way to my heart than telling me my favorite words: *You win.*

When we rearranged to practice solo forms, I was relieved to have some space from Chase, who joined the newer students (and to answer the obvious question—yes, my chest puffed out that I was in the more advanced group). I used the alone time to clear my mind from lingering bits of banter. (Jesus, what was happening to me?)

Marcin ended class with a bow and a whistle. "Welcome, Chase. You certainly brought a new energy to class. We're delighted to have you with us."

As soon as Marcin and the other students left the practice hall, Chase and I collapsed into two sweaty heaps. The frayed brown carpet millimeters from my nose smelled (and looked) like years of hard work and perspiration. The musty scent always filled me

24

with a confusing combination of disgust, respect, and comfort.

The lights flicked off, but I was too tired to move.

"Come to dinner with me," Chase's disembodied voice called out.

I was so shocked I started coughing.

His clothes rustled. "Never mind," he said, his voice bouncing around the empty room. "I shouldn't have said that. I think . . . I'm desperate for a friend. So far in Indiana, the only things that have been not crappy are meeting you and the view of the weeping willow from my new bedroom window."

Even though the sentiment was supposed to be nice, I could only focus on the bizarre comparison to a goddamn willow tree.

"I fucking hate it here," he continued. *No shit.* "You know how I knew your name? Because the second anyone saw me, they asked if I knew you."

I held back a groan. If I made a noise, it could change the course of conversation, and I wanted to hear more. I pictured what I looked like to him—silent, stoic, calm—and almost burst out laughing at how differently the world sometimes sees us versus how we see ourselves.

Eventually, he said, "I grew up in Flushing, Queens—as in Asians everywhere you look, and plenty of other Taiwanese immigrants. We were completely entrenched in the Chinese community, to the point where I could barely remember all the aunties' names."

I swallowed a chuckle.

His voice grew small. "My parents just picked everything up and moved us here, of all places—we even live on White fucking Lane. No one asked me—about anything, really, ever. Why does it have to be so secretive and uncomfortable and hard?" *Join the party no one wanted an invite to.* "Whenever I try to talk to them, they just always say, 'Focus on your studies and be a good kid; just—'"

"Tīnghuà," I finished for him. "Except that phrase is more for little kids and makes me want to punch something every time my mǔqīn says it."

"You call your mother 'mǔqīn'?"

"Only when she deserves it." What else was I supposed to call her when she was being distant—too distant to be "Mǎmá"?

The early fall breeze from the open window carried his laugh into what felt like infinity. Maybe I was being dramatic, but he was the only one to have ever understood my Chinese jokes. This was brand-new territory for me with two languages. Usually those jokes stayed in my head, or I said them out loud to my parents with mild success. Even though my dad used to be goofy before we moved here and I'd never had to call him "fùqīn" (the formal version of "father" akin to "mǔqīn"), he only understood my jokes half the time. And of course, even if my mǔqīn understood, she wouldn't laugh.

"How many times have you moved?" I asked.

"Just this once, why?"

"Darn. I thought maybe I'd cracked it: that your parents moved three times to follow Mengzi's advice on how to find the best school. But I guess it's weird to do that your senior year; wasn't Mengzi like five when his mother did that?"

"I dunno," he said. For some reason, I pictured him shrugging. "I didn't actually pay attention in Chinese school."

"Chinese school? What about life? He's, like, the second most famous Chinese philosopher."

Something nudged my foot and I jumped in surprise. "Nerd," he said, his voice closer than before.

I rolled my eyes even though he couldn't see me. "You're the one in six AP classes."

"So are you!"

I laughed, more bells than witch. I hated it. "What's so bad about knowing a Li Bai poem or two? 'Chuáng qián míng yuèguāng...'"

He joined in. "'Yí shì dìshàng shuāng. Jǔtóu wàng...'" And then, somehow, we both finished the joke version of the poem: "'hēibǎn, dītóu sī biàndāng'"—replacing "glancing up at the moon and lowering your head to reminisce about home" with "glancing up at the chalkboard and lowering your head to think fondly about lunch." I mean, it wasn't very funny, but it was the only chuckle I'd had in my Chinese lessons ... and apparently Chase had experienced it too. I had learned it courtesy of my dad, of course. I wondered who had taught Chase. . . .

"Do you even remember the original version?" he asked me.

"*Duh*, you don't? Shameful."

"Nerd," he said again, then paused. "You know, I didn't want to take kung fu at first. I was only six. My parents wanted— demanded, really—me to learn so I could be the lion's butt to my brother's head during Chinese New Year performances."

I laughed, unable to hold it in. He would be a cute lion butt.

"And I didn't want to," he continued. "And I don't even know why. Maybe because it felt like I didn't have a choice. Just like with Chinese school. And everything else. Maybe I'm tired of being the butt."

God, it was like he had wormed into my brain and plucked those words out one by one. How funny that kung fu for him was losing, yet for me it was winning. I wanted to tell him I understood, but the damn words were eluding me. Maybe because I hated talking. Maybe because I hated him at the moment because he was unhateable.

"Having you in kung fu made it better," he said. "Maybe even changed my mind a bit . . . because you're so annoying and competitive. Makes me work harder."

By now my eyes had adjusted to the dark, and I saw him roll onto his side to face me.

"Come to dinner with me, Ali." The way he said my name gave me goose bumps. "I'm pretty sure you want to, seeing as how you spent the whole class chasing me around the playground and yanking my pigtails or whatever."

I forced a chuckle. "Stop flattering yourself—I'm competitive with everyone."

Marcin flicked the lights on and left sans words. Without the cover of darkness cloaking everything in mystery and possibility, the moment passed.

With one swift movement Chase was in push-up position. "Contest. If I win, we go to dinner." Before I could respond, he was already going: ten, twenty, forty.

"That's the most chauvinistic, pathetic ploy." I hauled myself up, put one foot on his back, and pushed, hard enough to take his arms out from beneath him but not hard enough to hurt him. "Is there anything more barbaric than using a manly competition to take away a woman's freedom of choice?" I leaned down so close I could smell his sweat (unfortunately). "You should thank me," I whispered. "Because you would've lost."

I sashayed out of that room. When I turned to salute Beardy, Mole Hair, Baldy, and Grand-Shīfu, I peeked down to see him gaping at me, a puzzled expression on his face as if he couldn't figure me out, like he had several pieces but couldn't quite fit them together.

Neither could I, buddy. Neither. Could. I.

CHAPTER 4

MISALIGNED

The house was silent and dark when I returned home. My parents were experts at avoiding each other (and me) in such a tiny amount of space. Sitting down at the kitchen table in my mostly air-dried kung fu clothes, I removed the Saran wrap from my plate of egg rolls and dove in sans chopsticks, stopping only to dip the crispy deliciousness in black vinegar.

To be completely honest, I was shook. At the start of this day, I'd been resigned to always being different. The universe had beaten into my head that this was just how it was, a misaligning of stars for Ali, the lone-star weirdo.

The defining blow had come two months earlier, after which

it no longer felt like coincidence that my name was smack-dab in the middle of the word "misaligned." A family friend and his son, neither of whom we'd seen in more than a decade, were passing through Indiana on their way to tour colleges. The visit in and of itself was quite the aligning of stars, given that we had met in Boston during my early childhood and they now lived in Shanghai. My mother had been *giddy*, cleaning the house until you could lick the toilet seat and splurging on the expensive sauce with more kick. It had been a kick to my stomach seeing how lonely she must've been, and how a visit from a family friend could bring even her out of her self-imposed shell. Her giddiness had unexpectedly rubbed off on me, and I found myself thinking (hoping, really) that Yun might finally be the one to understand me, given our similar backgrounds.

As my mother had dusted, straightened, and cooked up a sweet-and-sour storm, I had continually glanced at my father to see if he would notice the woman he had fallen in love with and perhaps find a way to keep her here.

But he had holed up in other parts of the house as usual, and when he passed her in her frenzy, he seemed sad, so hopeless he couldn't even enjoy this moment, let alone find a way to make it stick. Perhaps he felt guilty, since he was the reason this was such an event in her life.

When the hot, sticky summer morning of the Kaos' arrival finally came around, my mother had shooed my father out of the house.

"Why don't I get to stay?" he had asked.

"You never bothered to meet them before, always too busy with your research, and where did that get you? It got us here." My mother gestured to our home as if it were smeared in poop. "If you want to be helpful, go to the office and do more research to get us *out* of here."

Covered in shame, my father had slunk out of the house, no attempt to save face. Given that our culture emphasized mìanzi, I had almost reached out and hugged him.

Almost.

When I had returned from kung fu that afternoon, Yun and his father were already there.

"Shǔshú hǎo," I had said immediately to the stranger sitting on our couch, instinct from when I was little and family friends would frequent our house.

"Ah, so polite!" Yun's father had exclaimed. "Wonderful, wonderful. So good to see you again, Ali. You can call me Uncle Kao."

A tall, handsome boy in fitted navy shorts and a cream-colored T-shirt emerged from the bathroom. He smiled nervously at me. "I'm Yun," he said, pronouncing it *ryuing*, meaning "cloud."

"Ali, you remember Uncle Kao and Yun, of course," my mother said as she waved me over to join them. "Remember when you were little, you and Yun used to play together? You know, Barbie, trucks, everything."

I didn't remember, but I nodded since it was easier. Besides, pre-Indiana, when we lived in Boston and my father was still a promising assistant professor, we used to spend every other weekend at Asian potluck parties filled with cold sesame noodles, dumplings, and, of course, the obligatory almond Jell-O/mandarin orange/maraschino cherry dessert. So many children had rotated in and out of the lineup that I couldn't remember most faces, and it had been so long that even if I had, I probably wouldn't have recognized them today.

"Why don't you two go out for ice cream and get reacquainted?" my mother had suggested, handing me a twenty-dollar bill.

"Like we're children," I'd mumbled, even though there weren't really any other options around here.

We drove in mostly silence, with Yun piping up only when we drove past the deli/hardware store with the GRAND OPENING sign still flailing in sync with the inflatable wavy-arm tube guy. "Happening town, huh?"

I chuckled.

We continued in silence, but now we both had faint smiles on our faces.

I took him to Shady Pines, which sounds like a retirement home but was actually a local farm that gave tours and sold homemade (farm-made?) cheese, ice cream, and chocolate milk, as well as other random stuff like honey, salsa, and cow mugs that said—I kid you not—UP TO UDDER NONSENSE AT SHADY PINES. When we pulled onto the dirt road and into the massive parking lot adjacent to vast farmland, Yun started laughing.

"Guess we're in Kansas, huh, Toto?" he said while shaking his head at the kitschy signs and giant plastic cows.

"Hey, don't knock our most popular date spot," I joked before realizing what I'd said. "I mean, uh, not that we're . . . not that you're not . . ."

Yun rolled his eyes at me. "Relax. That won't be happening."

Well, all right then.

As soon as we opened the car doors and the heavy scent of cow manure hit (it was so bad I could F-ing *taste* it), we booked it into the *cow*feteria on each other's heels. Seriously, had the cows all decided to take a huge dump at the same time to drive the humans away? Because it was working.

Cones in hand (strawberry and chocolate fudge for me, coffee for him), we settled into a booth painted black-and-white with cow spots, then watched the workers clean the production-line machines through the clear glass wall.

Except Yun wasn't watching the same way I was. While I was wondering what muscles were needed to be the best scrubber (biceps and triceps?), he was checking out the closest guy bending over the machinery. I didn't have the heart to tell him that Steve the Sleaze always had his hands down his pants in class and that instead of admiring his pìgu, we should be worrying about our ice cream (and yes, I knew everyone here).

I briefly wondered whether Yun was attracted to just guys or guys and girls before reminding myself it was none of my business.

Between licks, I asked, "What brought your family to China?"

"My dad's bank job. It was a great opportunity for him but hard for me." Sounded familiar. "I'm at an American school, but I just, I don't know, always feel like a foreigner? I'm not Chinese enough outside school, but I also don't fit in with the American students."

Were Chinese Americans doomed to feel like foreigners no matter where we went? He was a lone wolf in a sea of Asians, and I was a lone wolf in a sea of Caucasians. Even though I completely felt his pain, I couldn't find any words.

Lick lick lick. More silence.

Guess this wouldn't be a fast-friends situation but instead maximal awkwardness, our past almond Jell-O bond be damned. And for once I wasn't the only one to blame. Maybe we were too similar after all.

"Do you like it here?" he asked. "Must be better than Shanghai, since you share a first language with everyone else."

"Which do you think is better—looking or sounding like everyone else?"

He shrugged, then leaned back in his chair. "I tend to always want what I can't have."

"Like a boyfriend?" I blurted out, then immediately regretted it. In retrospect, I think I was trying to find a way to tell him I'd noticed and that I supported him whatever his preference was. Too bad I communicated it in the worst possible way.

Yun's face tightened with fear. "Why would you say that?"

"Oh, uh, I'm sorry? I didn't mean, er . . . I don't . . . I'm cool with it and . . ." Then I couldn't find any more words, because I'm me.

Yun's voice was as cold as his expression. "You better not tell your mom. Or my dad. Or anyone."

"Of course I won't!" I paused, but not for very long, because, to my horror, the words were spilling out like melted ice cream. "Have you tried talking to your parents?"

I wasn't telling him what to do or implying they'd be okay with it, but I was, believe it or not, trying to bond with him by finding some common ground. His hesitation had hinted at a strained relationship with his parents, and I thought maybe he and I could understand each other and share stories. I was trying to provide him with the support he seemed to be lacking.

My intentions obviously did not come through. His eyes narrowed at me. "Are you kidding me right now?"

I shook my head. "I was just . . . I thought you might be lonely . . . I'm lonely too—"

"So you thought it was fine to probe into something so personal for me? That's selfish."

Crappity-crap-crap. "I didn't mean . . . I wasn't thinking . . ."

"No shit."

"I'm really sorry," I said as sincerely as someone as awkward as me could manage.

"Maybe you should examine your own situation first. My dad may not know I'm gay, but at least I don't interact with him like we're strangers. Did you know you and your mom never looked at each other once, even while conversing? What kind of messed-up—"

"Stop!" I yelled, fighting the urge to cover my ears with my hands like a child. "Please stop," I said, quieter this time. "I feel so bad about what I said. You didn't have to . . . to . . ."

Then silence. For the rest of our short-lived Shady Pines visit. I bought him an UDDER NONSENSE mug filled with chocolate milk, hoping it would say all the things I couldn't.

It didn't.

Because of Yun, because I had foolishly allowed myself to hope, I had resisted all the signs that had been there with Chase: the familiar anger he wore on his sleeve, the parallel way he seemed to be struggling with his identity. Chase understanding me was much too good to be true and too misaligned with my life thus far.

But . . . did two misalignments equal alignment?

CHAPTER 5

RABBLE-ROUSERS

The following day, I couldn't get away from Chase even if I'd wanted to. Not only did we have the same schedule, but by mid-morning the teachers had already lumped us together a handful of times (barf), either with clueless comments or by making us sit near each other. With each incident, I wondered why he didn't say anything. Had I rubbed off on him? Was I right that silence was the only way to survive a place like this? For the first time in my life, the prospect of being right left a horrible taste in my mouth, like I'd eaten stinky tofu, then fallen asleep without brushing my teeth.

In AP English—my "throwaway" class, according to my mǔqīn and her belief that "all the money is in math and science"—I pretended to read the open book on my desk while actually thinking about how I couldn't be with Chase, not just because I refused to give this town what it wanted, but also because I didn't want to prove my mother right, that dating a Chinese boy was the one right choice for my life. It had never been a thing before, since my dating pool had been a mirage in the desert, but now that I had an option, I didn't want to give in to her unreasonable demands and reward her for being overbearing. But that was also a terrible reason *not* to go after someone who intrigued me, right?

Everything gnawed at me like a tapeworm I couldn't get rid of. (Instead of hearing about trudging uphill through the snow, I grew up with stories about fishing through poo to see if you had passed your parasite.)

And suddenly I realized the room was dead-ass silent. I heard a few classmates fidgeting in their chairs. They were uncomfortable, but evidently I should be the most uncomfortable of all because clearly, I'd just been called on.

What were we reading again? My gaze shifted from the cracks on my desk to the beat-up public-school paperback in my hands. Right. *The Joy Luck Club.* I had flipped it open last night and read one rando excerpt, which was more than I usually did. First I'd been intrigued by the Chineseness of the book, and then, because this was our one assigned novel not written by a white dude, I'd wondered: Had the school board added this to the curriculum to make themselves feel (undeservedly) good about checking its diversity box? Had they picked it in honor of their one Asian student (now two)? Was this also the reason why Mrs. Finch had chosen to call on me?

I continued to stare down, waiting. I knew Mrs. Finch—she'd crack before I did.

A throat clearing, old and withered. "Allie, why do you think the characters communicate with stories instead of direct statements?"

Predictable Mrs. Finch. Too lazy to come up with profound questions, and too old to realize everyone had internet and thus SparkNotes. She once told us to look up an interview with Richard Russo on this website: "w-w-w-dot-youuutube-dot-com." She had dragged out the "you" as if that would clue in someone who didn't know. Then, when we all burst out laughing, she had insisted, "No, really. That's a website. Look it up."

I usually read the answer off my SparkNotes printout (all thirty of us had them hidden in our notebooks), because to Mrs. Finch, that was the one right answer. Why murder the bird in your hand? But this question struck a messed-up chord inside me.

Good-bye, white toast. Good-bye, socially acceptable, PC Allie who blended in with the rest of the crowd.

"Because Chinese people don't know how to communicate with direct statements, at least not the ones I know. They barely talk, period." Out of the corner of my eye I saw Chase's head pop up. "It's just the way it is, the unwritten law, and since no one talks, I have no idea why or how it started. And so Amy Tan uses stories because otherwise there wouldn't be a book at all. The characters would just be staring at each other across the mahjong table like my family does every Thanksgiving. Just that goddamn silence, all the time, filled with secrets and anger and miscommunication."

"Language!" Mrs. Finch screeched.

"She's just telling the truth," Chase said as our eyes met over the heads that had magically shrunk down toward their desks. "It isn't easy to explain what it's like, especially to a room full of white people with parents who want to talk things out, keep an open door, all that nonsense, and when I say *nonsense*, I mean awesomeness, because I'm so fucking green with envy I'm—"

"Both of you! To the counselor's!" Mrs. Finch pointed at the door with a shaky finger, then muttered to herself, "The mouths on these young people. No respect at all."

I snapped my notebook shut and rolled my eyes. If Mrs. Finch could be the stereotypical high school teacher, then I would play my part too, even though I preferred Mr. Laurelson to Mrs. Finch, always.

In the front office the sixty-year-old secretary, Mrs. Dumas, greeted us with a shake of the head. Beneath her breath she whispered, "Rabble-rousers," her greeting for every student sent to the counselor. As Chase and I took the two rabble-rouser seats (what happened if there were three?), I asked him, "What was the end of your sentence going to be? So green with envy you, Mr. Yu, are . . . now a piece of yù?" From beneath my sweater I fished out the jade necklace my mother had given me for my fifth birthday. After flashing the green stone at him, I returned it to its hiding spot.

Chase laughed, his amusement reaching his eyes. "That, Ms. Chu, is quite the classic Chinese play on words."

It took me a moment to remember how to breathe.

"And . . . I'm not as clever as you," he added. "I had no clue how to finish that sentence, so I guess it kinda worked out that we got sent here."

His response caught me off guard and my laughter came out loud and genuine, neither witch nor chimes. It made me laugh harder, just so I could hear it longer.

Mr. Laurelson opened the door and motioned Chase in as he gave me the Look, his one and only tactic to try to tame students. It involved narrowed eyes and a tight jaw, aka a look of straining on the toilet.

I winked at him, knowing it was all an act.

Right before the door shut, he smiled at me.

Eventually I grew so bored that I pulled out *The Joy Luck Club*, telling myself the nerdiness of doing homework right now was canceled out by the fact that I was in the rabble-rouser seat. Literally—the words were carved into the back of the chair. I wondered why Mrs. Dumas had never noticed. Or maybe she had and loved it. Maybe *she* had put them there, making *her* a rabble-rouser!

I stared at the *Joy Luck Club* cover, the Asianness of the flower petals and leaves, the oh-so-Chinese shade of red. For some reason it irritated me, even though I felt like the Ali in me should've clutched it to her chest. Instead I just wished I had other homework here, homework that "mattered," as my mother would say. I fingered the greasy, weary, dog-eared paperback and wondered who else had trodden through these pages. Any Chinese Americans like me? Knowing this town, probably not.

Sighing, I began reading, starting a book from the beginning for the first time in God knows how long—ten years? Since my last *Baby-Sitters Club* book?

Annnd I snapped the book shut. I'd only read two paragraphs, but this old woman who actually *wanted* her daughter to assimilate, to speak perfect English? I was so fucking green with envy I . . . Speak of the buzz-cut, khaki-wearing devil.

Chase exited Mr. Laurelson's office with a funny smirk on his face. He waggled an eyebrow at me as I passed him on my way in.

As I took my seat, I smiled at Mr. Laurelson. Sweetly. Well, as sweetly as someone like me could muster. I'm guessing it looked creepy, with a dash of constipation.

He gave me a mini Look as he closed a blue binder that was, somehow, larger than mine (he filled out paperwork for every parent meeting, and that alone added hundreds of pages to my battered, overstretched file). Since all his binders were green, the blue one was obviously Chase's from his old school. I wondered if his thick file was because his parents were just as overbearing as mine or if he was a *real* rabble-rouser. And suddenly, because of the latter, Chase looked a little shinier, a little hotter in my head, even though it made no rational sense whatsoever.

My eyes followed Mr. Laurelson as he placed the blue binder in his cabinet under lock and key. Chase's past, typed out and summarized, ready for judgment. It was beckoning to me, an Ali magnet, but before I could do anything (yell *look behind you!* and swipe it, like in a cartoon?), Mr. Laurelson asked, "Anything you need?"

I shook my head at him, not able to say what I was thinking—how I appreciated his quiet, persistent support, and that I felt connected to him because he was one of the few who (sort of) knew what my mǔqīn was like.

He nodded, and I knew he was telling me he was always available.

At first, when I'd been a fledgling freshman, he had wanted to dissect me, figure out how my neurons connected and whether or not he needed to reroute anything. But by my sophomore year he'd realized my problems stemmed from my mother, and just like me, he had no idea what to do with her. It had taken a grand total of fifty-two meetings for him to figure that out, and yes, I counted. I tallied them up in my notebook the American way, with four vertical lines and then a diagonal. I'd refused to do it the Chinese way, writing out the character zhèng (正) in correct stroke order (which I of course knew, but that wasn't the issue).

I nodded back at Mr. Laurelson and tried to leave before my emotions could surface. But right as I was about to open the door, he said, "Wait," and I turned back.

"Be careful with him. Chase, I mean. Your . . . mother . . . has concerns."

My face scrunched in shock and confusion. I'd barely talked to Chase and my mother was already looping the counselor in? How did she even know about him?

I just shook my head because I didn't know what else to do.

Mr. Laurelson gave a nervous laugh, then shrugged as if to say, *Your mother. I know, right?*

When I left the counselor's office, Chase was still in front of Mrs. Dumas's desk, blocking my path to the exit, and for a second I wondered if he was waiting for me. Maybe my meeting had been so fast he was still there for some other reason. But duh, no, not unless he was trying to hit on Mrs. Dumas.

He was leaning against the wall, one foot propped on the peeling wallpaper and arms folded over his chest. I told myself he looked not hot at all. Downright shaved-ice chilly. I shoved him aside, congratulating myself when I managed to knock him off-balance despite the fact that it felt like throwing myself against a brick wall.

Chase squinted at me, curious, then shook his head in disbelief. "My meeting was like fifteen minutes. How'd you get out so fast?" Despite my accelerated pulse, I shrugged, my face neutral. Then I left without glancing back, but I could sense he was following close behind. "You've got secrets. Gonna let me in, Chu?" Surprisingly, disappointment shot through me when he didn't call me by my name, my real first name.

I paused in the hallway, hugging my books to my chest.

From behind he nudged my shoulder with his. "Don't want to go back to English, huh?" He shifted so his lips were right beside my ear. "Me neither," he whispered, sending chills down my spine. In response my shoulders rose toward my ears, knocking him in the jaw.

"Sorry," I said, flustered. Then, before I could filter, the truth tumbled out. "I don't want to go back and hear those people dissect our culture like they know anything." *Our culture.* It was the first time I'd ever said that.

He touched my elbow, and I turned back toward him. "Hey, I get it," he said, the gentleness of his voice slipping past my defenses. "What gives them the right to judge us, yeah? They have no idea what it's like." He paused. Scratched his head. And suddenly his face shifted as though a mask had come off. "What you said in class resonated with me. And . . . um . . ." The wall completely disappeared and he looked vulnerable, younger. "To be honest, I could only get through the first page of the book. It was too hard . . . it hit too close to home, and . . ."

I have no idea why I did what I did next. Maybe it was Ali rearing her rebellious head, or maybe I was sick of faking it, especially when it was clear I was not going to "make it" anytime soon. Maybe my armor was fractured, and the fact that he understood me in a way no one else did turned me into a puddle.

Whatever the reason, I dropped my books on the floor, grabbed his shirt with both hands, and yanked. Right before our lips touched, I paused, waiting for a sign of consent, and he leaned forward.

But then I snapped my head back and let go. Because . . . *yes, yes, they belong together.*

"Don't you care that this is what everyone expects?" I blurted. "That this is fulfilling every stereotype? You said yourself you hated how they all asked if you knew me."

He spoke carefully, calculated. "I don't care . . . anymore. Because it's you."

Fuck. "I'm not who you think I am."

"Oh?" His eyebrows shot up. "You're not a stubborn, incredibly strong, hot-when-you're-mad, perhaps slightly confused high school student named after, I presume, a mountain? Please, tell me, who is it you think I'm looking for?"

"Ali."

"And who am I talking to right now?"

"Allie . . . Alie . . ." I stumbled, pronouncing both names

exactly the same but seeing them differently in my head.

He leaned over like he was about to tell me a secret. "They're all the same person."

Even though I knew he was going to say that, even though my mind was telling me it was kind of a cheesy line and I'd set him up for it . . . I was melting, both figuratively and literally (in my armpits).

He tilted his head to one side. "Why don't you correct people when they pronounce your name wrong?"

Because I'm a coward. "It's hard being different," I admitted, craning my neck so I wouldn't have to look at him.

He swiveled so my eyes would have to meet his. "Better than being the same as everyone else, as boring and dry as toast."

The second the words "dry as toast" came out of his mouth, I grabbed his shirt again, but this time I pulled his face to mine. (Really, what were my options here? I basically had no choice.)

As soon as our lips met, all I could think was, *Why did I wait so long?* I'd barely known him a minute, yet it felt like I had waited an eternity—the same way I'd felt on day one of kung fu.

I pulled away first. I told myself it was to stay in control, but deep down, my churning stomach was trying to tell me I was overwhelmed: with his citrusy scent, the way I already knew his mouth was slightly lower on the left side than the right, the way he looked at me—Ali—as if he wanted to help me fit the pieces together. . . .

Cheeks flushed, Chase panted, "So, uh, is that a yes to my dinner invitation from last night?"

I left without answering. I was scared that if I spoke, I would say yes.

CHAPTER 6

EW

After the kiss that made me remember my name and forget everything else, Chase and I went a whole period without speaking or making eye contact. But on the way to the cafeteria, he caught up to me and our strides step-step-stepped in unison, the only sound between us. By understanding my need for silence, he was saying so much with nothing.

Some random girl who'd never bothered to speak to me before passed us in the hallway and yelled, "You two are so cute together!"

"Fuck you!"

Okay, maybe I was being a little harsh.

But then another guy I didn't know called out, "Way to go, you two—perfect match!" and I didn't feel as bad when I told him to shove it up his pee hole. (Chase raised his eyebrows but said nothing.)

Step-step-step.

Why did I let them get to me? People I didn't like or respect—how did they worm their way so deeply under my skin?

As we neared the table by the trash cans that was perpetually empty because there were more misses than hits from the annoying students free-throwing their garbage, I assumed Chase would settle there as he had yesterday, but nope. He headed for my usual table, where Kyle, Ava, and Brenda were so obviously talking about us (and not very subtly).

He's got balls, I couldn't help thinking, but the thought of him sitting anywhere else, especially at the trash table again, also made me nauseous.

Lukewarm introductions were made. I pulled out my peanut butter and jelly sandwich while Chase pulled out some Tupperware . . . and I immediately knew it was a biàndāng. The phrase brought back warm memories of reciting the joke Li Bai poem on the floor of the practice hall, and my stomach growled. Or was it completely in knots and trying not to empty its limited contents?

Kyle pointed to Chase's lunch box, the lid now off and the white rice, beef, and bean sprout deliciousness displayed for everyone to see. "Ew. What's that?"

I looked to Chase, expecting his Dave-Matthews-and-buttholes side to bust out, but he was silent, pressing his lips together so hard they were white. And his eyes were locked on mine. The three-second silence that followed felt like a year.

When I spoke, my gaze was glued to Chase, waiting to read his reaction to my words. "It's Chinese food, Kyle. And it's delicious."

Ava cringed just as Kyle responded, "Looks weird."

"You look weird!" The comeback burst from my lips before I realized what I was saying, which also explained why it was so pitiful.

The girls dissolved into giggles, probably because they felt like Allie Pot was calling the porcelain black.

"Is this the first Allie-plosion you're witnessing, Chase? Buckle up," Kyle warned.

Ava started laughing. "Remember that time Allie overreacted in seventh grade because George F. did that presentation on China, and he adopted that accent?"

Kyle laughed as Brenda imitated me, yelling "Stop it" over and over while covering her ears.

I took several deep breaths, but my mind wasn't shutting off like it used to. Chase was staring at them with his mouth open as if his mind couldn't make up whether this was actually happening.

"It was so cute," Brenda finished, flashing me a smile. "You used to be so dramatic. Now you're all quiet and dead inside . . . I guess until today."

Ava hunched over and made the motion of whispering but kept her voice at normal volume. "Maybe she's just flustered because she's been hit by Cupid's arrow."

Kyle faux pouted. "Aww, is Arrie rovesick?"

Even though I'd been around this for years, when Kyle's fake accent hit my ears, I dropped my water bottle on the floor, spraying liquid everywhere. Ava screeched, but the sound barely registered because my ears were buzzing with a loud ringing.

Normally I would have made myself gloss over their comments by remembering that first time they'd shared their lunches with me after noticing I'd thrown away my congee post-bullying. But today I was overcome with hurt. And rage. So much rage. At them, at myself, maybe even at Chase? Because before he came along, things had been fine. Not great by any means, but I'd at least had a system.

"How could you guys . . ." My mouth went dry. I didn't know what to ask.

I'd been Allie for so long, playing by my survival dry-toast rules, that there had never been an incident to spark something of this proportion with my white squad.

"It was just a joke," Kyle said in her bossy tone, with a splash of exasperation, as if *I* were the one who was being awful here.

"Can't you see how saying that is just so . . ." Why couldn't I find my voice? "That was a really shitty joke." I used air quotes around the last word.

"Okay, c'mon," Brenda chimed in. "That's not fair, Allie. Give Kyle the benefit of the doubt—you know us better than that."

I forced myself to keep my head up, gaze directed and stern. "I'd appreciate an apology, Kyle."

"Allie, what's gotten into you?" Kyle was peering at me like I was a specimen under a microscope. Which, well, I basically was. Always.

I was so, so tired. The past years of pretending and eating my feelings (and PB&Js) were suddenly so very present, and . . . God . . . I was going to explode or throw up or something.

Kyle leaned toward me. "Allie?"

When I didn't answer, she wrinkled her nose, and suddenly all I could think about was how, years ago, during that first lunch together, when I had tried to tell her how to pronounce my name, Kyle had scrunched her nose and said, "Ew, no, it's Allie."

"My name is Ali, you ignorant xenophobes," I declared, standing.

Silence. As in complete, utter silence in the *entire* cafeteria.

Then, a whisper from the next table over. "Leave it to the Asian to use big words. Probably studied way too hard for the SAT."

Chase slammed a fist on the table.

His voice was completely calm when he spoke, as if that one motion had let all the steam out of the pot. "They don't even deserve your anger," Chase said, standing in a hurry, maybe to show everyone he was on my side? "C'mon, *Ali*," he said with emphasis, before using his chopsticks to dish some of his food onto a paper towel. "Think they'll at least give it a taste," he asked just me, "or are they so racist they won't even try it?"

As soon as the *r*-word came out, the three of them—along with the rest of the cafeteria—froze. Chase either didn't notice or didn't care.

I smiled at him, then turned to Ava, Brenda, and Kyle. "I'm ashamed of so many things I don't even know where to start. I probably should've said something at the beginning, with George F., explaining how you were all being disrespectful, harmful, and, yes, racist. How do you feel about white American stereotypes? Would you be okay if someone did a presentation on the US and wore a fat suit and shoveled hamburgers into their mouth?"

"I'm not fat," Ava said immediately.

Kyle shrugged. "I think it would've been funny."

I nodded slowly. "What if the presenter spoke with an exaggerated Midwestern accent?" I said, mimicking one myself.

"Are you *trying* to sound like my mom?" Ava whispered. I wasn't. Her voice rose. "That's so incredibly mean, Allie! Not all of us can have fancy professor fathers!"

"Allie, get out of here," Kyle ordered. "You were never one of us, and you never will be. We were just being *nice*." Ava nodded, and Brenda kept staring at the table, as she'd been doing for the past five minutes.

Kyle's words, though meant to hurt me, actually enlightened me. My friends' actions might have included kindness over the years, but that didn't mean they could treat me however they wanted or that I should feel indebted to them.

Confidently, I handed Chase his biàndāng and left my gross sandwich behind.

As we exited the cafeteria, steadfastly ignoring the piercing gazes following us, I heard Brenda mutter, "Oh damn, that's delicious."

No shit.

"Tastes like ass to me," Kyle said, purposely loud.

No surprise there, I guess. I almost turned to chuck something at her, but I made myself keep walking; they'd already taken up too much of my time.

Chase and I settled in the grass beside the parking lot, and even though we weren't technically supposed to be eating outside, I wasn't all that worried, since the "punishment" would be a visit with Mr. Laurelson. Chase brought out an extra pair of chopsticks, and I wondered whether they'd been packed with me in mind.

As we dug into his biàndāng with gusto, we enjoyed the silence for a moment. It didn't feel like a win—there was never *victory* in situations like these—but I felt an odd sense of peace at having stood up for myself, finally. It was mixed with rage and shame and everything else, but for the first time there was a sliver of underlying calm.

"Why didn't you say something sooner?" I asked out of curiosity.

"They were your friends; it didn't feel like my place. And you didn't need me. Why, would you have preferred I said something? Because believe me, I had plenty loaded up."

I laughed. "I could tell. You looked like you were about to explode."

"If you ever need me, just say the word; I'm on your side."

"You surprise me sometimes: so sweet on the outside, thinking to share your food with them when they didn't deserve it, but then underneath, you're this hard-core"—*literally*, I thought—"badass martial artist."

He nudged me with an elbow. "Compared to you, I'm a giant pink teddy bear."

"With ruffles."

He smiled. "I'm glad you finally told them your name. It always pisses me off when people don't make an effort. It's not even that hard! Like, what the fuck is up with 'kowtow' being an English word . . . is everyone really so incompetent they can't say 'kētóu'?"

"Well, even if Racist Robinson knew it was supposed to be 'kētóu,' he'd still say 'kowtow.'"

Chase sighed, then jabbed at a piece of beef with his chopsticks. "I don't know how you've survived this town for . . . wait, how long has it been?"

"Too long. Eleven years." *And that's all I've been doing—surviving.* "The truth is . . . I don't feel like I've been present until recently. Until, um, yesterday. When you showed up. And now, suddenly I care, and I'm feeling everything I worked so hard to push away before." I couldn't look at him as I bared my freaking soul.

He put the food down. "I get it. I, uh, may have done things I normally wouldn't have, because this place is just messed up, man."

I raised a questioning eyebrow. "Does this have to do with the fact that someone told me you smoke, yet I've never smelled it on you?"

He flushed, and I leaned closer and sniffed.

He waved me back. "All right, all right, I'll tell you! Do you have to be so goddamn perceptive all the time?"

Through the teasing, I saw the admiration in his eyes and soared just a smidge higher.

He scratched the back of his head. "I, uh, went out with some kids for a smoke break yesterday, but I didn't do anything because I don't smoke. They were just the first people to talk to me who didn't say, 'Do you know Allie Chu?'"

I smacked his arm. "Aha! You were trying to blend in too! Jeez, and that was like, after first period—how many people said that to you in just an hour?"

"Too many. Enough to make me cave in to peer pressure for the first time." He tapped my knee twice. "But I don't feel the need to do that anymore."

"Me neither. Taiwanese pineapple cake instead of dry toast?"

He nodded. "Taiwanese pineapple cake."

We toasted with chopsticks full of beef and bean sprouts.

That night I reveled in my mother's home cooking. The tomato, scallion, and egg stir-fry no longer looked embarrassing and out of place in our cornfield-adjacent duplex, but homey and hearty. I wondered what Chase was having right now before it dawned on me that I would probably know tomorrow; the leftovers would likely be his—I mean, our—lunch.

I picked up my bowl and put it to my mouth to hide the ridiculous, goofy grin that had just surfaced. As I shoveled rice directly onto my tongue with wooden chopsticks, I heard my father in my head telling me in his professorial voice how this was perfectly fine etiquette in Chinese culture. Before, I'd just taken his word for it, but now I made a mental note to ask Chase.

As I put my bowl back down, I realized I didn't have to hide my grin. No one was paying any attention to me. *Hoosier Millionaire* reruns blasted in the background for my father, and my mother had the *World Journal* (the Chinese newspaper and her Bible) open in her lap. And me? I had a physics textbook laid out in front of me, more for them than for me, because how weird would it have been if I had nothing, as if I wanted to talk?

The silence crept around my throat and squeezed.

After dinner I wandered into my parents' bedroom, not sure

what I wanted to say but wanting to say something. The *pshhh* of the running shower flooded relief through me. I paused next to the perfectly made bed, which was beautiful on the outside, but I knew it was a secondhand mattress many years past its prime. When the water shut off—only three-minute showers to keep the water bill down, house rule—I hastily turned to retreat . . . and came face-to-face with a shiny, brand-new safe tucked into the corner. A mess of clothes cluttered the floor, thrown aside to make room in the tiny closet, which was barely large enough to house half one person's wardrobe.

Jesus, what kind of secrets did Liang, Chu, and the park hold that my mǔqīn needed a mother-effing safe?

I was still frozen there when my mother walked out of the bathroom, toweling her hair. We stared each other down for a few seconds, her daring me to say something and me trying to keep myself from drowning in disappointment.

Why? Who are you? What are you so afraid of? All the words caught in the giant lump in my throat.

Her eyes turned sad for a moment before she left to blow-dry her hair. I glanced at the safe again, still not fully believing she had really gone that far.

Sometimes I wondered—if I somehow had the superpower to see secrets as color, maybe blue, like some new type of synesthesia, would our entire house drown in a deep cobalt sea?

Zhu Yingtai
Hangzhou, China

So many secrets. Where do they congregate? Perhaps they're in the cloth that binds my chest flat, and one day there will be one too many and the cloth will fall, spilling the truth all over the floor for everyone to see. Worst of all, for my roommate to see.

Planning ahead, I made sure to arrive first, stake out the room, tuck away whatever lies I could into the crevices.

A slim man with hair as dark as a moonless night entered, only a tiny cloth bag slung over his shoulder. Like a newborn calf feeling out its shaky legs before taking that first terrifying step, I reached up to confirm my new hairstyle: front half shaved, back half long and braided, just like every man around.

He nodded toward me. Speaking in a local accent, he introduced himself: Liang Shanbo. As if in a Chinese opera, I responded with a rehearsed, perfectly timed smile to cover up how I already knew his name, not to mention how many siblings he had—four—and where he lived, and how his family had lied to marry off his hunchback of a brother.

Continuing the performance, I told him my name, and, just as practiced, it rolled off my tongue, smooth as polished jade, sounding as if it truly belonged to me, not my maid's son, who had passed last year from cholera. Shanbo's eyes barely registered me or my features, and I let out the breath I'd been holding since I chopped off half my hair and left everything I'd ever known to take the first step of my thousand-mile journey.

Maybe one day girls like me wouldn't have to pretend to be boys just to receive an education. I was ready to fight for them all.

Incoming text from Chase

Tomorrow night, after kung fu? First date of sorts?

Me

Who dis?

Chase

Don't make me chase you.

Me

Don't you mean Chase Yu?

After a minute,

Chase

I am truly quite embarrassed I didn't think of that. And no fair . . . your name isn't easy to make a pun with. But Chu already know that, don't Chu?

Me

I'll stop Yu right there because you've bitten off more than Yu can Chu. But don't go crying in an Allie about it because I won't Chase Yu in there. If you're lucky, maybe I'll yell Ali Ali oxen free to get Yu to come out.

Chase

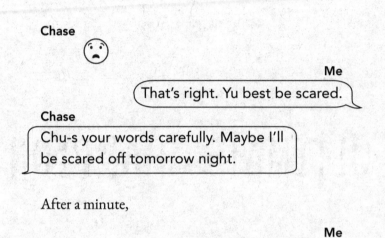

Me

That's right. Yu best be scared.

Chase

Chu-s your words carefully. Maybe I'll be scared off tomorrow night.

After a minute,

Me

I know Yu don't scare that easily.

CHAPTER 7

ULTIMATE CHAMPION

Great.

I woke with a giant, honking zit at the side of my mouth. A whitehead. Of course. It couldn't have been just slightly less conspicuous, and it couldn't have come, like, two weeks before.

Guess the gods were bored and wanted to see me self-destruct. Because like every other teen in the world (at least I assume so—everyone does this, right?), I squeezed it. I thought I had sound logic on my side: Wasn't all red better than red *and* pus in the center?

It imploded. Now it was red, white, and going to be crusty—I could feel it. It looked like I had a giant cold sore, which, ughhhh . . .

herpes was clearly worse than a whitehead, since that shit was contagious. Why did I never learn?

I broke out my concealer (a gift from Ava) for the first time. The liquid was on my finger, about to be smeared on, when I realized it would only clog the pore and add oxygen to the dumpster fire. If I was going to put any on, better to wait until later, closer to date time and potential make-out time. So I wiped my finger on a tissue and slipped the tube into my backpack.

The day passed by in an angsty blur, my leg jiggling away with a mind of its own.

Just enjoy this moment, I tried to tell myself. How often were there days like this, full of hope, anticipation, excitement? All butterflies and rainbows, before the shit storm of life rolled in?

Chase dutifully came to my locker after each class (making me wonder why he never had to go to his—then I noticed his backpack stuffed to the brim). Normally, this kind of thing might have bothered me because, you know, gender roles, et cetera, but with Chase it wasn't about that. I would like to think he simply couldn't get enough of our special brand of light conversation:

Him: "Do you eat chips with chopsticks?"

Me: "Of course, who doesn't?" We bumped fists.

"Stinky tofu: love or hate?"

"Hate," I said at the same time he said, "Love."

Me: "Tiger Balm or VapoRub?"

"Tiger Balm," we answered in tandem.

I was in such a good mood that I didn't even care when Ava made lewd movements behind Chase's back in the hallway. Air humps were never funny, but I found myself smiling anyway.

"So what do you want to do tonight?" I asked after physics.

"Leave that up to me." He nudged me with his elbow.

I sighed. "Why, because you're the guy? Give me a freaking break, Yu."

"Were you saying my name or 'you'?"

"Whichever one you thought it was."

He laughed. "You're weird." I had never been so happy to hear that before. "I'm into it."

I gave him a look like *Duh*, but really it was so not *duh*.

"Ali, just let me take care of tonight, okay? Not because I'm the guy, but because I really like you, probably more than you like me, and I think I've planned something you'll enjoy. And if you don't, then you win"—I smiled, maybe a little creepily—"and you'll plan all the future dates, okay?"

"Okay," I relented, feeling bad for not saying more.

At kung fu that night, the matching form felt different. Instead of a bout, it felt like a dance. Banter. Flirtation.

Our date had already started.

I wondered if others could sense the shift. I hoped Marcin wouldn't make some comment about how it was supposed to be rougher or else we wouldn't be fully satisfied or something.

After class I retreated to the bathroom to wipe with a towel (and maybe for a quick pit check-and-refresh . . . a "pit" stop, ha-ha). I paused when I saw myself in the mirror. After a moment I boldly shoved the concealer tube back in my pocket and decided it was fine. Mini Ali Mountain had calmed down somewhat during the day, and, well, if he was grossed out and didn't want to get near me or kiss me over something so human, it was his loss, not mine.

I had decided not to bring a change of clothes because I wanted to be myself tonight, all versions of Ali and Allie, and I was closest to her in my baggy Aladdin pants and unisex T-shirt.

When I exited the bathroom, he was still in his kung fu clothes too, standing in front of the door, a single plum blossom in his hand. "It's Taiwanese and resilient, just the way I like it."

So, years ago, when Ava had dragged me to the library's rom-com night, I had been the only one who hadn't *aww*-ed once (partly because I couldn't see myself in those white actors' shoes and partly because rom-coms just weren't my thing). But this, right here, with Chase praising me for my anti-manic-pixie-whatever? I was lapping that shit up.

I took the flower and twirled it between my fingers, rewarding him with a sincere smile.

He leaned closer and whispered out of the side of his mouth, "Sorry it's fake. They're not easy to find around here."

He held an arm out and I hesitated for a moment, then looped a hand in.

He led the way into the brisk fall night. "I'd cover your eyes, but I have a feeling that would end with me knocked to the floor under your foot."

I feigned shock. "Where did you get this violent image of me? I'm quite offended, good sir." I pinched my poofy kung fu pants between my left thumb and forefinger, pretending to be Cinderella waltzing into the ball.

He laughed so hard my hand slipped from his elbow.

I crossed my arms over my chest. "Are you done?"

"No." He forced a few more laughs, but they were pathetic. "Okay, yeah, I guess I'm done."

I stuck my elbow out this time, and he looped his hand in. And all was right with the world for that one beautiful, měi moment.

Except I didn't know where we were going, and it was difficult being led in that position. Eh, worth it.

We awkwardly made our way to the library across the street, through a door that probably should have been locked but somehow wasn't, and up a narrow staircase.

At the top, I expected the door to swing open again, but Chase knelt by the doorknob and retrieved a small black cloth from his pocket.

No freaking way.

After discovering the safe, I had spent last night reading up on lock-picking, and now I was staring down at the very stainless-steel tools I was coveting. Shoving him aside (but gently—it *was* a date, after all), I snatched up the doodad and thingamabob (clearly I was already an expert).

After struggling for a few embarrassing minutes, I took a breath, rebooted, and kept going, just like when I was winded in kung fu or stuck on a math problem. And finally it clicked. My forehead was full of sweat (and I was again happy I hadn't put on concealer, which would have been streaking by now), but we were in.

"So many secrets, Ali," he whispered as he held the door to the roof open.

"I could say the same about you. Those lockpicks aren't easy to come by."

"I'll show you mine if you show me yours." His breath tickling my ear sent a thrill through my entire body, and, so embarrassing, I found myself kissing him.

He made a low, guttural noise in his throat and pulled me closer. And suddenly it felt urgent and heated and, gah, how I wanted him.

His hand caressed my neck, then trailed down my back. I clutched his shirt. I could feel every muscle beneath.

We leaned against the door we had just come through, and something about the contrast of the cold metal and the heat from Chase's lips ignited my nerve endings. As our bodies curved around each other, his shirt lifted slightly, and the feel of his skin on mine shot a surge of adrenaline through me, like when I lost my balance mid-sweep.

Another growl escaped Chase's throat, and I thought I might combust on the spot. I reluctantly pulled my face away just long enough to say (pant, really), "Isn't this part supposed to come at the end of the date?"

"Haven't you ever had dessert first?"

I gagged. Quite dramatically. "Of course, all the time, but—"

He beamed. "Why not start with the best stuff?"

"Because we're not barbarians."

"No, we're teenagers. It's allowed."

"Ha-ha." I pushed him away and he flicked on the lights, drawing my attention to a towel on the other side of the roof. It was covering an oblong object. "When did you do that?"

Before he finished saying the word "yesterday," I started running to it. But Chase sped up and reached it first, blocking my way. He started a drumroll on his thighs with his palms.

"Is it dinner?" I asked excitedly. "I'm starving."

He shook his head. "It's better." He whipped the towel off with a flourish of the wrist. "Ta-da!"

It was a ninja doll nailed to a two-by-four.

I leaned closer to read the jagged words carved into the wood. "'Ultimate champion'?"

He grinned and seemed so proud that I didn't want to tell him the ninja actually looked quite creepy. "Yup. For our first date, I'm challenging you to a push-up, sit-up, sprinting, and panther-walk contest. You've got to earn your dinner."

I smiled so wide I worried my tender, swollen lips would crack. "You are *so* on."

As if choreographed, we dropped at the same time, counting our push-ups out loud. After thirty, we began trying to one-up each other by doing variations of increasing difficulty: knuckles, one-handed, Superman.

I was reaching my limit; I could feel my muscles tightening. And this was just the first part of the contest! He had an unfair advantage: his center of mass was better suited for this event. I decided to concede this one to save my strength and wallop him with sit-ups. I had confidence in my abs; I had gone through a period (of time, not menstruation) where I was obsessed with my core because it was so essential to every kind of movement.

We switched over.

Annnnd it worked. I was barely starting to feel the burn when Chase held up both hands in submission. He then brought them up and down a few times, faux worshipping me. I started laughing, and he joined in for a split second before grabbing his abs and yelling, "Ow!"

Here was my shot. I got up and bounced on the balls of my feet even though it was killing me. I had to get in his head. "C'mon, slowpoke." Too bad I was so tired my words were slurring together.

He groaned as he pulled himself off the floor, but as soon as he yelled "Go!" he was off like a bullet. I had to win this one. Because I knew I was going to lose the panther walk on account of my useless sandbag boobs. I told myself to give this one my all, that it was okay if I didn't have a drop of energy left for the last event because it wouldn't matter.

The wind breezed past my ears. My shoulder-length hair flew straight out behind me. *Thank you, kung fu gods, for the clear vision.* Yet another hindrance my gender and gender roles caused: I'd been wanting to chop off my hair for a while, but Jimminy Bob forbade it.

Halfway, Chase started to slow, but I kept pace and reached the other end of the roof before him. Too tired to jump up and down, I was pumping one arm in the air when he planted left, then charged straight for me. I (embarrassingly) yelped as he scooped me up and threw me over his shoulder, but after a second I got my bearings and twisted in his grasp so I could fling myself to the ground. Using the momentum from the fall, I tossed him straight overhead. He landed in a graceful, infuriating somersault. After some entangled limbs and messy couples-rolling, I ended up on top. I only had a moment to catch my breath before we were kissing again.

But this time, after a few seconds, we broke apart out of necessity. I crumpled forward and he nestled his face in the crook of my neck. I could hear and feel his heavy breathing.

"We'll share the trophy," I said. "It's a tie."

"Don't patronize me; you're one up right now."

I shook my head. "I've got nothing left."

"Okay, right. I guess I win the last event because I still have tons of energy, so that's fair."

I shoved him playfully. Then, shocking myself, I admitted, "I don't really want to know who wins."

"I already know you're a bigger badass than I am. I say you get it for winning two out of three."

"Why'd you pick four events? Because you were hoping we'd tie?"

"Um . . . because I'm incompetent and didn't think about it?"

We laughed together, both guffawing for only a second before gasping for breath.

From the other side of the roof, a voice called out, "Uh . . . hello?"

I sat up swiftly, then immediately regretted it when all my muscles screamed at me.

Chase pulled out his wallet and winked. "Dinner's here."

As I chomped into my slice of meat lover's, I told him, "My first time eating pizza was at school—that gross French-bread-and-cheese blob they try to pass off as pizza. So when I discovered toppings three years later, I felt cheated."

"For me, I had Hawaiian pizza first, and as a kid, blech, I just saw the fruit, and I hated fruit. I mean, *hated*. But I eventually came across a sausage slice, and we've been inseparable since. It's getting serious." Despite having his mouth full, he flashed me a smile.

I nudged him, trying to ignore the (very bizarre) inkling of jealousy that had surfaced (how can anyone be jealous of food?). "Didn't your mother tell Yu not to Chu with your mouth open?" I wasn't sure if he knew I was throwing our names in there, but sure enough, he widened his eyes at me, impressed.

Then he shrugged. "Nah, she mostly just told me not to go to sleep with my hair wet."

I grabbed his arm, my pizza momentarily abandoned in my lap, which, translated, meant my mind was utterly *blown*. "What is up with that? Why do they talk about wet hair like it's as bad as licking a pigeon? And wet hair plus a breeze—the ultimate killer, am I right?"

"Don't chuī fēng," he mimicked, wagging an index finger. His pinched expression looked nothing like either one of my parents, but his words sent an eerie chill down my spine as I laughed— quite the odd combination. He rolled his eyes. "There's something about the moisture wetting the inside of your bones—the shīqì or whatever—and then you get sick."

I nudged him with an elbow. "Look who's finally embracing his nerd side."

He lowered his voice. "Maybe I just feel like I don't have to hide that side of me with you."

I felt the exact same way. But I didn't know how to verbalize what he seemed to be able to so easily. So I kissed him.

This time was different. Instead of feeling frantic, passionate, and hungry, this kiss was . . . sweet. Vulnerable. The kind I'd dreamed about but had never thought I would get to experience (especially not with mini Ali Mountain in the way).

It was absolutely perfect.

Until my mother showed up.

CHAPTER 8

SHIT

And double shit.

Well, at least I was with a Chinese boy, right?

Except from the look on my mother's face, that was *not* what she was thinking.

Why, Fate, why must you do this to me? Despite our being confined in a boring-ass town whose main attraction was the fucking *hardware store* because it had begun serving steak-and-cheese sandwiches, Chase had planned the perfect date, only for my mother to Avada Kedavra it. How the hell had she even known I was up here? Did she have a mǔqīn-bloodhound nose?

When she spoke, her voice was so cold and dispassionate I found myself wishing she would scream instead. "Ali, zěnme gǎo de?" She folded her arms across her chest, then made me regret my wish. "I called because I couldn't remember which friend you were studying with; then you didn't answer! I spent the last thirty minutes trying to find you, only to see you here, doing . . . *that*! How could you lie to me after everything I've sacrificed for you? Are you punishing me for being absent by being as loose as possible?"

I wished it were just anger that flashed through me, because that I knew how to deal with, but I mostly felt shame. "He's Chinese," I eked out. I forced myself to regain some (faux) confidence. "You said I could date if the boy was Chinese."

Her expression was so unfamiliar I couldn't read the details in it. But it was obvious to anyone that this was *not* going my way. Was it because we'd been kissing?

"It's nice to meet you, ma'am. I mean Ǎyí. I mean . . . Mrs. Chu," Chase blathered. "Duìbuqǐ," he apologized, red-faced.

"Why did you move here?" my mother asked him. "No one comes here, especially not people like us."

I cringed even though I knew why she'd said it.

When Chase didn't answer, she raised her eyebrows, and I knew she was wondering why he seemed to be holding back information. Way to call the kettle black, Māmá Pot.

She opened her mouth, and I braced for more questions (and I told myself it was okay because soon she'd get her answers and give her blessing), but she shocked me by saying with finality, "You two can't be together. I forbid it. Ali, do you hear me? You're coming home with me right now."

I was completely frozen in place. I mean, I knew she couldn't have been happy about the making out, but this was kind of extreme . . . wasn't it? We'd never really talked about guidelines beyond *only Chinese boys*, so maybe there was a no-kissing rule I didn't know about, since there had never been any Chinese boys to kiss before. . . .

No touching, no exceptions rang in my head, the words my mother had said to my ballet teacher years ago when I was supposed to waltz with Thomas for ten seconds during the *Nutcracker* party scene. But I'd assumed it was because I'd been so young. . . .

"Ali!"

Crap. That tone wasn't one to mess with.

"Chu Ǎyí, please, if you just give me a sec—"

The glare my mother shot Chase was so stern I half expected him to turn to stone. Her dèngyiyǎn was legendary, honed over the past eleven years of fighting with my dad.

"No." My voice was so small, but there. I'd said it. "No," I repeated, slightly louder this time.

My mother turned and left, but I chased after her into the parking lot. I knew down to my (very strong, very tired) core she wasn't bluffing. (Chase yelled another "duìbuqǐ" after us.)

As I nipped at her heels like when I was little, my mouth couldn't stop running, keeping in time with my feet. "You can't just say you *forbid* it, no reason given, and expect me to follow," I told her. "You said I could date if the boy was Chinese, and ta-freaking-da, Mǔqīn—I did the impossible and found a Chinese boy in the middle of Whites 'R' Us. One I actually like!"

"Aren't you going to bask in being right?" I pressed on. "I bonded with him *because* he's Chinese, just like you predicted. You win!" It pained me to force those words out. "So what's the problem?"

She halted and turned back to me. There was so much swimming beneath her hard gaze that I sent a silent prayer up to a god, any god, for a peek beneath. Then the . . . wistfulness? . . . in her eyes disappeared, leaving behind only coldness and determination, and, well . . . shit.

"You don't even know him," I whispered.

"*You* don't know him, Ali! Or his family!" Her voice was as sharp as a saber. "If you don't come home with me right now, it means you don't trust me to have your best interest at heart, in which case you don't need to live under my roof. Your choice."

My next words flew out faster than a tornado kick. "Does this have something to do with the park? With Chu or Liang something? Is the Chu from that article someone from our family?" When she didn't answer, I kept rapid-firing. "Why is this so serious you feel you need a safe to keep Bǎbá and me out? You already do a good enough job with your face and personality."

Her only response was to slam her car door. For a brief second I considered not following her home (I could take my dad's car and run), but I didn't really have a choice, did I?

Zhu Yingtai
Hangzhou, China

Shanbo cleared his throat, which he did often, but this time it was on purpose—one of many habits I could read after spending several weeks on high alert as his roommate.

"How do you do it?" he asked, his pitch too high, as if his taut nerves had also tightened his vocal cords.

I slowly shifted my attention to him, scared he knew my secret. Had he noticed how often I wore a hat, sometimes even to bed, and subsequently inferred that it was because I was too uncomfortable with the foreign draft on my newly half-bald head? Or had my womanly bleeding left a spot somewhere, and he hadn't been able to find the source wound and consequently deduced my true gender?

"I spend all my time studying, yet I am always behind," he continued. "How are you soaring? I mean, I am overjoyed for you"—he scratched his scalp, his braid shifting back and forth with each stroke—"but I don't know what else to do." He chuckled.

"*Perhaps you are just smarter than me, gentle Shunan.*"

Would he still admit that if he knew my true gender?

Instead of saying the first few thoughts that had formed in my head, I asked, "*Why does it matter? As long as you are learning, understanding the information, isn't that most important?*"

Shanbo sighed, so heavily that it dragged me down too. "*My family is struggling,*" he said. "*We have made . . . some mistakes.*" His already-faraway look grew glassier, and I pondered whether he was seeing his hunchback brother in his mind's eye. "*I need to do well to raise my family's status. My parents have been trying to match me with a woman from a prestigious family, but there are no takers.*

"*There is just so much pressure,*" Shanbo continued. "*I want to honor my parents and ancestors, of course, but sometimes I worry I'm not the man for the job.*"

Yes, this I understood. My mother was constantly pressuring me to be someone I never could. Sometimes I was so weary; other times I was so angry I thought of burning the world down.

"*I also worry I'm not the man for the job,*" I said carefully, feeling each word with my tongue before it left my mouth. I amuse myself.

Shanbo's eyebrows drew together in surprise. "*What do you have to worry about?*"

"*Same as you, honoring my family in my marriage.*" I paused for a moment and came to a decision: I would let him in on one secret, the mildest one. Perhaps I shouldn't be helping the competition, but how well I tested would have no bearing on my *future, unfortunately.* "After the sun sets, I go outside and study by the outhouse where they leave the lanterns burning."

Shanbo chuckled. "And here I just thought you had a bowel issue."

Oh, how I wanted to laugh. If only my mother knew I was here, my head partly shaved, talking to a man about my bowels . . . I laughed with Shanbo—freely, as only a man could.

CHAPTER 9

PAPA BEAR

I followed my mǔqīn home in a haze, the aftershocks of the shit storm still rolling in. When we arrived, she came in just long enough to snarl "I wish you were a boy" to me, and "Deal with her" to my father. Then she left on foot to who knows where. (To the mysterious park, perhaps? To see Liang or Chu something?)

From his perch on the couch, my father patted the spot beside him. For a moment I longed for the bǎbá I'd known when I was young: clean-shaven, openly affectionate, finding any excuse to hug me. That vibrant, goofy version of him was now covered in apathy and salt-and-pepper stubble that would probably sting on contact (though I would welcome the pain, a reminder he was actually embracing me, near me, wanting me).

"What happened?" he asked, and my traitorous mind filled in the last two words for him: "niū niū," my childhood nickname, which he hadn't used in years. I wasn't sure if he'd stopped because it was a term for little girls or because he no longer talked to me enough to warrant a second way to address me. Or a first.

"Um, she's being really strict." I wanted to ask him why my mother was forbidding Chase and me from being together, but I couldn't bring myself to tell him what had happened. We'd never talked about boys before, and I had a feeling he wouldn't exactly be proud papa bear if he knew I'd been sucking a boy's face on the roof of the library a little while ago.

He nodded. "She's doing her best—you know that, right?" I said nothing, partly from shock that he was defending her but also because I didn't agree. "I'm . . . sorry . . . that she's constantly saying the thing about wishing you were a boy." I stiffened. "I don't want you to blame yourself. You didn't do anything wrong."

Obviously, I thought, but my father's assurance revealed it wasn't obvious to him.

I tried to make a joke. "If anything, you're the one most in charge of my gender."

He laughed, and I felt safe . . . until he said, "That's not what I meant, but yes, you're right about that. I meant you shouldn't feel bad about causing her infertility."

My entire body and even my mind froze for a moment. "What?"

His eyes widened. "Oh! I, uh, thought you knew. Your mother

became infertile giving birth to you. So she never got to try again, and . . ."

He didn't have to say it. I heard the words as clear as cooked glass noodles: *she never got to have a boy, and she blames you, Ali.*

Was this why she treated me the way she did? Was there so much resentment that she couldn't see past it to the child who *did* exist, the one who was more than ready to receive her mother's love? Why did having a boy even matter?

"She loves you even though she doesn't say it," he continued. "That's not our way. We show our love by sacrificing so you have food in your belly, a roof over your head. You don't see everything she's given up for you—did you know she used to be a brilliant painter? But she gave that up when you came along."

But why? No one asked her to, certainly not me.

Then, slowly, as if he wasn't sure whether it was okay for him to voice it aloud, my father said, "Your mother is headstrong. She knows what she wants and she'll do what it takes to get it, even if . . . it means forsaking her parents. Life has been unkind to her, and she's doing the best she can. I'm glad we're here, in America, Ali, because you take after her. If we weren't here, you'd probably never fit in, just like your mother never did."

I shifted away from him, unwilling to let him see in my eyes how he was wrong: I still didn't fit in, even here in America.

"What happened with Mā?" I asked quietly, not wanting to spook the truth away. Because I had seen a glimpse of it in his eyes—there was a lot to my mother's story I'd never heard.

"It was a long time ago." He opened the book in his lap, signaling an end to the conversation.

It was how every discussion about the past ended. But just because they didn't tell me didn't mean I had to stay in the dark. And regardless of what I discovered or what my mother said, I'd find a way to be with Chase. After all, what was one more secret in this family of hidden truths and buried emotions?

Unfortunately, it wasn't just up to me.

Hours later, when my mother returned, she made a beeline for me. And from the stern, constipated look on her face, I knew what was coming was going to require all the humor I had.

"You cannot get involved with the Yu family. They're no good," she said.

I was *stunned*. That was not what I'd been expecting her to say (yet after it came out, it felt so perfectly Mŭqīn). "How could you *possibly* know that?" I asked.

She ignored me.

"What about their family?" I pressed.

Instead of answering, she stated with authority, "You need to go to China." The time of asking was apparently over.

"What about Chase's family, Mŭqīn?"

She flinched, then continued on about the China trip in rapid, clipped sentences. "You don't have to worry about the money. We're not paying. There's a program: they want to help Asian Americans connect with their roots."

Her focus on another topic enraged me, as if my feelings for

Chase had no meaning to her, which, well, I guess was true given everything she'd done.

I took a stand. "Since you haven't even bothered to tell me why you don't like Chase's family or why you don't want us to be together, I don't need to listen to you. You can't stop me from seeing him; I'm not a prisoner."

I thought I'd won and that I'd either force her to divulge what she knew or relent, but instead, to show me who controlled my world, she removed the bottom left piece from the haphazard Jenga tower that was my life.

"No more kung fu," she said matter-of-factly.

The words knocked the wind out of me like that time I'd bobbed left instead of right and met Marcin's punch square in the chest. She might as well have said *No more food* or *No more breathing*, the way my gut had sunk into my pelvic floor. It wasn't even about Chase anymore—kung fu was the one place I truly felt like myself.

"I'll do anything," I said softly as my eyes remained glued to the floor by her feet. "If I promise not to date him, can I have kung fu back?" I was ashamed by how quickly I'd caved, but I was also desperate and completely at her mercy. I could see Chase behind her back, have my cake and eat it too. What was she going to do, make me wear a body cam?

She lowered her eyes and shook her head, only a slight jerk of the chin.

"What could possibly be so bad about his family that you would destroy me like this just to keep us apart?"

She didn't answer.

"Mǎmá, wǒ xūyào gōngfū," I begged.

"Why?"

Her use of English in response to my Mandarin felt like a slap. Was that what it felt like for her every time I spoke English? I never thought about it because her English was fluent, but of course she was less comfortable in it than her native tongue, just like I was fluent in Mandarin but strayed from it because it felt foreign in my mouth, like salt water coating my tongue.

She put her hands on her hips. "Why do you need kung fu, Ali?"

Here was my chance to show her a piece of my soul. I could finally explain how kung fu filled in the missing piece of me, made me whole, and without it I felt weak, inconsequential, unseen.

But I couldn't get those words out. All I managed was "I just need it. This isn't even about him, Mǎmá. Please."

Of course, just like everything else, it wasn't enough.

CHAPTER 10

ALIGNED

At two in the morning, I was lying in my bed staring, at the lone glow-in-the-dark star on the ceiling, when I decided I would make my own fate. It was also no coincidence my name was at the beginning of "aligned," right?

Without bothering to change out of my oversize long-sleeve tee and sweatpants, I grabbed the Vaseline tub plus a flashlight and set them by the window. Then I snatched my Feiyues from their place by my gym bag, but I had to lean against the wall for a moment when I realized they were now apparently relegated to late-night trysts with Chase—no more butterflies or tornado kicks, no more panther walks on my beloved practice-hall floor, no more, no more, no more.

I used the emotion to fuel me. First I Vaselined my rickety, otherwise-noisy window with determination. Then, as slow as a sloth, I eased it open, using three fingers to create a gap big enough for me to squeeze through.

Once the in-case-of-emergency rope ladder was unfurled, I climbed out, then left the window ajar, just enough so my fingers could slip in on return. I scaled down easily thanks to my callused hands, strong (albeit tired) core, and trusty Feiyues. Instead of rushing, I took a moment to relish the burn creeping up my forearms, trying to savor it.

The autumn chill breathed life into my lungs, and I ran wild in the shadows, a caged animal freed.

On my way to Chase's house, I stopped to shove some pebbles in my pocket but otherwise kept a steady jog. Actually, it was more like a sprint, because I just couldn't wait. By the time I reached his neighborhood, I super regretted that (1) I hadn't brought a water bottle and (2) I hadn't looked up which house on White Lane was his. Curiosity didn't kill the cat; it was lack of planning.

But then I saw it as if a giant Chinese spotlight from God was shining down on the brick house with the upside-down *fú* character on the door, announcing to the entire neighborhood the Yu family's desire for luck as well as their ethnicity. What good luck for me.

I shined my flashlight on the house, taking care not to aim

directly in a window as I tried to figure out which room was Chase's. I circled around the backyard, and then there it was: a lone weeping willow. And only one window was facing it.

Okay, I'm calling it: two misalignments does *equal alignment.* If I could find a way to talk to my mother, maybe I'd show her all the proof that this shit was meant to be. *Willow tree, you are forgiven, and I am now honored to have been compared to you.*

I took aim and threw pebble after pebble.

After a couple of minutes, Chase's light came on and he appeared at the window, his clothes and hair disheveled. His face completely changed when he saw me, and he yanked his window up and basically parkoured his way down to me.

Um, so freaking, unbelievably hot.

I wanted to jump on him when he got close, but I held back. For some reason, even though our tongues had been in each other's mouths not that long ago, awkwardness stood between us.

We hovered like prepubescents scared of cooties before he patted my shoulder in the saddest hello.

"Sorry," he said sheepishly. "I guess I just . . . don't know where your head's at, and I don't know where we stand. . . ."

"We're in your backyard."

He laughed, and the bubble of tension burst.

"I'm so sorry about everything," he said, the sympathy in his eyes softening me.

"You didn't do anything wrong."

He peered at me curiously. "I just meant it was terrible, and I'm sorry you had to go through it."

"Oh. Thank you." I wasn't sure how to react; no one had ever cared about how things affected *me*.

"So what happened after you went home? How bad was it?" he asked.

"She said no more kung fu," I whispered reluctantly, almost as if saying it out loud would make it more official, even though it was already as real as it could get.

He pulled me into a hug. "That's so awful."

I felt my muscles relaxing of their own accord, and our bodies melted further into each other. A strong hand stroked my back up and down.

"Maybe it doesn't feel as awful anymore," I said into his neck.

He leaned back, making me wish I hadn't said anything. "Sorry, I couldn't hear. What'd you say?"

"Nothing," I mumbled, my face returning to its nook.

We stood like that for what felt like hours, though in reality it was probably five minutes. I'd never been able to just *be* with someone like this before, and instead of worrying what I should be saying or doing, I just *was*.

I savored the warmth of being cocooned and tried to store it up so I'd be able to dole it out later when I was alone again.

Eventually we untangled, but he had to initiate it. Part of me wanted to pull him back to exactly where our limbs and torsos had been, but I didn't.

He poked my pocket where the remaining rocks weighed it down. "How'd you find my window?"

I winked at him, then pointed to the weeping willow. "It's

now one of my favorite parts of Indiana: you, the tree, and . . . actually"—a light bulb went off in my head—"follow me."

His eyes twinkled with mischief as a huge grin spread across his face.

It was my turn to dazzle him, and I meant that quite literally.

I led him down the street, traversed a dirt path, then trespassed (just a bit) to reach our destination.

"Where are we going?" he asked for the fiftieth time.

"I told you—just wait."

"I don't need the surprise. I'll enjoy it more if I can know now and anticipate it."

I chuckled. "Trust me—for this one, it's better if you just see."

He finally quieted.

We were nearing the entrance to a cornfield. "I'm taking you through here for the full Indiana experience," I explained as I pulled him toward the tall stalks of my favorite crop.

We entered their shelter. I tried to put everything with my mother behind me to focus on the now: I was with Chase, we'd find a way, and *I* controlled my destiny.

Hand in hand we zigzagged through the neat pathways in the perfectly planted maize maze. The cornstalks danced in the wind, and I bobbed and weaved with them, sparring and high-fiving their giant leaves. Chase whooped and danced with me, and I could tell from the pure joy on his face that he was taking in every detail of the sky, the field, and me.

As we trekked deeper into the heart of the crops, journeying far-

ther and farther from the streetlamps, I retrieved the flashlight from my pocket and turned it on. Chase's hand tightened around mine, and I chuckled to myself. The city mouse in the dark, unknown country—I knew that kind of fear intimately. I'd never grown to love it here, but I had learned to appreciate one thing—something I couldn't wait to show him. Something I'd never shared with anyone else.

We stepped out of the corn into an open meadow. The night was so full of promise and magic that, for a moment, it felt like we were leaving the Triwizard Maze. The tall cornstalks looked just like the overgrown walls from the movie, except in our case there weren't any monsters creeping out to hurt us.

Just fireflies.

I shut the flashlight off, drowning us in darkness, and Chase's hand gripped mine even tighter . . . until a moment later I heard the sharp inhale, and he let go so he could turn in a circle.

In the empty field, thousands of fireflies flickered on and off, little pops of magic. We stood side by side, watching nature's light show in silence, as it was meant to be.

Eventually he took both my hands in his, facing me, but still neither of us spoke, like we didn't want to break the spell that was shielding us from reality. His lips found mine, and we came together naturally, softly, sweetly.

It was the stuff of epic romances, and if it hadn't been happening to me, I would've guessed it was fiction. Because how could something like that be real, especially for a lone-star weirdo?

Unfortunately, reality seeped back in as we made our way back to Chase's.

Nervously he asked, "So did your mom say anything else? Do you have any idea why she's so against us being together?"

It was like he knew.

You cannot get involved with the Yu family. They're no good.

"Um . . ." I hesitated a moment, but I eventually repeated her words to him, cringing as I said them.

His entire body stiffened.

I waited.

And waited. Waited for him to say something, to either explain her words or question them, but neither response came.

"No good," I repeated to nudge him. To ask again.

He flinched. "I heard you the first time."

"And?" I pressed.

"And it's a tough thing to hear. Did she tell you why she said that?"

I shook my head, unable to offer any theories because my brain was fully preoccupied at the moment. Was Chase keeping things from me? How had my mother found out whatever it was she knew? How had she known to look? Was it Mr. Laurelson?

Chase increased the distance between us—consciously or subconsciously, I wasn't sure. "Do you think she's just saying that as an excuse, a lie?" he asked. "Your mom might just not be ready for you to date . . . anyone."

"She used to always tell me I was only allowed to date Chinese boys."

"Well, maybe that was her way to keep you from dating—by

making up that rule because, conveniently, there were no Chinese boys around. Then when I showed up, she had to improvise. Maybe her objection has nothing to do specifically with me or my family."

That certainly sounded plausible. Maybe Chase was right. And maybe my mom's secrets were unrelated—she'd certainly had them before he showed up.

"Well, regardless of the why," I said, "how are we going to do this? Keep sneaking out at night? We'll have to plan so far in advance—she took my phone earlier." I grabbed his forearm. "Oh crap, you didn't try to contact me, did you?"

He covered his mouth with his hand. "Oh God, she saw my sexts?"

I shoved him playfully, and we traded a few jabs back and forth along the side of the empty street in front of his house.

"Don't worry, she has a soft spot in her heart for penises," I told him between kicks.

He gagged as he swerved left, then right. "Don't tell me shit like that. Gross."

I laughed as I easily blocked his punches, an instinct. "I was joking about how she wishes I were a boy."

"Ah, one of those situations. Sad." He stopped sparring. "Well, my parents have two boys. One's . . . gone . . . and they aren't too fond of me, so it's not all it's cracked up to be, is it?"

I waited, standing completely still, hoping he would say more, but speak of the devil . . . there was a throat clearing from the direction of Chase's house.

We turned at the same time, and as I came face-to-top-of-the-head with his mom, I crossed my fingers that she was nothing like my mǔqīn.

She looked weary in a different way than my mother, and I wondered what she had seen.

"Chase," she said, her voice pained, and I wondered if it was because of this moment or a long history. "Please."

And that was it. I had no idea what to make of it.

"We're just having a conversation," he said, completely calm. "No need to worry yourself. You should get some rest."

His mother wrung her hands. "Did you . . . you wouldn't . . ."

"Mā, there's nothing to worry about, okay?" He sounded as tired as she looked.

They spoke to each other as if they were strangers tiptoeing on eggshells—ones they had smashed onto the floor themselves a long, long time ago.

She nodded, then turned to me and introduced herself. "Yu Āyí."

"Yu Āyí hǎo," I said immediately. "Sorry to have interrupted your sleep. I had something urgent to talk to Chase about, and my phone broke. I'm Ali. Chase's . . . friend."

"I know who you are," she answered. Then she scrutinized me. As her narrowed eyes traveled up, then down, I was just waiting for her to ask me if my mother knew I was here. I had the lies already loaded on my tongue, but she merely nodded before retreating back into the house.

"What the hell?" I whispered, searching Chase's face for some answers.

He didn't say anything, just stared after his mother.

"Is she going to tell my mom I was here?" I asked as my mind pictured her looking up the only Asian name in the school directory this instant. I also wanted to know what Chase had told her about me, but this was more pressing.

He shook his head. "You definitely don't have to worry about that, I promise."

"How can you know that?" When he didn't answer, I said, "I get it in some ways—the distance, the unfamiliarity—but how did you get so much control? Tell me your secrets."

A darkness crossed his features. "It's not like that."

"If I could figure out how to have that kind of relationship with my mom, we wouldn't be sneaking around, I'm just saying."

His eyes grew watery, which stopped my running mouth cold. I completely clammed up, unsure how to turn the oncoming tide.

"Are you absolutely sure I don't have to worry about my mom?" I asked again, quietly this time.

He nodded. "I'm a hundred percent positive. Trust me." Then, his voice still among the eggshells, he said, "C'mon, I'll walk you home."

I didn't protest, mostly because I couldn't find any words, but the entire walk back, all I could think about was how he hadn't told his mother where he was going, she hadn't asked, and, overall, there was something there I didn't understand.

I needed to know what he was hiding. And since he wasn't telling me, a Swiss-cheese plan with gaping holes took shape in my head, an idea so terrible it was irresistible. And I would need a partner in crime—one who, unfortunately, would have to be kept in the dark about my true intentions.

CHAPTER 11

ADD FOOD

Since I had flopped face-first onto the bed at five in the morning (falling asleep before my nose made contact), it felt like I'd only slept ten minutes when my alarm blared.

Given our late-night tryst, it was no surprise that Chase and I both fell asleep at school the next (the same?) day. And in Mr. Robinson's class, to boot . . .

"Oi!" he yelled, snapping his fingers. "You're *both* asleep? Been sneaking out late at night?"

I wanted to chuck my pencil at him, even though he was right (for once).

"Everyone saw that one coming, *whaaaaaat!*" some douche yelled from the last row.

Robinson chuckled, then turned back to the board. "This is your one and only warning. Enjoy the rice paddies on the weekends, okay, kids?"

Every last fuse of mine lit. As they crackled to the root, I knew this would blow up in a nuclear meltdown of swears, insults, and who knew what else.

But before I could find my words, Wendy Pemberton, of all people, jumped in. "Jesus, Mr. Robinson, can you give it a rest already? If you want to be funny, at least come up with something original."

I don't think Wendy and I had spoken since . . . fifth grade? When I'd told her I'd never had brownies before. I think she had side-eyed me in response?

That plus the fact that she was one of the more popular kids left me speechless.

Chase, however, did not know the social hierarchy and was not fazed, calling out, "Rice paddies, really? It's racist but so lazy. Should I assume all of you are hanging out at the hot dog factory this weekend?"

I racked my brain for something to say, but all I could think about was how Robinson hadn't been that far off, since cornfields were essentially the American analog to rice paddies. The anger bubbled up and erupted as I yelled, "Wángbā dàn!"

I hadn't meant to say it in Chinese—it was just how the thought had formed in my head.

Mr. Robinson's face finally turned serious. "What did you just say?"

"She called you a turtle's egg," Chase answered honestly, leaving out that he was giving the direct word-for-word translation and not what the term actually meant to Chinese folks, which was, for some reason, "son of a bitch."

Chase and I burst into laughter. I couldn't get over the irony—how the very thing that had led to our discrimination had become our secret weapon—and I just kept going until tears pooled in my eyes.

"Allie's lost it—boning Chase must've flipped some switch in her," someone whispered from the other side of the room.

I gave them the finger. With both hands.

"Counselor's office," Robinson said calmly, pointing to the door. His voice was even, but his face was flushed and his eyes tight. Chase and I air high-fived, then left the room holding hands as a statement. Everyone else could suck it.

As we journeyed to the other end of the school, we walked in silence until one of us couldn't take it anymore and whispered "turtle egg," which would result in us doubling over in laughter. Rinse and repeat. It didn't seem the joke would ever get old.

And then I almost peed myself when Chase turned to me and said, "What do you think that one asshole turtle did in ancient China to fuck it up for the rest of them?"

I think we might have stopped in the hallway and laughed for a minute straight, me bent over at the waist, supporting myself on my knees, and Chase leaning back, clutching his belly.

When we reached the front office to find it empty—even Mrs.

Dumas's post—I clapped my hands, shocking Chase. Finding a time when the office would be vacant had been one of the Swiss-cheese holes in my scheme, and bada bing, bada boom, Fate was handing it to me on a silver platter, maybe as recompense for Racist Robinson.

I grinned mischievously. "This is perfect. You see, I have this plan. . . ."

I was crouched beside Mr. Laurelson's locked office door.

"Jiā yóu, jiā yóu!" Chase chanted while waving imaginary pom-poms.

"You're supposed to be keeping a lookout, not telling me to add oil," I murmured, not taking my eyes off Chase's lockpicks in my hands.

He laughed. "I never thought about that before. Funny how that works, you know? You memorize that 'jiā yóu' is how you cheer people on, and you never stop to think about what the words mean."

"Emphasis on the *you*, Yu. Some of us think about it."

I imagined him rolling his eyes but didn't look up to check—I didn't have much time, especially since Chase had to run to his locker earlier to grab the lockpicks.

"Isn't it funny that they chose 'add oil'?" he continued. "Or I guess it could be 'add gasoline,' which makes a little more sense. But why not, like, 'add food,' especially when we're cheering on a human? Jiā fàn! We can say 'jiā yóu' if we're cheering a car on."

Well, I knew what phrase I would be using in the future to

encourage Chase. I peeked at him for a moment and saw that he was staring at me with a lopsided grin on his face. "Eyes on the front door!" I admonished. "Mrs. Dumas could be back any second!" Seriously, he had *one job*. But I couldn't keep from smirking as I turned back to the lock.

"You should've let me do this part," Chase said as he nudged my foot with his.

"That's the thanks I get for making sure your fingerprints aren't all over this?" I didn't voice the real reason, which was that Mr. Laurelson would be easier to deal with if I was the one most at fault for the B&E.

I was after Chase's shiny blue binder, which I was convinced held his origin story. And this would also give me access to my own file, which might very well contain some answers, given the buffet of notes I could sample from and the fact that my mother had, for some reason, spoken to Mr. Laurelson about Chase even before she'd caught us attached at the lips.

Of course . . . I'd only told Chase about my desire to dig into my own files. When he had followed up with "What do you think you'll find?" I, in full spy mode, had answered smartly and slyly, "I don't know. How about we remove the interrogation light from my eyes now?" Too bad the spy I'd been channeling was Mr. Bean's Johnny English. Like I said earlier, it was a Swiss-cheese plan, okay?

If Chase noticed something was off, he didn't say anything. Probably because he'd just assumed the weirdness was me being me. Who knew that would ever serve me well?

My palms sweated like an Asian American art major at Thanksgiving dinner, but finally, one more twist and . . . click. I had so much adrenaline coursing through me I couldn't believe I'd fallen asleep in class a short while ago.

"Stay out here," I whispered to Chase as I ducked inside.

"I'm familiar with the plan," he said as he took his rabble-rouser seat—fittingly, I might add.

"Always has to get the last word," I muttered even though he couldn't hear me anymore.

I *did* feel terrible going behind the back of the one adult in this school who trusted me, but I also reminded myself that I was keeping Mr. Laurelson from having to make a tough decision. Better for me to steal the information than have him break any rules to give it to me—so, really, I was doing him a favor.

No time for this. After breaking into the filing cabinet, which only took a couple of seconds because the lock was ancient, I went straight for the lone blue binder. Then I snatched up the bloated green binder that stuck out like my thumb after my last butterfly twist attempt gone wrong. Both so easy to locate among the rest, just like me and Chase.

As soon as the binders were open, side by side, on the desk, I switched to turbo mode, snapping photos of each page—with Chase's cell phone, since my mom still had mine. It was quite the wrench in my not-at-all-thought-out plan, since I was lying to him and thus would have to transfer and delete his files before I returned his phone.

Yes, it bothered me that he was trusting me with something as personal as his phone and here I was, liar liar pants on . . . smolder, but he was the one being so cagey about his weird relationship with his mom. And if my endgame was to find a way for us to be together, that nullified any wrongdoing, right? Right.

Just as I was reaching the last few pages, I heard three cacaws from the other side of the door. That lovable weirdo. Chase had insisted on birdcalls, but I'd told him to cough or talk loudly—you know, normal things easy to cover up. I thought we had agreed on mine, but apparently not.

I rushed through the last bit, but I got what I came for and more.

After putting everything back in place, I glided to the door and tap-tappity-tap-tapped—our secret code—before hearing the tap-tippy-tap response that signaled the coast was clear.

"What was the 'cacaw' for?" I asked as I slipped out and fiddled to relock the door.

"Nothing. You can go back in if you need to. I just *really* wanted to cacaw. I still believe it's the better signal."

I finished and we moved toward the exit. "Except they cacaw in comedy and use coughs and other *actually* stealthy signals in serious spy movies, so I guess that means I'm the James Bond and you're the Johnny English."

He laughed. "Fair enough. And . . . maybe I cacawed because I missed you."

The twinge of guilt I felt for lying to him was fleeting, because he wrapped his arms around my waist and kissed me until I could no longer feel my lips or knees.

Once we left the scene of the crime, I led Chase to the poorly lit, ancient computer lab, which was (shocker) empty when we arrived.

Chase drew a smiley face in the dust on one of the screens. "So, uh, why are we here?"

I pointed to his phone. "Uploading the photos to my Dropbox so we don't lose them."

And because I don't know if I'll be able to look at all of yours before I'll need to delete them.

He tried to clean off the nearest station but ended up generating a dust storm. As he dissolved in a fit of coughs and struggled to pull his shirt over his nose, I used the distraction to hurry and get everything in motion. When the upload progress bar appeared, I relaxed slightly, then scanned through the files on his phone in an attempt to sneak a couple of his pages in.

Chase used his sleeve to wipe the monitor in front of us. "Do you want to pull them up on the screen?" His voice was muffled and slightly nasal from the neckline pressing down on his nose.

Hello, Swiss-cheese hole. Of course he would ask that. I hesitated, continuing to read as fast as I could while the other half of my mind worked to plug up the hole.

"But we don't have to," he added quickly. "You don't have to share your files with me if it makes you uncomfortable."

I felt like the disgusting human being I was. I briefly considered just spilling it all, but then I saw him gazing at me with that kind, hopeful look he reserved for me; I couldn't say anything that would jeopardize that.

He'll never know, I reassured myself.

Or you could just ask him about his family, a tiny voice said, but I had already thought this through. If the shoes were reversed, I would rather he find out about my family from anywhere but me.

"Let me just weed through these useless pages," I stalled. "Just . . . trying to find something . . . interesting."

I had no clue what I was looking for—it would've been nice if there'd been a big red arrow pointing to exactly what I needed—but there had to be *something* in my files that was related to my mother's objections. Something I could pull up on the screen so I could stop acting as shady as Shady Pines on an overcast day.

Most pages were Mr. Laurelson's notes about my mother with some thoughts scribbled on the side.

Monthly meeting to discuss Ali's progress. Expressed my concern of too much pressure. Do not think I communicated effectively; she kept mentioning shame, Ali's future prospects, her husband's failure. Worried she is increasing the pressure on Ali because of Mr. Chu.

Note to self: check in with Ali.

Note to self: Isn't Mr. Chu a professor?

But then I reached the date around the time Chase first showed up.

> Mentioned Chase to Ali's mother during monthly
> progress meeting, thinking she might be friends with
> Mrs. Yu.

My fists clenched; I thought Mr. Laurelson was better than that.

> Not only did Mrs. Chu not know her, but she seemed
> concerned. Asked me personal, in-depth questions about
> Chase and the Yus (which of course I did not answer
> because of confidentiality).

> Note to self: don't bring up the Yus in the future. Keep
> an eye on Ali and Chase.

Hmm, so it sounded like my mother first learned about Chase from Mr. Laurelson. I wasn't sure what to make of that.

I swiped until I found the note from my rabble-rousing:

> Ali and Chase sent to the office today. Coincidence
> because of the race-related incident in class, or
> something else? Was Mrs. Chu right to worry since Ali
> has not been sent here in a long time?

Well, that sucked. Chase wasn't making me more of a rabble-rouser—well, he was, but it wasn't a bad thing.

My swipes grew jerky with anger.

Then, finally, I paused on the second-to-last page of my file as if there *were* flashing red lights on it, not just because it would plug the hole, but also because I was genuinely onto something. I pulled it up on the monitor so Chase could look too.

Mrs. Chu called three times today and left messages asking to transfer Chase Yu out of Ali's classes.

I checked the date and time. Early this morning. I continued reading.

Called back and explained this was not possible without a legitimate reason (which she did not provide—she just said "it's important"). Tried to bribe me with homemade scallion pancakes. I refused. She proceeded to threaten me, and I gave her another warning. Warning 2 (this week).

Oh, Mǔqīn. That was like trying to bribe a lactose-intolerant person with a trip to Shady Pines. My mother's scallion pancakes were the best in a hundred-mile radius, but they would've given Mr. Laurelson diarrhea since, by his own admission, he was used to boiled chicken and sandwiches, not something called "scallion *oil* pancakes" in their native language.

Because my mind was functioning at max capacity, it took me a minute to realize Chase was silent. When I finally broke away from the screen to look at him, his expression tugged at my heartstrings.

"Why does she dislike me so much?" he whispered. His words

were questioning, but his tone gave them a hypothetical edge, like he already suspected something.

I placed a hand on his. "We'll get to the bottom of it." His look of both hope and fear was not lost on me.

I picked up the phone again (with no explanation to Chase of why I wasn't using the monitor), and I didn't have to scan much further to locate another flashing-lights page. At the end of the binder, from later this morning, was this:

Mrs. Chu called about the best timing for Ali to miss school to visit China. When I suggested waiting until the summer, she grew upset and huffed that that was "no longer an option." When I asked with concern whether there was a family emergency, she said something confusing about how her family was from Hangzhou, where Ali would definitely not be visiting, and that I would never be able to understand.

Well, shit. Why was waiting no longer an option? Did this have to do with Chase?

"Your family's from Hangzhou?" Chase said, reading over my shoulder.

I jumped in surprise and just managed to avoid banging Chase in the chin with my shoulder.

"Sorry," he said sheepishly.

"Good job, Agent English," I said, even though I was the true Johnny English here. And actually, he *was* onto something.

"You know, I never knew we were from Hangzhou before."

I pulled up a window on the computer and searched for "parks in Hangzhou, China, Liang, Chu."

Chase pointed to the "Chu." "If this is in China, the pinyin spelling would be 'Z-h-u.'"

"Brilliant, double-oh-seven," I said as I made the change and hit enter.

Two hundred fifty-one thousand hits, down from several million. Progress!

And at the top, through whatever school-library database we were connected to: a book and movie not available here but stocked at the Chicago Public Library.

The Butterfly Lovers: Liang Shanbo and Zhu Yingtai.

"That sounds vaguely familiar," Chase said, pointing at the screen and leaving a smudge in the dust from excitement.

I nodded slowly, thrilled we were finally moving forward but clueless as to how everything fit together. "My mom used to tell me the story all the time when I was little."

"It was a tragedy, right? Star-crossed lovers?"

"Aren't all Chinese folktales tragedies?" I typed in "Liang Shanbo Zhu Yingtai Park." Together, Chase and I read about the park dedicated to the Butterfly Lovers—yes, located in Hangzhou—with a temple, fountain, and garden. Nothing matched the photos I'd glimpsed from my mother's stack, but that didn't mean much, since I'd barely registered anything that day during the frenzy.

I refamiliarized myself with the "Liang Zhu" epic love story: families don't approve, boy dies from heartbreak, girl goes to his grave on her wedding day, and then the usual—grave opens up, girl jumps in, boy and girl turn into butterflies to live happily ever after together as insects. The Chinese *Romeo and Juliet*.

Nothing felt even remotely related to me (except for the obvious, that Chase and I were star-crossed lovers of a sort, but that clearly had nothing to do with my mom's motivations, since we were star-crossed because of *her*).

"I feel like we could find out more if we could type Chinese characters," I said, closing the tabs in frustration. "Have you ever tried looking this kind of stuff up? It's impossible. Although we're making strides. At least there are translation options, even if they aren't great. And there's definitely entertainment value there."

Chase sat up straighter. "'All your base are belong to us'?"

"I was thinking more along the lines of how I once saw a picture online of a Chinatown store called Fuck Goods because they translated 'gān' wrong." That dried-goods store probably attracted the wrong kind of English-speaking customer.

He laughed. "You win."

I looked at the familiar tilt of his lips and the crinkle in his eyes that showed up only when he was amused or happy. Or looking at me. "Yeah, I really did win, didn't I?"

We didn't get much sleuthing done after that, and we certainly dusted off a fair share of the table.

Zhu Yingtai
Hangzhou, China

My gargantuan, non-lotus steps banged onto the rigid, unyielding floor, little jolts of satisfaction that, though painful, reminded me how immensely lucky I was. Still, as the class discussion of Su Dongpo's poem grew into a broader analysis of foot-binding, it had taken every last drop of self-control to keep from voicing my unpopular opinions.

"Shunan," Shanbo said gently from behind me as I reached the door to our room.

Stuffing my anger back into its box—a skill that I, as a female, had been forced to deftly hone through the years—I turned to him and responded to my fake name with a fake smile. "What can I do for you?"

"What is troubling you?" The genuine concern in his eyes was as frightening as his ability to read me so accurately.

A deep laugh made its way out of my mouth, slightly strained from the revelation that Shanbo saw more than he let on. "Nothing is troubling me. Don't waste your time worrying about matters that do not exist."

Shanbo put a hand on my shoulder, and I just barely fought off the urge to shrink away.

"You can tell me," he said, entering our room and perching on his bed such that his right ear seemed to be leaning toward me, waiting.

My mind churned, struggling to stay one step ahead of my mouth. "I have a sister. We're close." Almost one and the same, in fact.

And before I knew it, almost as if I had become a puppet and somewhere there was a god manipulating me for his amusement, I was weaving Shanbo a tale . . . except it wasn't a tale in the least. As I told him about how my "sister" with a warrior's spirit had refused to bind her feet into "tiny deformed claws," I glanced down at my gigantic, twenty-three-centimeter feet, so many lengths larger than those of every other girl my age. Eight centimeters: that was what the men preferred, half the length of my hand. They liked them dainty and monstrous, a weapon of submission and humiliation.

I hadn't begged to get my way, but I had manipulated. Even though I hated the different places women and men had in society, I knew how to use that same separation to my advantage.

"They have to break my bones," I had cried to my father, adding extra tears to gain sympathy. "Please save me, Fùqīn. You are the only one who can. Surely someone as wealthy and successful as yourself will be able to marry me off without difficulty regardless of the size of my appendages. I throw myself at your mercy, Honorable Wěidà de Fùqīn."

It may have been hard to stomach, but I had saved my feet, and even though I hadn't known it at the time, my life. Otherwise I could never have passed for a man, could never have snuck my way in here.

"Your sister sounds wonderful," Shanbo said, his eyes unfocused, dreamy. "Quite the spirit."

My mask dropped for a moment and a tiny gasp escaped from my lips. Obedient, sān-cóng-sì-dé kind of women were the coveted brides, not boisterous women like myself, whom my mother deemed too manly to be married off. (The irony of that comment was not lost on me—she didn't even begin to understand just how manly I could be.) I was already breaking the first third of the three obediences—I wasn't obeying my parents before marriage—so how could my future husband expect me to obey him in matrimony, and then my son after his death?

"You're lucky we're rich," my mother would always say, meaning that at least some poor family—poor both in wealth and in luck— would maybe accept my disobedience for the large dowry that would accompany me. When my father had told her we wouldn't be binding my feet—yet another obstacle in her life goal to, essentially, sell me off to another family—she had fainted. I wondered if she had always had that instinct, or if she had developed it because of society. I wondered if, like me, she wanted to scream and stomp and fight. She had tried to manipulate my father by stroking his ego, but he was wrapped around my finger, not hers.

Which was why I was here, and my mother didn't know. She believed I was away learning how to be a better bride, if a place like that even existed. The irony of it all almost felt like a farce.

Shanbo scratched his face with twitchy fingers, and his eyebrows furrowed as he stumbled to find a way to take back his blasphemous words about a non-sān-cóng-sì-dé woman being wonderful.

Before I could think too long and ultimately change my mind, I smiled at him, genuinely, a smile that reflected the inner warmth his words had created. My voice cracked as I said, "My sister . . . she's one of a kind. Ahead of her time."

Shanbo nodded in agreement, then turned away and opened a book, completely oblivious to the pitter-patter pulse on my side of the room. Alas, I couldn't decide if I was happy or disappointed that he hadn't noticed. Or had he?

CHAPTER 12

SANTA SLAYER

Even though I had successfully uploaded the files to my cloud, James Bond–style, I still had to delete them from Chase's phone. Meaning I needed to find a way to sneak off while conveniently "forgetting" to return his phone.

I shook my head as I darted to the girls' bathroom, asking myself if I had to lay it on *quite* so thick. With my use of words like "emergency" and "oh God, it's bad," he probably thought I had explosive diarrhea, which actually didn't upset me as much as it might someone else, because I personally felt the world was way too shy about something *everyone* did. I mean, how many things like that were there in the world? That was one thing Chinese culture got right—

I'd seen the pictures of the Taiwan toilet cafés and poop toys. And my parents, who barely talked about anything, were totally fine discussing (sometimes in great detail) the taboo subject.

I, unfortunately, had learned of the American stigma the hard way, in fifth grade, when I had declared at Suzie's birthday party that I needed to go poo.

Anyway, better for Chase to know about my openness now. And since he nodded seriously and called after me to feel better, I was pretty sure we had an understanding. At the very least he knew I pooped, which sadly, was not a given with some high school boys.

So there I was, in the girls' bathroom, about to wrap up my Swiss-cheese plan, when Brenda came out of one of the stalls. She froze for a second, then washed her hands without meeting my eyes. She wasn't looking at me, but she started talking.

"I'm sorry."

I was so shocked I almost dropped Chase's phone in the sink. So many thoughts: *It's okay. It's not okay. What exactly are you sorry for—just lunch the other day, or the past few years?* But I said nothing.

"Look," she continued, "I'm not going to make excuses, but if you want to know about it from my side . . ." Did I? "I grew up here, and so much of high school is just going along with what everyone else is doing. . . ." I folded my arms across my chest. "So I never really thought about it before. You say what the others say, you know? And you don't really think about the meaning beneath."

"Maybe *you* don't," I muttered, even though I had done the very same thing in my own way.

She placed both palms on the sink as if supporting herself. "Do you remember . . . that time . . ." She was talking so slowly I wanted to tell her to just spit it out, but I waited patiently (on the outside). "When you wanted us to go see that corn maze at that farm and we said we couldn't go? Well, we didn't tell you then, but we were all at Olivia's birthday party. You weren't invited, and Olivia said it was because she didn't think you'd have any fun. But now I'm wondering if it was because she just . . . didn't want you there. You know, because you're . . ." She gestured to me, unable to say "Chinese," like it was a dirty word.

I shrugged even though I swear my chest suddenly hurt. "Who knows what it was," I said, my voice a lot calmer than I felt. "It may not have had to do with my race. Maybe she didn't like how weird I was, or how I didn't like to sing karaoke or ogle the Shady Pines work hands with the rest of you." Whatever it was, there was no denying that Olivia hadn't wanted me there because she didn't like something fundamental about me I couldn't change.

Sometimes race felt muddled in with everything else, just one more thing people could not like about me, just like my personality, but other times it felt like it was on its own level, maybe because it was so inescapable. Before anyone had even talked to me, there it was—*bam!*—in everyone's face: my black, chopstick-straight hair, dark brown eyes, my not-yellow-but-also-not-white skin. When I was little, I forgot I was different because I hardly ever saw myself, and when I was in a group, I gazed out at all pale skin and non-black hair and assumed I mirrored them. It had always confused me when other kids asked about the shape of my eyes, my coloring, and it would take me a minute to remember: *oh yeah, I don't look like them.* But now, it hovered over me like a perpetual rain cloud, and when I was with my (ex-)friends, I'd constantly notice Ava's blond hair, Brenda's freckles, Kyle's green eyes, and I'd wonder what part of me they were noticing. Even now, as Brenda and I stood over the sinks, I couldn't help staring at my reflection and hers, comparing everything. If I lived elsewhere, would I feel like this?

"There was also that other time," Brenda continued, and part of me (Allie) wanted to ask her to stop, but the rest of me needed to know what was coming next, "when Julie told us her dog had never come home and she was pretty sure you'd eaten him."

The urge to hunt Julie down overwhelmed me, but a memory also niggled at the back of my mind, unwelcome. What did it mean that this had actually happened to my mom? I'd found a picture of her, five years old, chubby little arms around a husky larger than her, and when I'd asked for stories, all she had said was, "Jīli was eaten. We left the fence open while moving and she disappeared, and since she never came back, someone probably ate her. So ironic that I named her 'lucky.'"

There were cultures that believed cows were sacred—to them we were barbarians for eating beef, but that didn't seem to bother any of these hamburger scarfers. It all came down to familiarity, which resulted in a fairy wanting children's teeth and a gift-giving fat man being "normal," while my Chinese New Year red envelopes stuffed with money were "weird."

As if she'd read my mind, Brenda said, "Remember when your father came and gave us that Chinese New Year presentation, and you ruined Santa Claus for the class?"

I burst out laughing. Couldn't help it.

We'd just arrived in town, and my father was still excited about teaching, about Chinese culture, about life, and he'd come to my first-grade class to teach the young 'uns about Chinese New Year customs and food. My classmates had picked at the dumplings my mother had labored over, made fun of traditions that until that moment I'd loved, and, worst of all, they had snickered at my father's accent. (Later George F. would say in defense of his China presentation, *How come Mr. Chu gets to speak like that but I can't?*) The snickers became the loudest when my father described setting off firecrackers during New Year's to scare the monsters away.

What monsters? whispered Nick, who everyone looked up to because he was the best at four square. *I stopped believing in monsters when I was three.*

When my father asked me to hand out the chocolate-coin-filled red envelopes, I had yelled, "No! They didn't earn them!" Then I glared at all of them, especially Nick, and said through gritted teeth, "You think you're so smart? You still believe in Santa Claus! *He's. Not. Real.*" When I'd yelled those last three words, most of the class had burst into tears.

I maintain they got what they deserved.

"I'm sorry I laughed at your beliefs," Brenda said quietly.

Ignoring my inclination to shrug it off, I said sincerely, "Thank you for saying that. And for the record, I didn't eat Julie's dog." Though part of me wanted to tell her I did, just as a weird *fuck you.* But I couldn't perpetuate that stereotype further.

"I know."

She laughed, and we shared a nod before parting. It wasn't exactly a touchy-feely moment, and I had no desire to wrap my arms around her or say how much her words had meant to me, but I'd given her all that I could at that moment. I hoped one day she would remember me when she was off in college, maybe meeting new people with a slightly more open mind and heart. I could dream, couldn't I?

CHAPTER 13

ORIGIN STORY

I was *finally* ready to delete Chase's files. And to make sure I had privacy, I was locked in a stall. I'd been in here so long my nose had grown accustomed to the underlying stink of pee and used pads.

Since I was pressed for time, I told myself not to read anything until later. But once I opened the first photo, I couldn't help myself. I skimmed each page before deleting it, learning about how young Chase and not-so-long-ago Chase loved to argue with his teachers about any grade below an A. What an adorable uber-nerd.

As the dates grew closer to the present, I began reading every word.

Chase still won't talk about his brother.
When I ask questions, he stares out the
window.

After several entries along these lines, I came across this one:

Chase finally opened up about Yang
today. It's been one month and three days
since Yang fled and the lawsuit was filed.
Chase finally managed to name one of his
emotions: sad.

His parents are still refusing to meet, either
just with me or with Chase in the room, even
after I stressed how much he needs it.

One week later:

Admitted he was angry today. Progress.

Two weeks later:

All he talks about now is his family's
shame and 面子.

And the last entry from his Flushing school:

Chase informed me of the move. He seemed
very reluctant but couldn't voice it out loud.
Perhaps he's still in shock? Gave him my
contact information.

What did Yang do? Also, why did his brother have a Chinese name while Chase was Chase? And he hadn't been kidding when he said he grew up in a mostly Chinese community—even his school counselor knew Mandarin.

I swiped right, hoping Mr. Laurelson's notes would illuminate things even more.

Shit. The last few photos were blurry—I must've been moving too fast because of the cacaw. I zoomed in and tried to at least pick a few words out, but it was like reading a few errant characters from my mom's article: useless.

Shit . . . this time, literally. Someone had taken up residence in the neighboring stall and was having a much worse day than me. Even though I had been in her exact position many times before (especially in this very same bathroom—like I said, my mom's specialty was *oil* pancakes), the smell was so bad I was having a hard time finding my empathy.

My fingers fumbled as I rushed to delete the rest of the photos, my digits flying faster than Yo-Yo Ma's in concert.

Jeez, what did she have for lunch? I assumed it was all white bread and deli meats for these people, but maybe this was the universe sending me a lesson through this girl's bowels: *Do not judge others by stereotypes, you hypocrite, or you will be forced to smell poo.*

I bolted out of there . . .

. . . and ran right into Chase.

He scratched the back of his head. "Sorry, I just wanted to make sure you were okay."

His face scrunched the second the smell wafting from the still-closing door hit him, and I instinctively yelled, "That wasn't me!" before reminding myself I shouldn't care. "I mean, it would be fine if it had been—everybody poops—but I lied. I was trying to get some privacy to, uh . . ." It was my turn to scratch the back of my head.

I ran through possible excuses but in the end (surprise, surprise), I said nothing else.

He gave me a kind smile. "I know all this is overwhelming. I'm here for you."

All I could think was *What did your brother do?* And *Is this what my mother is so concerned about?*

Since I couldn't ask about any of that, I instead blurted, "Why do you have such a white name?" The remaining words died on my lips: *especially when your brother has a Chinese name.*

His face turned down—quite the rare sight. "My parents didn't, uh, give me much thought," he said, looking straight ahead. "I came along five years after my prized older brother, and they gave him the honor of naming me. He thought it was pretty funny for me to be Chase Yu."

I waited a beat, hoping he'd say more (not just about his name), but nothing came.

"Um, it could've been worse?" I offered.

He laughed. "I guess I could've been Chuck or Dick if he'd been older when I was born?"

"Exactly." I thought for a moment. "If I had the opportunity to name a younger sibling, I would've gone with Pika. Pika Chu."

He burst out laughing. "Okay, maybe my name isn't so bad after all. And . . . maybe Chase Yu doesn't bother me so much anymore, in light of recent events." He winked at me, and I made a mental note to keep up the puns.

"I get it," I said. "I may also know a thing or two about changing how you feel about your name."

His smile was brighter than I'd ever seen, stretching from one side of his face to the other—no tilt.

I wish I could have just enjoyed the moment and basked in his warmth, but all I could think was, *What are you hiding?*

CHAPTER 14

NO GOOD

With so many unanswered questions about Chase swimming around my head, I could barely sit still in my next class. So I did what any other person would do (I'm guessing): I made another show of desperately needing the bathroom. Chase raised an eyebrow at me and I couldn't quite read if he was questioning whether that smell earlier had really been me or if he knew I was up to something.

As soon as I was in the hallway, I ran to the computer lab and googled the shit out of Chase and his family. I didn't have much to go on, but I did have his brother's name, their hometown, and the fact that there was some kind of lawsuit.

After searching for "Yang Yu, Flushing, Chase Yu," and "fraud" on my tenth try (I was quite relieved when "murder" yielded nothing on my sixth try), there it was: a local newspaper article that detailed everything down to what the neighbors had said and how shocked they were.

If my mǔqīn—an ex-believer in true love who blamed her current misery on financial troubles—knew about this, she would definitely see it as reason enough to keep Chase and me apart.

The Yu family is no good.

Why didn't Chase trust me enough to tell me about this? How had he lied so easily to my face, coming up with other suggestions for why my mother disapproved when the most plausible answer was right there in his back pocket?

And what the F was I supposed to do now that I knew?

THE PARK

AS SEEN FROM AFAR

At the center of the park, shrouded by shrubbery—the most popular rendezvous point due to the surrounding tree cover—a woman with a red briefcase met a man with missing teeth and a long, lucky mole hair.

They conversed in Mandarin.

"You haven't told me anything substantial about her," she accused, pointing a finger at the paper in the man's lap.

How could he, when he knew nothing? The man looked down at the two-dimensional face staring back at him, trying to feel the blood bond between them, but all he could think about was his own mission and how she was a means to an end.

I will need to ask for more information, he realized, dreading his next phone call to that woman he feared—also a stranger, just like the girl.

When the man still hadn't said anything two minutes later,

the woman snapped her briefcase shut and stood. "I'm sorry, this isn't going to work."

Though he was frustrated in the moment, unbeknownst to him this was a turning point, and not just for his faded, withering soul. Yes, he was soon to remember what it was like to have loved ones, and his heart would bloom as it hadn't in decades, but his actions would affect others all the more.

As the woman floated away and the butterfly hovering just outside the entrance of the park flapped its wings, several lives on the opposite side of the world took the next step of their thousand-mile journeys.

CHAPTER 15

DONG'S

The new knowledge about Chase's family gnawed at me the rest of the school day and into the evening. For the first time, I was thankful I didn't have my phone so I wouldn't have to explain via text why my awkwardness had been dialed up to eleven that afternoon. At one point Chase had asked, "Are you okay?"—to which I'd responded, "No I'm not; you are." Even when he told me he was going to get a new email address in honor of our puns, I couldn't manage more than a sad "okay." Sigh.

I was fully prepared to hole up by my lonesome with just my glow-in-the-dark star to keep me company, but two strange things happened that night. (Was it a full moon or something?)

First, my mother *initiated conversation* with me, even if it was about nothing. (She asked if I'd heard from Yun recently, and I felt a little sorry that she was so desperate for family friends she had deigned to talk to me.)

The second strange thing happened soon after the first: there was a knock at the door. We rarely had visitors, and the rap-rap-rap resounding through our hallway was as out of place as we were amid the cornfields.

I opened the door to a familiar yet unfamiliar face. The East Asian man vaguely resembled my father in the curve of his lips and the bend of his nose, but was otherwise another strain. As I stared rudely, all I could see was the dark mole on the lower right side of his chin and the—wait for it—extremely long, single hair coming out of its center. I felt terrible for noticing it even though anyone who grew up here would have. Wasn't I doing the exact same thing I had just accused Brenda of not that long ago? Was the universe going to make me smell poo again?

My eyes (reluctantly) drifted away from the mole hair and landed on the spiderweb of wrinkles surrounding his face, deep enough to imply he'd spent his whole life in the sun. I wasn't sure, but he looked at least a few decades older than my father. Maybe seventyish? The tattered clothing, bloated fingers, dirt-encrusted nails, the teeth missing every few steps like mid-game Jenga blocks—I couldn't understand how he and my father could look so similar at their base yet so different elsewhere, like the prince and the pauper.

"Ali, we finally meet!" he exclaimed in Mandarin with a mainland Chinese accent, confusing me even more. Maybe he wasn't related to us at all and I was being racist. Maybe the cornfields were getting to me.

He swept me up into a hug, and though I stiffened and held my arms out like a zombie, he continued to squeeze.

I heard footsteps in the hallway, then a crash as my mother dropped the bowl she was holding.

"Aiyah, bad luck!" the stranger exclaimed in Mandarin, again with that mainland accent (obviously, but it was so out of place I couldn't help noticing it every time he spoke).

He let go of me (thank God) just as my father appeared.

"Hello?" my dad said in English, a confused smile pasted on. "May we help you?"

The stranger's eyes grew as wide as the broken shards of porcelain, then darted from the mess to my mother, who somehow seemed more surprised by the hug than the stranger.

The visitor forced a smile. "I'm your bóbo," he said to my father, who was squinting as if trying to place him, "and your bógōng," he said to me. He didn't seem to speak English.

I didn't know the word "bógōng," but since he was my father's uncle, that made him my . . . great-uncle? So, my grandfather's brother.

My dad stiffened, his knees locking and spine straightening. After a moment he took a step closer, his gaze glued to my great-uncle's face. "It's you," he whispered, tracing the slope of Bógōng's nose with his eyes. He swallowed so hard his Adam's apple bobbed up and down. When he spoke, it was in Mandarin. "How did you find us?

Not that I'm not happy to see you," he added quickly, his face flushing. "I just mean . . . I don't know. How are you? Do you want some tea? Can I get you a pair of slippers?"

Bógōng laughed, then pointed to the coarse, gray mole hair and winked. "Don't you know these are lucky? I came into a bit of money and"—his tongue flicked over a couple of his teeth—"I poured everything into tracking you down. It's all I've been thinking about for years."

My mother clapped her hands, the act startling me even more than the sound. "We should celebrate!" she said, a cheery smile on her face that made me shrink away, wondering what she was covering up.

"Yes, of course," my father said, snapping out of whatever he was in. "You're family," he said to Bógōng with a heaviness that made me wonder if he was trying to remind himself of the fact. "How about Chinese food?"

We piled into my father's fifteen-year-old, almost-falling-apart car and trekked more than an hour to the closest Chinese buffet. And to give you an idea of just how desperate we all were, this one was named Dong's Number One Seafood Palace. I should've told Chase about that one earlier.

The only bright side of driving this far out was that I didn't know anyone here. And I wasn't thinking that because of racism or stereotypes or anything obviously predictable—I was thinking it because my family was especially cringeworthy at buffets.

Case in point, we'd barely been shown to our seats when my father ordered hot waters for the table, then ran to load up on the most expensive items—crab, steak, fish, and oysters. God, so many oysters. He had an entire plate dedicated to them.

The mortifying part was that the seafood he was practically snatching out of other patrons' hands wasn't even appetizing. The fish had a gray tint (and had clearly been stir-fried with a thousand other things to hide the fact that it was probably a week past its prime), the oysters were dry and withered, and the steak didn't look like prime cuts even to a noob like me.

Okay, *and* it was embarrassing that he was trampling others. For Dong's.

I reached for the fried rice and my mother slapped my hand. She didn't say anything, but I heard her words in my head. *Not expensive enough.* I waited for her to move on before grabbing three scoops (one for spite).

When I turned to the next aisle, I saw my great-uncle frozen in place, his body shaking. I hurried over and reached out to pat his shoulder, but my arm only hovered before dropping.

"Are you okay?" I asked in Mandarin.

He startled, almost dropping his plate, but I grabbed it in time.

"Yes, yes," he said uncertainly. "I'm just feeling lost."

I followed his gaze to the mayonnaise-honey-walnut shrimp. "It's Americanized Chinese food," I tried to explain, "and it's all we've got around here. Sorry."

He shook his head. "No, I wanted to come to America, and this is part of the experience, right?"

He started to relax, only to seize up again as a busser wheeled a cart of dirty dishes to the back. Most of the plates were still half covered in food.

"So wasteful," he whispered, walking toward the cart as if he was going to finish the leftovers.

Oh, my heart. I gently took him by the elbow and led him to the safest entrées.

"Here, try this," I said, motioning to the fried rice. We rounded the rest of the buffet in silence, with him periodically sticking his plate out for me to spoon my favorites on.

When my great-uncle and I made our way back to the table, my parents were already eating in silence. Bógōng picked up his fork and stared at it; I passed him the snap-apart chopsticks I had grabbed earlier.

"So, um, Bógōng, what do you do?" I ventured, since *no one was saying anything* even though a *family member* had just shown up out of nowhere. I wanted to shake everyone and ask what the hell was going on.

My father shook his head at me. "Did you have a good trip in?" he asked, patting me on the wrist as if that would explain everything. "Tell me more about this lucky money." His eyes shifted down to the mole for a second, and I hated that I had to wonder whether my dad actually believed in mole-hair luck.

My great-uncle's eyes flicked to my mother, and if I wasn't mistaken, she dèng-ed him a yǎn. He flinched, then looked at me, and finally returned his gaze to my father. "It's not important. As I always say, focus on the future, not the past. That's the only way I've made it this far."

My father's eyes lowered to his oysters. Bógōng pretended not to see.

Annnd silence.

"What's it like . . . where you're from?" I asked, my instinct to be the buffer kicking in.

But it had been a while, and I was as rusty as the Dong's fork in my hand.

My father patted me again and said to me, in English, "Now, now, let the grown ups talk."

Except you're not talking! I wanted to yell, but that would make me look even more like the child he already saw me as.

It was so quiet I swore I could hear the oyster dying a slow death in my father's mouth, then sliding down his throat.

I bit my lip to keep the questions from bursting out. *What happened to your teeth? How come I didn't know you existed before tonight? What is wrong with all of you?*

Eventually my father asked my great-uncle, "Why are you here now?" His tone was curious, but his words oozed suspicion.

Bógōng started to respond, but, surprisingly, my mother jumped in. "Let him eat in peace," she said to my father. "Aren't you happy to finally meet? Are you going to pry into how he earned every penny? Are you going to tell him what your salary is?" A cloud immediately covered my father as he shrank down in his seat. She turned to my great-uncle. "We're happy you're here."

With his eyes on my father, Bógōng cleared his throat, then asked, "What do you know about me?"

My father's eyes ping-ponged between Bógōng and his plate.

"So, just that I exist," Bógōng said, his eyes falling to his own plate. "And, I'm guessing, the letter." After a pause he asked, "Did he ever speak of me?"

"For a long time, he assumed you were dead," my father whispered.

Complete silence.

All the muscles in Bógōng's face tensed. After cycling through several emotions—frustration, confusion, exhaustion—he settled into sadness.

My mind buzzed as I tried to piece everything together. My father's cheeks were flushed, his forehead covered in sweat, and I worried he might pass out.

"One too many oysters, Bā?" I said with a forced laugh, but he ignored me.

"Please excuse me," Bógōng said quietly, grabbing a crab Rangoon off his plate before leaving the table.

I imagined the entire restaurant drowning in a deep, deep blue sea of secrets, with my parents at the epicenter.

CHAPTER 16

CERULEAN BLUE

No one offered me any information. I knew this wasn't about me and I was selfish to even think about myself right now, but how could my parents leave me so in the dark and not care? Could we even be classified as a family anymore?

Many others might have lost their appetite, but my parents scarfed down three plates of Dong's Number One Seafood—more a consequence of being poor than anything else. If they were going to pay for dinner, they were going to eat their money's worth, god-damn it, and part of me suspected that since my great-uncle hadn't eaten that much, they were, ahem, eating that cost.

The ten-year, I mean eighty-minute, drive back drowned in cerulean blue and silence.

When we arrived home, I thought for a second that my great-uncle might just disappear as quickly as he came, but then my mother handed him a used set of pajamas, and I realized he was here to stay, at least for a short while. Seeing him caress the bargain-bin pj's made me want to reach out and slip him my meager savings, maybe find a way to fix his teeth.

As my mother left the living room without another word, I saw my father stare after her, his eyes cloudy with a wistfulness I'd never seen before. It stirred up memories long buried, and as flashes of his laughter and her smile whizzed by in my head, I tried to figure out what had rebirthed this tonight. Maybe it was seeing her kindness to one of his family members? Except . . . there was something sinister beneath the oddball bond my mother seemed to have with Bógōng—I could feel it from the shared looks between them, even her unexplained compassion.

My father noticed me watching him, and the longing gaze disappeared, leaving behind first embarrassment, then shame.

How could anyone be ashamed of admiring his own wife? I started toward him, hoping to maybe find a way to keep that door open, but he cowered from me, then ran into the bathroom.

Damn it. I hadn't known what I was going to say, but I was never in the mood for yet another reminder of how he'd rather hide on the toilet than be around me.

I turned and saw my great-uncle looking at us curiously. For some reason—maybe because he was family—I wasn't embarrassed. I shrugged, trying to tell him this was the usual. He patted the couch beside him and I took a seat next to my mysterious bógōng.

One of my hands hovered over his but never managed to land. "I want to know your story," I told him.

His head turned toward me, and when our eyes met, it felt like he was staring into my most inner self, all the way to Ali, and even though I wanted to know him, I found myself itching to leave. How could I expect him to show me who he was when I, who barely had a story to tell, didn't want to reciprocate?

"You know, you're lucky, Ali," he said, "to be born here, to grow up not seeing the things I'd seen by your age." He scooted forward and smiled widely so I could see his gray teeth, and then he waved a hand in front of his face quickly, back and forth, as if he were trying to wipe something off. When his hand came away, he smiled again, revealing five more teeth missing.

It was morbid and terrible but also so incredibly heartwarming that, whatever he'd gone through, he hadn't been broken beyond repair. I could almost feel his fighting spirit, like the battle aura from Japanese manga that grew to be ten sizes larger than the body.

His tongue clicked his partial denture back into place. "Why so serious? That was a joke. You were supposed to laugh."

"How can I laugh about something like that?"

He leaned closer to me. "I'm going to tell you a secret, Ali. Humor is one of the greatest weapons the world has to offer. If you can hang on to that, you can make it through anything."

I shook my head. "That can't be right. That sounds too simple."

"If it were simple, then more people would do it."

Deep in my bones, in that area that was supposedly susceptible to wind and water and whatever else my ancestors believed, I understood what my great-uncle was saying.

"Ali." My mother's voice was level, but I knew her well enough to parse out the underlying urgency. "Time for bed. Wǎn'ān."

"Wǎn'ān, Māmá and, um . . . Bógōng." That last word was so foreign in my mouth, as foreign as I felt in Plainhart, Indiana, but maybe I'd been focusing on the wrong thing all along. I couldn't help running my tongue over my teeth, which, yes, were crooked, but intact and pain-free. As the tip of my tongue caressed my right canine and felt smooth enamel instead of the jagged sliver that hung in my great-uncle's mouth, my stomach flipped, and I had to bend over to keep from hurling my gray fish.

Just as I was about to turn the light off and huddle under the covers, three gentle knocks sounded from the other side of my door.

My first thought: maybe Bógōng was coming to tell me his story. My insides churned with every emotion in the book.

"Qǐng jìn," I called out, doing what I could to steady my voice. But it was my mother.

"We need to schedule your China trip, and it needs to be soon."

Mr. Laurelson's note immediately came to mind. *Waiting until summer was no longer an option.*

"Why are we so rushed?" I asked. When she didn't answer, I tried to be even more direct for once. "Can we cut the crap, Mǔqīn? There's obviously more to this than you wanting me to 'find my roots.' If you're going to lie, can you at least try a little harder?" She ignored me again, so I dropped the bomb I'd been holding on to for a few days. "I googled it and there are no programs like you described."

She wasn't fazed. "You must have misunderstood me. It's not exactly a program—more like a benefactor who will fund your trip."

"Who is it? Why would they do that?"

"It's anonymous. Stop asking so many questions. It's rude."

She flicked the lights off without giving me the chance to uncover whatever she was hiding. I was close; I could feel it. Or maybe that was just the Dong's oysters having a party in my gut.

Zhu Yingtai
Hangzhou, China

By the yuèguāng, Li Bai's beloved moonlight enhanced by the outhouse lanterns, I let my mask slip slightly. Since Shanbo and I were straining to see the calligraphy in our books, I doubted he would be able to see past my veneer.

As we recited Qin Guan's "Immortals at the Magpie Bridge" into memory, I had to distance myself from the words to avoid thoughts of my unwanted future. How was it possible that a culture so steeped in matchmaking also indulged so many poems and tall tales of true love?

Shanbo's voice switched from cadenced to speaking, startling me as much as his words. "My parents made a match."

I swallowed hard, convincing myself that the bitterness I suddenly tasted was not bile. "Oh? And?"

"She is . . . a good match." His pitch and the way he prolonged the sentence spelled out his reservations in clear calligraphy strokes.

"Is she attractive?"

"I guess in a conventional way, yes—she is petite, feminine, with bound feet and a small guāzi liǎn."

My words came out without passing through my filter—a curse of the moonlight's bewitching, perhaps? "I've never understood why having a face shaped like a melon seed is so desirable," I said.

He laughed, startling me. "I agree. I've never understood why people even bother to look at the physical. It doesn't tell you how you will get along, how you will communicate."

I could hardly believe my ears. All the men in my life treated their wives as showpieces to be paraded, ogled, and impregnated on occasion, but otherwise expected to blend into the background.

Shanbo's gaze met mine, and his eyes widened when he realized the blasphemy of his words. "Of course, it doesn't matter what I think. The matchmaker has spoken, and I am happy to honor my family." He sat up a little straighter. "And this match will elevate my family's standing, which we need. There was so much shame after the . . . incident . . . with my brother."

"Why did your parents lie?"

He didn't ask me how I knew; he was presumably used to everyone knowing. "You're familiar with how things are—they wouldn't have been able to find him a spouse otherwise."

His eyes unfocused, suddenly dreamy. "Do you ever think about what it would be like to fall in love?" He pointed to the poem in his lap as if to say that if Qin Guan spoke of it, we could entertain the thought as well, at least for a brief moment in time.

Yes, constantly, I thought to myself. "No. It's a waste of time."

I excused myself to the outhouse to tend to the pang in my stomach.

CHAPTER 17

TAP-TIPPY-TAP

I was lying in my bed, staring at the lone star, when I heard it. A tap-tippy-tap. Then silence. Then again: tap-tippy-tap. *Coast is clear.*

I bolted upright in an instant and rushed to the window. And there he was, illuminated by the moonlight and a little battery-powered lantern at his feet, throwing a pebble, then a shower of sand, then another pebble. I held my index finger to my lips, not wanting him to wake my mother or great-uncle.

After grabbing my trusty Feiyues, I repeated my Vaseline-rope-ladder-leave-the-window-cracked routine. Halfway down, I paused, realizing I'd have to pass directly by my great-uncle sleeping on the couch. I slowed, hoping to create less noise, but when

I passed by Bógōng's window, he was completely zonked out with his mouth wide open and a little drool coming out—guess that was in the Chu DNA, regardless of where you grew up. A partial denture sat in a glass on the end table—six teeth total, just on the one denture I could see. Most likely there was another beneath it.

Once my feet hit the ground, I hurried Chase away, whispering that I didn't want my great-uncle to see him.

"Your bógōng lives with you?" he asked, craning his head over mine to see.

I didn't think I'd ever get used to him speaking Mandarin to me.

When I was satisfied with our distance from the window, I answered, "He just showed up on the doorstep tonight. I didn't even know he existed until a few hours ago."

"Where was he before?"

"Mainland China, no clue what town or city."

"Wait, you have family in China still?"

"I guess so." He knew as much as I did.

In the back of my head, I was selfishly grateful for the distraction my bógōng created. Maybe Chase wouldn't ask what had been going on with me earlier, and maybe I could teach myself to be normal—my version of it, anyway—until I figured out what to do with the new information I'd gleaned.

The little lantern in his hand sprayed light back and forth over our path as it swung with each of his steps. Without thinking, I instinctively led Chase down the street toward the swings in the public park. As everyone, their mothers, their dogs, and their sheep would've guessed, as soon as our butts hit the seats, our legs

began pumping and pushing to see who could go higher.

I didn't *need* to beat him . . . not really. There was just something about our energy, our shared spirit, and I just pumped and pumped and pumped until, I swear, I was flying.

The swings had always been my favorite. My mom used to take me to parks when I was younger, and I felt drawn to them even now that I was too old. Before we'd moved, she would swing with me, push me higher, laugh with me. Once we came to Indiana, she stopped going outside (at least with me), and I found myself gravitating toward parks for no reason other than the fact that I craved a piece, any piece of her.

Eleven years later, even the ghost of her was gone.

Chase conceded the swing contest, scraping his feet against the dirt until he was low enough to be heard over the wind. "I've been wondering something. . . ." I dragged my feet in the dirt until I matched his height. "Do you think you're a descendant of—"

"Zhu Yingtai," we said at the same time.

"I've considered it, but she died young, remember?" I said. "She didn't have kids. At least, not that we know of."

"Don't you think it's a weird coincidence your family is from Hangzhou, where they went to school?"

I stopped swinging. I hadn't even known my family was from there until I'd read Mr. Laurelson's note. Honestly, it confused me, because I was pretty sure my mom used to tell me stories about her family living in the remote countryside of China, but that was from the days before plumbing, and of course people move, especially over a century of time.

Chase continued, "Doesn't it feel like it's all connected somehow—your mom's disapproval, Hangzhou being the common setting of so many things, your bógōng appearing out of thin air?"

Why was he busy coming up with other theories when he knew the real reason behind my mother's disapproval? And when would he put me out of my secret-keeping misery?

"Even if I am somehow related to Zhu Yingtai," I said, my feet gripping the ground and twisting my body such that the chain tangled around itself, "it still doesn't explain why my mom doesn't want us to be together—which is the only thing I really care about right now."

Please just tell me.

There was a brief pause. Then Chase pulled out his phone and started swiping. "Was there any mention of your great-uncle in your files? Because maybe—"

Everything stopped at the same time: his words, movements, the faint puffs of fog that had been accompanying his exhales.

"You looked through my files?" he asked, a chill to his voice I'd never heard before.

Crappity-crap-crap. I must've left one of the photos behind in my rush to delete because of my neighbor's crappity-crap-crap. In my surprise, my feet slipped, and the chain spun me into a dizzy haze as it untangled itself.

I jabbered for a bit before improvising, "Yes, I looked, but they didn't really tell me much?" And of course I held off from admitting I'd poked around further, because I couldn't stomach the way his eyes were boring into me as if he wasn't sure who I was. What would his face look like if I told him more?

"So this is why you've been squirrelly since the computer lab."

I chewed on my cheek. "Oh, you noticed?"

"With you I notice everything." His eyes were sad. Hurt. He wasn't even angry. "Why didn't you just ask me about my family?"

"I did ask!"

"No, you never did. You just told me what your mom thought."

Was he serious? "How is that not asking? It was so obvious what I wanted to know!"

"That's not the same as asking, Ali. I'm sorry I didn't just tell you, but maybe you can try to be a little better with your words? You make it so difficult sometimes."

"Me, difficult? You're the one who made me break into Mr. Laurelson's office by not telling me!"

"Don't you find it ridiculous that *that* was your first instinct instead of just asking?"

"Would you call James Bond ridiculous?" I retorted.

"Yes."

Silence.

Confidently I said, "You made me show you Ali and you still refuse to show me . . . Chaz? Ace? Retreat?" He looked at me questioningly. "'Retreat': the opposite of 'chase.'"

He chuckled as I'd hoped, but it was strained.

"I just wanted to know you better," I told him quietly.

"You want to know me better? You want to know about the horrible mistake my brother made that sank our family? About

148

why my parents went from living in their HARVARD MOM and HARVARD DAD sweatshirts, even when it was eighty degrees out, to never speaking of my brother? He defrauded our family and friends, Ali! Got us driven out of Flushing! When the people he hurt came for what they were owed, he ran, and we haven't heard from him since. And my parents are so consumed by shame they can barely function. It's all they care about, all they think about, and it drives everything they do, including how on that night she saw you, my mother's only concern was whether or not you knew our dirty secret."

As he spoke, his face morphed from narrowed-eyes anger to clenched-muscles pain to utter defeat. And underlying every expression were the two phrases from his past counselor's files: "shame" and "mìanzi." The irony was not lost on me that the latter meant both "face" (more literally translated) and "reputation," and its weight was what was dragging Chase's face down.

"It all happened so fast," he whispered, his tone also defeated now. "When Harvard accepted him because of his high school wrestling achievements, man, I mean, my parents acted like he had cured cancer, which, I think, they believed was also now in his cards. He was always their 'number one son,' as they called him, yes, out loud"—shit, that had to hurt—"and even though I knew they were technically referring to the order in which we were born, it wasn't just that. The little money we had was spent on him: his wrestling, his tutors, his viola lessons to help his college application stand out. Our worlds revolved around him."

And it had started before Chase was even born, with his name. By entering the world second, he was doomed to be second place forever, the afterthought, the lion's butt.

He sighed. "Anyway, I'm getting off track." *No you're not,* I couldn't help thinking. These details, his side of the story, were exactly what I was looking for. "When the neighborhood's golden boy"—he said the nickname in a sarcastic tone—"graduated and returned home, crimson scepter in hand, all the other parents swarmed us, begging my brother to help their precious Mei or Ling or Jessica follow in his footsteps. My parents, with their bloated heads, would respond, *Of course, our son can do anything. I'm sure your brilliant Ling will have no trouble, but we're still more than happy to help.*"

I braced myself, waiting for the roller-coaster car to crest past the apex and free-fall to the ground.

"And then . . ." He trailed off. After a breath he held a finger up, asking for a minute.

"I already know," I whispered, wanting to take away his pain.

Chase stiffened and he stared at me—no, *through* me—and it felt like the surrounding air suddenly dropped ten degrees.

"I saw the newspaper article," I clarified.

"Why didn't you just say so earlier?"

I opened and closed my mouth before shrugging.

"God, Ali, it's just one thing after another with you—what else aren't you telling me?"

His words made me want to curl into a ball and disappear. But

I also wanted to dig in and fire back. Neither emotion was foreign, but the combination was.

When I didn't answer, he continued, "Why did you go looking in the first place instead of just asking me?" His voice was low and distant, almost unrecognizable.

"I didn't know what to do when you didn't tell me—I did what I thought was best for both of us. This way, I would know, and you wouldn't have to face any demons to tell me. It's what I would've preferred."

He shook his head at me in disbelief. "Come on, Ali. *Of course* I would've preferred to tell you myself."

"Well, you didn't—is that because you don't trust me?"

"Of course not!" His face looked as bewildered as mine felt. I was used to being on a different wavelength from most people, but not from Chase.

"Then why didn't you tell me, especially when we were trying to figure out why my mǔqīn was so against us being together? You practically lied to my face by withholding information, not that I'm not guilty of the same, but you're being a little hypocritical getting mad at me for doing exactly what you did first."

Chase's eyes widened in what felt like slow motion. "Are you seriously comparing what you did to what I did?"

Um, yes? But I knew enough not to say anything.

"Jesus, I can't believe you right now," he huffed.

His little jabs had poked this bear one too many times, and even though I knew I'd made mistakes too, I was tired of taking all the blame. Couldn't he see I was trying?

"I can't believe *you*," I threw back at him. "You obviously withheld this from me on purpose because you're as burdened by the shame as your parents are. I've been away from the Asian community long enough to gain some perspective, and I think our culture can sometimes push us to assign meaning to the wrong stuff. Miànzi is such a messed-up thing, the anchor that sinks you when you should be focusing on what's important—moving on, helping Yang, making amends—not escaping because you can't show your face anymore."

Chase flinched at the sound of his brother's name. I'd done that on purpose after noticing he couldn't say it; I wanted to push him one step in the right direction.

Except . . . his jaw flexed as he said, "I open up to you about my family, and this is what you say to me? That we just have to fucking get over it, like it's no big deal? What if I said the same thing to you, that you're being a coward with your mother and all you need to do is talk to her, stand up for yourself? Just get over it, Ali!"

Hearing my name perfectly pronounced in that harsh tone pierced my heart as much as his words had.

"Jesus, Chase, what the fuck," I whispered, my voice barely audible.

I still stood by what I'd said to him, but when he turned the tables and fed me my bitter medicine, I wanted to kick and scream and do anything but what he said. Perhaps we were more on the same wavelength than I'd previously thought, except we had given and taken too many punches to feel anything but anger and feel anything but pain.

For your reading pleasure before each flush.

Daily Flushing

All Your Flushing News

We're not afraid to get down and dirty.

VOL. 123 No. 181   Flushing, Queens, New York   June 30

Ivy Dreams Dashed as Families Go Bankrupt

By Emily Chen

Our beloved community was shaken to its core recently by a scandal that has been infamously dubbed "Ivygate." Innocent hopefuls dreaming of the best future for their children threw their life savings to Ivy Guaranteed, the recent start-up promising to help students gain acceptance into their dream colleges for a hefty fee that would be refunded if the students didn't get in.

Only, none of the company's clients were accepted into Ivy League schools, and none of the money was returned.

"My little Kimmy only applied to her three top choices—it was supposed to be a guarantee," said former client Shen Liu. "We gave all our money to Ivy Guaranteed, then could only afford three application fees. Now Kimmy, a top-ten student in her class, is not going to college!"

When the clients demanded their refunds, the Ivy Guaranteed

He turned away and closed his eyes. "Ali . . . I . . ." He sighed. "I need a little space, okay? I'm too upset right now. . . . I just need to breathe."

Since shutting down was what I knew and what made me feel safe, I said nothing.

Then I turned and ran home in the dark, stumbling a few times, just like I was constantly doing with all my decisions, with every word out of my mouth.

When I tucked myself back into bed under my lone glow-in-the-dark star, I was exhausted down to the parts of my bones supposedly susceptible to shīqì.

founder, Yang Yu, was unable to pay and fled town. The former clients have now banded together to sue the company for fraud.

"We had no choice," former client Hom Wang said. "Most of us gave all we had; we're left with nothing! Bankrupt! And our children's futures are now also in trouble."

"We just want our money returned," Liu said. "We did not want it to come to this."

Ivygate was especially shocking given the young man at the center of the controversy. Not long ago, Yang Yu was his neighborhood's golden boy, the first of the blue-collar community to attend an Ivy League college. His Harvard acceptance had sent waves through the neighborhood.

"Every child wanted to be like Yang Yu," a former family friend, Jeff Pan, said. "Every parent wanted their child to follow in Yang's footsteps. He was living everyone's dream."

Several members of the community remembered Yu's celebratory Good-Luck-at-Harvard party with fondness. It had been held at the Happy Garden Restaurant, where the Yu family has worked for decades: Shui An Yu, father, as chef; Xin Jie Yu, mother, as bookkeeper; Chase Yu, youngest son, as a busboy; and Yang Yu himself as a waiter.

"We threw [Yang Yu] a top-notch banquet," Happy Garden owner Peter Ho told *Daily Flushing*. "Everyone chipped in. The entire community, all of us, we were cheering for him."

Another former family friend described Yu as the "king of the neighborhood," returning home every college break to fanfare and excitement.

So what happened? A source who wishes to remain anonymous speculates, "Having that kind of pressure on your shoulders, it can be too much to bear. I believe [Yang Yu] started out with noble intentions, wanting to help his community while also helping his parents get a better life, but things fell apart so fast. He should not have made promises he couldn't keep. He should not have spent the money so quickly."

In recent months, after Ivy Guaranteed started and before the clients received rejections from top colleges, the Yu family swapped their apartment for an upgraded four-bedroom home in an upscale neighborhood. Clients also claimed to have seen the Yu family sporting new clothes and accessories, as well as a shiny new Camry coming in and out of their two-car garage.

A class-action suit against Yang Yu has been filed, and criminal charges of fraud could be made as well. Yu disappeared before he could be served and has not been located since. His parents told the court they are unaware of his whereabouts and have not heard from him in weeks.

The Yu family declined to comment.

CHAPTER 18

ROH BOY

I woke somehow feeling worse than I had last night. How had our fight escalated so quickly? Oh that's right—because it was one of life's sad ironies that it was easier to hurt someone you cared about, someone you knew so intimately you could go straight for their Achilles' heel.

Even though it was Saturday, even though I had climbed through my window around three in the morning (and yes, almost slipping and falling straight down into Bógōng's open mouth), I rose before eight, most likely because one can only take so much tossing and turning before their unconscious gives up.

With thoughts of turning this week's leftover rice into breakfast congee, I padded downstairs, off my game, and, lo and behold, I almost ran headfirst into my father.

"Oh! Uh, Ali, zǎo'ān."

"Good morning."

We hovered on the stairs, my socks rubbing back and forth on the ancient hardwood despite the threat of splinters.

He pursed his lips to one side. "Okay, well, I have . . . stuff today, so . . . have a good day, okay?" He patted me on the head like I was a stranger's dog, and I heard him exhale as soon as he had moved past me.

My mother was, of course, already gone, sans car, walking to who knows where to avoid the rest of us, and Bógōng was still asleep on the couch.

So what's a kid to do with a house all to herself? I had no choice, really. The second my father left, I attacked my mother's safe with everything I had: Chase's lockpicks (borrowed yesterday after the Laurelson B&E), a nail file, even one of those Asian earwax scoopers. (Did we get more earwax than other races or something? Or were we more obsessed with cleaning it out?)

I was looking for confirmation—some kind of proof that my mother had dug into Chase's family history—along with an explanation as to how everything connected to the mysterious park (or how it *wasn't* connected—maybe my mother's secret cup simply overflowethed). Also? I wanted a clue into what the bejesus was going on between my mother and great-uncle. And maybe . . . I just wanted to see a piece of her, the one from my childhood, somehow, somewhere, because I'd never felt as alone as I did right now.

After watching enough YouTube tutorials to ensure I was on some government watch list, I *did it*. I was in.

I wiped my cut-up fingers on my jeans, trying to soak up the droplets of blood.

Okay. I swung the door open. The inside was stacked with papers. Upon first glance, they appeared different from the ones I'd seen on the kitchen table. But on the top, almost floating, there it was: the picture of the park. *Roh boy*, had I earned my Scooby snack. I fingered the edges as if I needed to confirm it was real, and then I examined every last detail.

I'd been in such a rush last time that I'd missed the trash. There were so many scraps of paper tangled in the trees and littering the walls that at a quick glance, they appeared to be a part of the park, as if they'd fused over the years to become part tree, part bench, part cobblestone.

I put the photo aside but within eyesight to remind myself this was actually happening: I had bypassed the obstacles to dive head-first into the cerulean, soon-to-be-clear sea.

My attention shifted to a bundle of photos. All front-facing portraits of a stranger, another stranger, and, yup, a third stranger, and then Yun. Aw, he must've overslept on picture day. His hair had a little untamed cowlick in the back and he still had a pillow crease on his cheek, but he was smiling so wide his eyes were almost closed. This wasn't the Yun I'd met. Since the photo was clearly old (I mean, he still had braces, for goodness' sake), I hoped this side hadn't been stomped out by something.

I thumbed through more photos until I saw another one of him.

This picture was closer to the Yun I'd seen recently, both physically and in stoic nature. For some reason (or I guess I didn't need a reason), I nodded at him as if he could see me, then pushed these off to the side while wondering: Did my mother also send photos of me to family friends? Which one did she use, the one where I was scowling or the one where I was mid-blink? Did these photos of her friends' children ease the loneliness or merely remind her she wasn't around to watch them grow up alongside me? Also, why were they in the safe?

More digging. The papers pushed up against the side were so stained, worn, and dog-eared I half expected them to turn to dust with my touch. Gingerly, I pulled the entire pile into my lap, but then my anticipation got the best of me and I hastily pawed through, hoping for something to jump out labeled THIS IS THE KEY TO EVERYTHING.

An old, dirt-encrusted envelope caught my eye. There were fingerprints on the edges implying that someone else had handled it recently, but the letter was resealed by decades of grime. I glanced at the unfamiliar addresses, only able to read that it had been sent from China to Taiwan, and from a Chu I didn't know to another unknown Chu. I quickly memorized the two names in case they came up somewhere else. Then, pushing the envelope aside because I didn't want to risk getting caught by reopening it, I dove back into the rest of the heap.

Gah, the loose newspaper clippings were in Mandarin. Of course. I knew I shouldn't have expected anything else, but it still shot impatience through me.

Channel your mother.

I downloaded a translation app, took photos, and began uploading. As the little wheel spun, so did my mind, trying to keep up. Between the mediocre accuracy of the app and my past education, I slowly began piecing together each phrase, then sentence, then paragraph—just getting enough words to be able to infer the rest.

The more Mandarin I went through, the faster the characters started coming back to me, the faster the picture began to form.

As I read about the famed Butterfly Lovers Park dedicated to Liang Zhu and located where they attended school in Hangzhou, Chase's words rang in my head. Was I somehow a descendant of Zhu Yingtai? Except . . . her kids, if she'd had them, would've taken on the last name of whoever her husband was. Shoot. Goddamn patriarchy. If I ever married, my husband would have to become a Chu. Or we could both become Feminist or Pineapplecake or Something.

As I stared at the fuzzy black-and-white photos of angled bridges and water-lily ponds, memories flashed through my mind. My mother, sitting on my bed when I was a child, telling me stories about a park in China. *It's moved too far from its original intention now,* she had told me in Mandarin, *but one day it will be restored into what it was meant to be: a celebration of love, real love, the kind captured by ancient folktales and poems and songs.* There had been so many fantastical creatures in her stories—a different one each time—that I had assumed it had been nothing but a figment of her imagination.

Another memory: my mother, teaching me to write Chinese

calligraphy, showing me how to hold the brush straight up and down, my index finger and thumb pinching high on the bamboo and the other three fingers resting below. As she held her hand over mine—the last time she would so openly guide me—she would tell me things. *I married for love, Ali, and had to lose so much in the process, but I don't regret it. My family believes in duty, honor, and legacy, but I sacrificed everything to come to America so you could have a different life. And one day, you will bring these ideals back to China, to Taiwan, to them, and that is why you need to know Mandarin and your culture. You are my little love product, the proof, and you will show them all how they were wrong about your father and me.*

I had been so young that her words hadn't carried much weight; my focus had been on the brush in my hand and the watery ink it left behind. Why hadn't I asked her more at the time? How was I to know that was the last time she'd ever talk about herself?

I heard my father's words from our almost talk earlier this week: *She knows what she wants and she'll do what it takes to get it, even if it means forsaking her parents.* Growing up, we rarely spoke of my mother's family. For a long time I had assumed they were dead, especially because my mother only referred to them in the past tense, but what about when she had said, *My family believes in duty, honor, and legacy . . . you will show them all how they were wrong*?

It was suddenly so obvious: my mother's family hadn't approved of her marriage, and she'd chosen my father over them. Was that why my parents were so broken now? Because she had given up too much, and it created a mountain of pressure impossible to surmount?

My palm swiped roughly at my eyes, and I forced myself to return to the safe so I could try to orient the puzzle piece I'd just discovered.

The next photo grasped my heart and squeezed, compressing until tears of longing were forced out against my rapid blinks. My fingers cradled the rare treasure, which in any other household would be proudly displayed, but in our house was buried and locked away.

My parents, faces plump with youth, smiles so wide I almost didn't recognize them. And God, the way they were gazing at each other? I couldn't remember seeing them look at each other or at me that way, with pure, unconditional love, where the mere presence of the other filled their hearts and lives so much they would never need to look at anyone else.

Was it better that they had once been so enamored? Or worse because they had fallen so far and lost something precious?

Part of me wanted to crumple the photo and destroy the proof that there was a happier reality they'd deprived me of. The better option had been within my grasp but slipped through my fingers before I knew to grab hold.

I frantically searched for more photos, wanting clues that could maybe tell me how to find our way back to this place.

But the next few pieces took my breath away in a completely different sense. And all the gushy adjectives that came into mind arrived in Mandarin, because my mother's paintings were so beautifully, richly Chinese—of bamboo, cranes, carp, and cherry blossoms, all painted with exquisite calligraphy brushstrokes, the perfect thickening and thinning of lines and dots in all the right places.

Did you know she used to be a brilliant painter?

No, Bǎbá, I didn't.

When I reached the series at the end of the stack, I had to wipe my cheek to prevent the tears from ruining these pieces of my mother's heart. Rendition after rendition of Ali Shān, my namesake and my mother's favorite place, painted during different seasons, at different angles, both close-up and far away, a different focal point per piece: sometimes the mountain itself, sometimes the clouds, other times the trees, the flowers, the sun. The one common thread? How much this place meant to her.

Suddenly I wanted to see Ali Mountain for myself, to fall in love with it the way my mother had and maybe see the person she had once been. Was this what she meant when she talked about finding my roots? Did I feel only a piece of the whole because I was missing this part of me? Was it possible that her intentions could be pure?

My eyes flicked back and forth between the paintings and the photo of my enamored parents. I barely knew the person who had made these careful, deliberate brushstrokes, the one who had lovingly brought these animals and objects, this scenery to life, shaded in each curve, feather, and petal. Yet, sitting here among all her secrets, I felt closer to her than ever before, despite the fact that I could never tell her about finding these treasures.

I mourned for her, for my father, for me. I would never know the depth behind these shallow findings, nor see the vibrant, creative life force she once was.

The heartbreak was almost too much, and I considered stopping my search for a moment, but that feeling was quickly replaced by the need to know more, the desperation for any answer, a way to make progress of some kind. Because there had to be a fix, right? And surely, it was buried in here among all the regret, pain, and missed opportunities.

I pulled out the paper that, in my excavating, had risen to the top. It was folded in thirds but sans envelope. A bank statement.

I blinked.

Then blinked again.

We weren't poor. We weren't rich, but we certainly didn't have to reuse the toilet paper, either.

Except, I realized slowly . . . the reason we probably had this little nest egg was *because* we'd lived this way.

And . . . the only reason my mother would put aside this kind of money was . . .

We're saving it for college, Ali, I heard her say in my head, repeatedly, from when I was a child and too young to understand.

I immediately began to bawl. The snot-dripping, can't-breathe, gasping kind of crying.

Every complaint about not getting something as meaningless as a birthday party or the toy of the month came tumbling into my head along with all the guilt. Why couldn't she have told me this? Then I would've had a different reaction.

She did *try to tell you.*

We'd been talking past each other our whole lives, eventually giving up so I'd be reduced to sneaking behind her back and violating her privacy to get answers.

As I stared at the statement through my watery, distorted gaze, my eye caught on a very large withdrawal. I yanked the paper closer even though I knew I'd seen it correctly; I just couldn't believe there was anything my mother would spend more than a hundred dollars on.

No details, just a wire transfer overseas. Maybe . . . to China? My mother's out-of-character kindness to my bógōng, their shared looks and whispers . . . Was my mother the source of the lucky money? She would never give so much out of the kindness of her heart; there had to be something bigger at play.

I was looking for answers but seemed to only find question after question, the blue sea turning darker with every discovery.

I thought I had figured it out, that Chase's family was at least in part to blame, but the wire transfer was dated seven months ago, and I couldn't fathom how all of this could tie together.

Maybe it didn't.

What if . . . going to China meant I could find a piece of myself *and* dig further into all of this? Even if my mother did have some unknown, sinister motive for the trip, that didn't mean I couldn't have one of my own.

I heard footsteps in the hallway and shoved everything back into the safe haphazardly. Shit, the lock was now scratched up from everything I'd done to get inside. But there wasn't much I could do about it, was there?

I'd just shut the safe and buffed the lock with my sleeve when my great-uncle's head popped through the doorframe.

"Ali?" he said, and even though his voice betrayed nothing, I knew he'd seen what I'd been doing.

What are you hiding?

But I said nothing. Didn't move.

He shuffled in and took a seat on the bed. "I saw you sneak out last night, Ali. And I saw him, the boy." It was stated matter-of-factly, and for some reason I found myself liking him more for not beating around the bush.

I just stared, daring him to do something about it. He stared back. I always thought this power of mine came from my mother, but maybe it was from both sides.

"You need to be careful," he said finally.

I responded in Mandarin to match him. "You don't know me." My tone was softer than my words, more sad than accusatory.

"I know more than you think. And I know you need to be careful. Someone's going to get hurt. Hearts heal, but I can't watch a train heading for a mountain and say nothing."

"What do you know? About the mountain?"

He sighed, then fingered his mole hair, a reflex. "I of all people am completely against taking away a person's freedom. But I am also very familiar with feeling trapped, with no easy way out." He paused. "Do you really want to know my story?"

"Yes," I answered immediately. "But not here." Not where my mǔqīn could interrupt. Besides, I had to get far away from the safe—it was taunting me from its hiding place, pointing a guilty finger and also laughing at how little I knew about my mother.

We made our way downstairs in silence. By the front door, I handed him a scarf—my favorite gray one, which reminded me of my long-lost dog and what my mother was capable of—and we ventured out into the crisp autumn air.

Side by side we trod the pebbled road, tracing the footsteps I had taken just last night.

"You hate it here," he stated simply. I frowned at him and he smirked a little. "You scoff at everything we pass."

"That's just my face." Similar to his partial denture joke from last night, I waved my hand in front of my nose, only I left behind the exact same bland expression. He belly-laughed, the rich sound eliciting a return chuckle from me.

"And you're wrong," I continued. "I do find some beauty in what's around me—the changing seasons, the abundance of nature." The—oof—fireflies. "I'm not made of stone, you know."

He clasped his hands behind his back as he strolled. "I was once forced to be in the countryside. China is quite beautiful, with lush green grass, mountains, and winding rivers, but it's hard to enjoy that when you're there against your will, forced to do manual labor and denied an education."

"You didn't get an education?"

"Not since the war." His voice still held no emotion.

"Well, if I compared my situation to yours, I'd be a fool, don't you think?"

He tilted his face up to the sky, basking in the sun. "Or you would learn to see things through a different lens, one with a more nuanced, optimistic slant."

"Like Botox for perspectives." I used the English word for Botox since I'd never learned it in Mandarin.

"Hmm?"

"Nothing," I mumbled, even though I had a feeling he might've appreciated the joke, bad as it was.

Bógōng stopped in front of a bench and tucked himself to one side of it. "My knees are struggling." *From what they did to me* went unspoken between us.

I scooted next to him, awkwardly pushed against the other side, leaving a gap between us. Like the gaps in his teeth.

I waited, hoping.

And hoping.

And finally, he sighed, super long (like ten seconds), with his cheeks and mouth puffed out, and with the weight of the world exiting his broken body in a gust of fog. "Aiyah, Ali, where do I begin?"

It was a dark and stormy night. . . .

I said nothing.

He folded his hands in his lap and thumbed a scar that ran from his knuckle to his wrist. "My father, your great-grandfather, was part of the Kuomintang Party. Quite high up."

I nodded. That part I knew, had heard a hundred times: how my great-grandfather had escaped to Taiwan by plane, where he'd met my great-grandmother, then had my grandfather.

And then suddenly, with Bógōng's mainland accent ringing in my ears, it hit me.

"He left you behind," I stated, my voice hushed. My great-grandfather had left his first family behind to escape to Taiwan, then started a new one, my dad's branch of the giant family tree I'd previously seen only a portion of.

He didn't ask me how I'd put it together; he just told me his past. "The day my father fled from China to Taiwan schismed my life into Before and After . . . and who I was Before died." He paused. "It may sound dramatic, but I'm not exaggerating. Sometimes a piece of you must die for the rest of you to survive, and for me, I lost so much I became a different person."

I know the feeling. On a much, much different scale, but definitely the same idea.

"I don't blame him for leaving, not completely," he said, his eyes not on me but not avoiding me either. He was just . . . absent. "Nobody knew what was happening. He claimed he was escaping capture and execution, and that after the Kuomintang regrouped in Taiwan, they would come back and fight. For us. For China. He said he could only get one seat on the plane, and that his life was most in danger. Which may have been true, but my mother and I weren't exactly safe either."

He used his tongue to click his partial denture off, then on again, telling me in that one swift movement what had happened to him After. I hovered a (supposedly) comforting palm over his clenched fists. He nodded at it, then eventually managed to say, "He didn't come back; no one did. China sealed the borders. My mother slit her own throat, and I was banished to a labor camp—" He broke off, overcome with emotion, and I grabbed his hand with mine. "All while he . . . he moved on so quickly. I used to resent him for everything: how he didn't save my mother or me, how he married and started a new family as if we could be replaced. And, according to your father, his new family didn't even know about us for a long time."

"How did Bǎbá find out? When?" I had so many questions in my head, but I limited myself to the most urgent.

"I don't know."

Of course. Our family had been drowning in cerulean blue for generations, playing telephone when we didn't have to and leaking truth with every person added to the chain. So much had already been lost; I wanted to plug all the holes and scream at everyone to just fucking learn to communicate . . . but I was just as guilty. I didn't know how to talk to any of them—except my great-uncle, apparently. The great-uncle I hadn't known existed and who felt more like a stranger than family. Was that why we could communicate? Was there something about family that made it impossible to express your thoughts, be yourself?

Bógōng continued, "I spent most of my life wondering: Did he ever think of me? Did he know I was being punished for his political allegiances?"

"Did he?" I whispered, choking out the words because I could barely breathe.

"Eventually. When I was becoming an old man myself. Granted, China didn't open the borders for many decades, but he didn't reach out as soon as he could have." He sighed. "He wrote a letter to the old address. It found its way to me. Quite a miracle, really."

He paused.

"And?" I pushed, needing to know.

"I unleashed all the anger I had bottled up. My last communication with my father, and all I did was pen my hatred and demand the money I felt he owed me. All because I didn't know how to forgive; I didn't know how to ask for love or comfort or an apology. And . . . he wrote a letter back telling me to never bother his family for money, that they were changing their address, and then . . . that was it. I'll never get another chance with him."

I swallowed the enormous lump in my throat. "How did you find us here?"

"Fate," he said simply. His eyes twinkled, but not with mischief or happiness. Perhaps sadness? Guilt?

How did you find us? my father had asked when Bógōng had shown up on the doorstep. So it wasn't Bǎbá who had reached out.

Then I remembered it: the dirt-encrusted envelope in the safe, sent from China to Taiwan—likely the very letter my great-uncle had just spoken of. The fingerprints on it had been small and dainty, clearly my mother's. I hadn't realized it at the time, because it hadn't felt like a significant piece of the puzzle. But now . . .

"Is Fate a tiny, scary woman who doesn't speak much?" I forced my eyes to stay on his so I could read any tells he might have.

The edge of his mouth twitched.

"Why?" I asked. "She paid you, didn't she? I saw the wire transfer. What did she pay you to do?"

He looked down at his lap. "I am still angry, Ali," he told me instead. "But I am not as consumed by it as I used to be. Before, I thought the rage fueled me, shielded me, and gave me something to grasp on to, but really it ate away at my soul until there was barely anything left. After dying another death, I woke up to realize I don't have much time left in this world." He turned to face me. "Don't let the same thing happen to you."

I wanted to ask him to tell me what he knew, but a part of me also felt like it was such a small thing now. How could I feel anything but grateful living a life like this one? He fucking Botoxed my perspective, all right.

"You are even better than I thought you would be," he continued, "but I can see that this place has taken some of your sweetness. What happened to the girl who didn't leave her father's side for two days after he was denied tenure? Who covered him with a blanket after he cried himself to sleep, then dozed beside him? I still see her inside your tough exterior, but she's too scared to show herself now."

My insides seized up. "How do you know about that?" My father would never have spoken of that time, and my mother had been too busy yelling at him to notice my presence.

My great-uncle's eyes tightened; he hadn't meant to show me how much he knew about my past.

"What are you hiding?" I asked, more demanding this time. "It's about me; I deserve to know."

Instead of answering, he reached into his oversize, pilled sweater and then hovered his enclosed fist over mine until I opened my hand. Penny-size origami turtles swam through the air into my palm—four brilliant patches of red, green, orange, and blue, so bright against my sun-deprived skin.

"Are you trying to insult me? Or wish me death?" Because of the *turtle egg = son of a bitch* deal, turtles were an offensive symbol, and the number four represented death due to the two words being homophones in Mandarin.

Bógōng chuckled. "I don't believe in luck anymore—not even

mole-hair luck—and I like to focus on how turtles are so resilient. Always determined to persevere. Thinking of them this way doesn't take away the negative connotation, but both can find a way to coexist, no?"

I stared at the little fighters nestled in the crease of my palm. Looking from them to my great-uncle's sad, weary eyes, I said softly, "I'm sorry about everything that happened to you."

"You didn't do anything."

"That's not the point. Sometimes you just need to hear the word 'sorry,' and that someone else knows you've gone through hell and back."

"Then I'm sorry, Ali. In more than one way. Please remember that for the future." He stared straight into my eyes, into *me*, as he said in a clarion call, "You've been given a gift—your life doesn't revolve around surviving. You can *live*. Sometimes it's hard, but you have more choices than I did. So live."

Before I could question him further, he rose from the bench and padded home, leaving a trail of cerulean blue in his wake.

CHAPTER 19

ALI-GYVER

My bógōng didn't just Botox my perspective—he Hulk-smashed everything I thought I knew, leaving a million broken pieces I didn't know how to rebuild. I spent the rest of Saturday feeling overwhelmed. Then, by Sunday morning, I was deeply regretful but couldn't pinpoint why.

Was it wrong that my first instinct seemed to be to find the answers myself instead of asking, even if it meant violating someone's privacy? Then again, how could my instincts be any other way given how my family operated?

Conversation had never been our answer. With my mother, the most extensive dialogue we seemed to have was her telling me over and over, *You know I want the best for you, right?*

At first I used to sit in my room repeating "the best" over and over to myself in her voice, trying to feel the threads of love that should have reached out to embrace me. But every time, without fail, the doubts would take over. Because how could someone who thought penises were the best have good judgment? How could someone who barely saw me know what the best was?

Then, after a while, it became that thing where I heard the words so often they lost meaning, and when I opened my eyes, I saw them for what they were: a blatant lie and an excuse to run my life. And eventually it became easier to simply take matters into my own hands. Except . . . was Bógōng right? If I continued this way, swimming through the deep blue secrets without coming up for air, would I wake up old, still angry, and full of remorse?

I was already regretting how everything had played out with Chase. And I couldn't just sit here and let it stew, not after the Hulk smash and learning everything my bógōng had gone through.

I dragged myself out of bed and snuck the family laptop into the bathroom, not worrying about getting caught since my mother was swishing away at the stove and wouldn't come upstairs because my father was on this floor.

When I turned the computer on, I was shocked but not shocked to find it was fingerprint-password protected. Now it made sense why the laptop was in its usual spot on my father's nightstand and not in the safe. I retrieved some glue plus the transparencies from my father's graduate-school days that my mother wouldn't throw out because "you never know when you'll need them" (which, yes, was making me double over from the irony). After an hour of playing Ali-Gyver, I was in.

Instead of logging into my old email, I made a new one based on our name puns to match Chase's. Ignoring the pang that surfaced, I clicked the compose button. Immediately my fingers started flying of their own accord; apparently written word was easier for me than spoken.

Chase,

I'm sorry for how things devolved. For what I said. I should've been more sympathetic about your family situation, and I now remember what it was like, how deep the shame can sink its claws in, and how it's not something you can just get over. I should've been more supportive.

You hurt me, too

Shit. I deleted that last line. This was an apology, not another confrontation.

I will try harder.

Hmm. I deleted that and replaced it with:

Let's be better about communicating. I now
know your preferences, and when I'm not sure,
I'll ask. Maybe via email, but I'll find a way.

Okay.

Ali

My finger hovered over the send button.

I wanted to throw up.

Just do it.

Damn it, I couldn't.

I closed out the unsent email, the (1) by my drafts folder taunt-ing and haunting me as it would for days to come.

What was wrong with me?

I stared at my inbox for a long time, trying to dissect myself. When the screen darkened, I didn't recognize the face staring back at me.

At some point I numbly pulled up a new message and typed an email I *could* send—to Yun, to say all the things I hadn't been able to two months ago. I didn't hesitate before firing this one off, because with Yun it didn't feel like my glass heart would shatter depending on how he responded.

From: AliAliOxenFree@gmail.com
To: Yun.C.Kao@gmail.com
Time: 9:25 a.m. EST
Subject: Udderly Sorry

Um, hey, you. As the subject of this email clearly states: I am udderly sorry. I should've tried to explain myself better before, which was that I was trying to bond with you and tell you I support you. (Really.) Look, I'm sorry it's been sucky for you and I can't understand, but I do support you and want to give you a hug from afar (and only from afar because I don't like to be touched . . . nothing personal). Anyway, I'm trying to tell you a little about me in the hopes that you can maybe understand a smidge better how I mean well but don't know how to show it sometimes. Oftentimes. And I know I have shit with my mom but I'm not ready to face it and maybe I overreacted. Hope you can forgive me.

Yeah. That's all. You don't have to respond if you don't want. If you can't forgive me, I hope this email at least amoosed you.

Yeah I went there.

From: Yun.C.Kao@gmail.com
To: AliAliOxenFree@gmail.com
Time: 10:17 p.m. CST
Subject: Re: Udderly Sorry

Moooo.

Okay fine I guess you're forgiven, but it's only because you said udderly.

.

.

.

.

.

.

.

.

And if you scrolled down this far, then we can be friends because you'll know the previous line was a joke. I forgave you only because you said amoosed.

Okay, no seriously, I'm sorry too, Ali. To be honest, I've been in a bit of a haze for the past couple years and there's just too much manure between my dad and me, just like at Smelly Pines. I may have even taken some of that out on you, though, no, now that I think about it, you were quite abysmal in your social skills (please imagine me with a monocle and top hat pursing my lips as I say "abysmal"). But now that you've explained yourself, I'm sorry I reacted the way I did. Thanks for reaching out and apologizing. That, my friend, means you're not even the same Ali from the cowfeteria. Kudos to you.

And thank you for your words of support. Since you're the only person who knows about . . . me . . . it means a lot.

All right, enough cheese. I'll smell ya later, my favorite cowgirl. Don't be a stranger.

← correct cowgirl

← incorrect cowgirl

CHAPTER 20

GO BACK

When Chase passed me in the hallway the next morning, a hesitant smile on my face, he gave me a sad upward tilt of his lip and kept moving, taking my heart with him.

That was why I used to keep everyone out: because once someone gained enough of a hold on you, they had the ability to crush you so small you disappeared. But even knowing that, I didn't regret letting Chase in.

I wasn't sure what he was doing that lunch period, but he wasn't in the cafeteria, and I couldn't stomach being in there without him. So I made my way to the parking lot to execute my sad plan

of munching on a gross PB&J while running through my favorite barehand forms.

No Chase, no friends . . . I was so embarrassed I wanted to disappear for real. Could I just dig a hole and be swallowed up to the other side of the world?

Which was . . . China . . .

Shit. I mean, why not? I couldn't bear to be here right now, and maybe I could learn something about the park.

So there I was, adjacent to secondhand Chevys and Fords, a soggy piece of sandwich in my mouth, when my thousand-mile journey took a seven-thousand-mile turn toward China.

Mid-hamstring stretch, I noticed a familiar outline hovering at the edge of the parking lot. I continued, not caring that she was watching, and after a few more stretches, my peripheral vision confirmed that it was indeed Kyle loitering there, her keys out and ready to insert into her Chevrolet but frozen midair as if someone had pressed pause. She was chewing her lip the way she always did when she was steeling herself for something. Then she marched over to me with purpose.

"Can't we just go back to the way it was?" she said, the sentence coming out more like a command than a question.

I didn't answer. Couldn't. Because a part of me wanted to yell *Yes!* and pretend like none of this had happened.

But then . . .

"Allie," she started.

And I cut her off. "It's Ali."

Silence.

"If it weren't for me, you would've been alone the past few years," she finally said.

Quietly I responded, "Meaning I should be so grateful it doesn't matter how you treat me?"

"I didn't treat you badly." Her voice and stance were completely confident.

It wasn't my job to make her understand, and could someone like her even be swayed?

"I deserve to be myself," I said finally, with confidence.

"Well, then maybe you should go back to where you came from, *Allie*," Kyle snapped at me.

"You mean Boston?" I yelled after her, but she didn't seem to hear.

I took her words as a sign from the universe that I should do it: go to China, escape from this wreckage, and find out more about my mother's secrets—all while sending Kyle a twisted Ali-style *fuck you*. No more steps backward—only forward from here on out.

Zhu Yingtai
Hangzhou, China

"Can I share another secret with you, Shanbo?"

He smiled. "Nothing would please me more."

Swallowing the last of my doubts—this was merely a moment between good friends, I assured myself—I led Shanbo between abandoned buildings to the hidden gem I had discovered weeks ago during one of my many explorations around the school grounds to locate hiding places and escape routes for if/when my skeletons came to light.

"Are you sure we're allowed in there?" Shanbo whispered as we approached the gate. As usual, the rusted padlock was hanging open like a snoring lion's mouth, vines dripping down like strings of saliva.

Shanbo's innocence was endearing; he could use a little more color in his life, and who better to paint it than me, the rebelliousness to his tīnghuà?

We entered silently, reverently, as a place such as this compelled. Our feet trod side by side along the cobblestone path.

Shanbo was walking with his hands clasped behind his back and his head toward the ground, drowning in his thoughts as usual. I grabbed his arm, reveling in the freedom of my men's haircut, and then I swung him in a graceful arc. He tripped over the cobblestones slightly, but I held tighter, righting his balance.

"Shanbo! You always have your head down, lost in your thoughts. Don't you realize you're missing the world? We're outside, the sun is shining on us, and just look!" I reached over and gently directed his head left, then right, first toward the rock sculptures in the center of the big pond, and then toward the stone wall. "Look at where we are!"

With a smile, he answered quite literally: "A butterfly garden." He pointed toward the entrance at the faded HÚDIÉ HUĀYUÁN sign partially covered by foliage and time. I hadn't noticed it before, but now it was clear as day. And here I had been poking fun at him for not noticing things. Perhaps we noticed different things— yin and yang.

"Alas, there aren't any more butterflies, at least not that I've seen." They had all moved into my stomach, perhaps.

"I may have a tendency to lose myself to my thoughts, but just because I'm not looking directly at it doesn't mean I don't see," he said. I stopped breathing. But then he continued, "I see the beauty here, yes, but I also think about how it must have taken quite the effort to create this sanctuary. I hope it's a labor of love, not just labor. Do you think anyone suffered to build it?"

"You were born to be a scholar, Shanbo. Such a pure, gentle heart you have."

He smiled, genuinely, showing me his crooked teeth. I hadn't seen him bless anyone else with that kind of unadulterated joy yet. Maybe he will smile like that for his bride, *I thought sadly.*

"You are wrong, Shunan," he said. "A true scholar would be wondering whatever it is you're thinking about. You are the true scholar between the two of us."

I laughed, the loud, hearty sound filling my soul and the grounds. It reverberated off the stones and settled in the pockets of the garden to dwell in secret forever, where Zhu Yingtai would live long after she would return home to become someone else, someone she wouldn't recognize or respect.

I took hold of his hands and started running, pulling him along, so free in this moment that my toe snagged on a misplaced cobblestone. In my efforts to right myself, my body flung left, then right.

And then the cloth binding my chest, wound too tight for too long, ripped, falling to the ground and freeing my womanly shape for the world—and Shanbo—to see.

CHAPTER 21

SHIT + FAN

Before committing to the China trip (because I knew the second I brought it up to my mother, it was happening), I wanted to talk to Chase.

The following day, right before lunch, I hurried to exit the classroom first, then waited for him on the other side of the door, my back against a locker. As I'd hoped, he immediately understood I was mimicking his stance from our non-meet-cute (meet-ugly?), and finally—finally!—there it was, that crooked grin.

"Lunch?" I asked.

He nodded.

We traipsed into the cafeteria in silence and sat at the garbage free-throw table, already covered in wrappers and crumpled brown bags.

I swept the trash off and settled in beside Chase as he brought out his biàndāng. I tried not to look too *I'll have what she's having* as I inhaled, savoring the smell of home, savoring the fact that I was enjoying this *here*, of all places. Mmm . . . scallion-and-egg stir-fry with breaded pork chops. My eyes popped open to confirm. I'd gotten pretty damn good at this.

As we dug in (and my heart had fluttered when he'd handed me an extra pair of chopsticks), I tried to focus on the task at hand: telling him about China.

But, no surprise, I was having a hard time finding my words.

As we munched in silence, Brenda made a point to stop by and say hello. Two minutes later, when Kyle accidentally walked by, she sniffed and scowled, as if reiterating that she had been correct to say "ew" that day. It took every ounce of self-control (and some qigong fist clenches) not to say "ew" to her judgmental face. To all those who say *they're not worth your time,* I say, *it depends what you do with that time* . . . but fine, I left her alone.

A green-eyed, strawberry-blond girl in a fitted sweater and jeans shuffled up to the table.

"Hey, Wendy," I said, greeting her first. I wanted to add *Thanks for standing up for me with the rice paddies last week,* but I couldn't quite get it out for some reason. I racked my brain, and the memory resurfaced: We were kids at a pool party, and she and her friends had been whispering right before their designated messenger (not Wendy, but how much does that matter?) ran over to tell me I couldn't go in the water because I would turn it yellow, "like tinkle water." I made fun of their use of the words "tinkle water," then cannonballed in. No one else joined me, and I spent the entire party in the pool in defiance.

Wendy scooted onto the bench opposite Chase and me with an expression like she'd just shit herself and was trying to keep everyone from noticing. She shook Chase's hand when he introduced himself but wouldn't meet his gaze.

"That smells good," she finally said.

"Do you want to try some?" Chase offered, holding his chopsticks out to her, then hesitating because, well, yeah, she probably didn't know how to use them.

But she gingerly took them and scooped a piece of pork chop into her palm, then popped it in her mouth. Well, that'd teach me to be the same kind of stereotypical ass I complained about.

She swallowed and grinned. "Yum. Brings back good memories."

"Yeah?" Chase said just as I leaned back in shock.

She nodded. "My stepbrother and his wife adopted a boy from China, and they work really hard to incorporate his culture into his life." She blushed as she said in a heavy accent, "Ní hǎo. Shuǐ. Xiǎo lóng bāo."

When I laughed, her face fell, and I explained: "Good priorities—learning how to order dumplings first. After you learn 'wǒ xūyào niào niao,' you're all set." I paused. "And then you can use 'niào niao' instead of 'tinkle water.'"

She flushed and cast her eyes downward, but she didn't apologize.

Chase, not knowing just how heavy the words 'tinkle water' were, said to me, "She could also learn 'Where's the bathroom?'

instead of 'I need to pee,' though, don't you think?"

I shook my head. "What if it's an emergency? Better to learn 'I need to pee.'"

Wendy smiled. "Thanks. Wǒ xūyào niào niao," she repeated. "I'll teach that to my nephew—he'll get such a kick out of it." She licked her lips, stalling, and then her face grew serious. "Look, it sucks that things have been tough for you." She paused, and I wondered if she was thinking about the parts that had involved her. "I didn't really think about it until that incident the other day, and I realized that if it had been my nephew, I would've wished for others to defend him. So I said something." She looked so proud of herself.

"Thank you," I said.

"You're welcome. Thanks for the food." She smiled at both of us before leaving to join her friends, no longer shuffling but with a bounce in her step. I couldn't help wondering if that conversation had alleviated her guilt more than it should have.

Once Wendy was out of hearing range, I steeled myself. If she could say all that, I could spit it out too. "So . . . ," I started.

"I still need some space," Chase said just as I said, "I think I'm going to be away."

We both paused awkwardly.

"In China," I finished.

"Oh!" Even though it was exactly what he had asked for, he seemed surprised. "Are you going to the park?"

I nodded. "And I also just feel like I need to get out of here for a bit, find myself, you know."

"I hope you do. That sounds great." We were speaking like strangers.

Chase started to say something else, but whatever it was, I didn't hear. Because out of the corner of my eye, I saw a familiar shape—one that made my heart stop beating for a second. I convinced myself it was just fear conjuring her. When I turned and saw my mother standing there with her hands on her hips, my vision blurred.

All my brain could come up with was *fuuuuck*. It took me a second to see Mr. Laurelson standing behind her.

My mother flicked her head to the side, and leaving Chase behind, I zombie-walked beside them to the counselor's office.

Step-step-step-step, *shit shit shit shit*.

My mouth opened to tell my mother Chase and I weren't really together (at least not right now), but it was completely dry and soundless.

Once we were seated with the door closed, she cleared her throat. "The counselor tells me you and Chase have made quite the spectacle of yourselves around school."

I glared at the traitor.

"Ali, listen," Mr. Laurelson said, his voice wavering. "You know I'm always on your side and only have your best interest at heart. I read an article recently—in a reputable journal—about how tiger parenting works, and how it comes from a place of caring. And it just got me to look at this whole . . . thing"—he gestured desperately to my mother, who was sitting completely motionless in her chair beside me—"in a new light."

"So you read one 'reputable' article, and now you're an expert on our culture, on what it's like to be the child of a Taiwanese immigrant growing up in a predominantly white Midwestern town?" It was easier to attack him than my mother, who I was avoiding eye contact with like she was Medusa.

Mr. Laurelson wiped some sweat from his brow with a wrinkled handkerchief—which, yes, was endearing, but not enough to excuse his non-PC meddling. "I was worried about you." His hand shook, and I wondered if he was scared of my mother or felt bad for what he'd done to me. Maybe now that she was here, he could see the extent of his actions. "You've not only been sent to see me several times, but you broke into my office—I saw the scratch on the locks and checked the security footage. You've never done anything like this before, and I see now why your mother thinks Chase is a bad influence."

"It wasn't your place to tell," I whispered, even though it didn't matter. Everyone in the room knew we were all just biding our time because my mother and I didn't want to actually—*gasp*—communicate.

"Stop blaming him," my mother said to me. "I saw the Vaseline on the window. Give me some credit, Ali."

I said nothing. She hadn't earned anything.

I spoke to Mr. Laurelson instead. "Did you also break student-counselor confidentiality"—if that's even a thing—"and tell her about Chase's family?"

"Whoa, whoa, whoa," Mr. Laurelson said frantically, holding both palms out. "I did no such thing."

"What about Chase's family?" my mother asked.

I stared her down, calling her bluff. But she continued to question me. "What will I find if I look into them?" She turned to Mr. Laurelson. "What's there to know? You have to tell me; I'm being a good tiger parent."

My confidence waned. "But *you* told me his family was 'no good,'" I said after a few seconds.

"I just meant that because they moved here, there must be something wrong with them," my mother answered with a shrug, implying that there was also something wrong with us.

Oh my God. I saw the truth in her eyes: she had lied to me all those days ago, implying things when she knew nothing. This was all. Her. Fault. It made me want to scream. It made me want to grab all the binders and chuck them across the room, send the sheets of paper flying in a horrible, beautiful mess.

"What is *wrong* with you?" I yelled at her.

Mr. Laurelson leaned back in his chair. *Yeah, you and me both want to get outta here, buddy.* It gave me a little satisfaction to see him so uncomfortable in the situation *he'd* created. Well, sort of.

I continued after her at the same volume. "Why're you so secretive all the time? Do you just derive utility from keeping stuff from me and Bǎbá since you seem to hate everything else in your life? What is so terrible about me and Chase being together?"

My mother took a deep breath. "Ali . . ." She paused, then repeated my name as if she were imagining herself back on the mountain, back in her old life. "Ali, I'm sorry this has been tough on you. I truly am. Everything I do is for you, with your best inter-est in mind—"

"Yes, exactly as the article said!" Mr. Laurelson interrupted.

She nodded politely to him, then continued. "I know it's diffi-cult to be missing so many details, but please trust me. It's for the best. I'm speaking from experience."

"How can I trust you when I don't know anything about you or your goddamn experience?" I turned away from her to face the kitten poster on the wall that said, HANG IN THERE! *You hang in there,* I wanted to scream at it; then I realized that the kitten was forever hanging there on that clothesline.

"I'll go to China," I said quietly. "Because I need to get away from you." *And I need to know what you're hiding. And I have nobody left here.* "But I'll go only if it's to Shanghai, where Yun is." *Which is also only a two-hour car ride to Hangzhou and the park.*

My mother's eyes brightened, but her voice came out strained, like she was trying not to show me just how excited she was. "Of course it will be to Shanghai—I can sleep at night only if you are with a trusted family friend. And I already bought your plane ticket and sorted your schoolwork out with Mr. Laurelson. You leave in two days."

Rage mixed in with my excitement. "Seriously, Mǔqīn?"

She flinched. "The money came in and there was a deadline to buy the ticket; I had no choice, Ali."

"No, I'm the one who never has a choice."

At that time, I had no idea how true that sentence was.

From: AliAliOxenFree@gmail.com
To: Chase.You@gmail.com
Time: 4:58 p.m. EST
Subject: See you when I see you

Just letting you know I'm leaving in two days. I'll
be back in a couple weeks. That's all.

From: Chase.You@gmail.com
aTo: AliAliOxenFree@gmail.com
Time: 5:33 p.m. EST
Subject: Re: See you when I see you

Have a good trip, be safe, and I hope you find
out a lot of stuff. If you're up for it, maybe we
can talk when you get back. Thanks for giving
me space.

P.S. Love the new email address.

From: AliAliOxenFree@gmail.com
To: Yun.C.Kao@gmail.com
Time: 5:36 p.m. EST
Subject: Moo, bitch, get out the way

. . . because I'm coming to Shanghai! In case
your father didn't already tell you.

From: Yun.C.Kao@gmail.com
To: AliAliOxenFree@gmail.com
Time: 8:22 a.m. CST
Subject: Re: Moo, bitch, get out the way

!!!!!!!!!!!!!

Shit's about to get shady up in here!

And no, he didn't tell me. I'm not that surprised,
unfortunately.

📎 MeWithShadyPinesMug.jpg

CHAPTER 22

ACHILLES' HEEL

The evening of my departure, my great-uncle and father wished me well on my journey. Meanwhile, my mother's mood swings from giddy to stern were just another shade of blue to color my world.

My father patted my shoulder—his form of a good-bye—as he said, "I wish you could have gone to Taiwan instead, to see where your mother and I came from and . . ." He hesitated, glancing over at her. "And where we fell in—where we met." He was sweating bullets. "You could've seen your namesake, Ali—how fun would that have been?" He rubbed his chin with one hand. "Why couldn't you go to Taiwan, actually? Where did the money for this trip come from again?"

"Not from you, that's for sure," said stern version of Mǔqīn. That, along with her dèngyiyǎn, shut him up.

It was the most my father had expressed in a while, with a rare mention of a magical time long past, and she'd extinguished the spark with an ocean of water just to ensure it would never burn again.

I tried to give my dad a sympathetic look, to find a way to show him I still saw him, but his gaze was now glued to the floor.

When my great-uncle pulled me into a hug, the room buzzed with shock, and my mother's dèngyiyǎn developed an ominous tint.

"Live *your* life, Ali," Bógōng whispered in my ear before slipping a handful of turtles into my coat pocket.

Gerald, Bernadette, Randolf, and Klondike, I named them immediately.

My dad came over and pulled me into a hug as well, but unlike my great-uncle's, his felt competitive, especially since he'd already said good-bye. I managed a smile at both of them before I climbed in the car beside my mother.

I wasn't sure why she was taking me to O'Hare when she avoided driving every chance she got. But then, I realized, my dad would have refused. Unlike my mom, he'd feel pressure to at least try to converse with me, and the two-hour trip was probably more than he could bear.

God, I couldn't wait to take a breath of clean, non-cerulean air. Why the hell did I have to travel to the other side of the globe to find it?

It was silent for most of the ride as my mother stared at the road and reacted too much to every car around us. But when we inched closer to the airport (and I really mean inched, because O'Hare traffic was the pits, man), she finally said, her hands gripped on the wheel and eyes not on me, "Thank you for agreeing to this trip and trusting me that it's the best for you. I want to tell you, Ali . . ."

I stopped breathing.

"I've put money away, all for you. I want you to go to whatever college you choose—in the top rankings, of course—without worrying about having to pay back a loan. Like I always say, everything I do is for you."

So much irony. I'd agreed to the trip not because I trusted her, but because I was planning to dig into her secrets, and I already knew about the college fund from invading her privacy.

"Thank you," I managed to eke out around the enormous lump in my throat.

"I've planned your whole itinerary for you and worked it out with Mr. Kao and his driver. Yun's happy to accompany you, of course. I want to make sure you see everything worth seeing without wasting any time." She was rambling a bit, and I wondered what she was covering up.

After a pause she jerked her head toward the back seat, and I reached over to retrieve a tote bag filled with Dramamine, a stainless steel water bottle, several magazines, and a pack of Trident.

"Chew the gum during takeoff and landing," she instructed me. "Swallowing helps your ears stay clear so you don't get that plugged feeling. I get motion sickness, so just . . . be prepared. If there isn't a motion-sickness bag in your seat, ask for one."

I hugged the care package to my chest, unable to get my thanks out this time.

We inched forward another block.

"Mǎmá?" I said hesitantly.

"Hmm?" Her eyes never left the road.

"Even if I do trust you, can we maybe still talk?" The words felt like sandpaper against my throat, the lie of my "trust" scratching the fleshy walls raw. "Why are you so against Chase and me being together?"

She sighed, huffing her breath out forcefully like I should've known better than to bring this up.

But I kept going. "You didn't want us to be together the second you saw us; you didn't even give him a chance." I felt utterly, completely naked.

"Your counselor told me about Chase as soon as he arrived," she stated, clipped. Then her voice dropped and she muttered, "Damn racists, putting us all together." I felt closer to her in that moment.

"That doesn't answer my question."

She cleared her throat. "Ali, sometimes when you are young, you don't know enough to make the right decisions."

That had as much to do with my question as I should've expected, but because I'd stepped so far out of my comfort zone, I had foolishly let a bud of hope bloom.

She continued, oblivious to what was going on in my head. "You know how in Chinese culture we revere the elderly? It's because of their wisdom and experience. I thought I knew what I wanted when I was young. . . ." She trailed off for a moment, and from the forlorn look that crossed her face, I knew she meant my father. "Did you know I was disowned for marrying him?"

Yes.

"Why?" I squeaked out, hoping I didn't look suspicious.

"Because they didn't think he was good enough for me. He didn't come from a good family with money—yes, he worked hard, but they didn't think he'd make it, not when so much luck is needed in this world."

I ventured a toe in the water. "But he's done just fine. He's a professor—isn't that respected? And you've been able to raise a family and put aside enough money for my college tuition—not many people can say that."

She sighed. "Yes, but at such sacrifices. If I'd married better, we would have been able to live more comfortably, with less stress." She pointed to her black hair streaked with gray.

"Marriage isn't a business transaction. Didn't you love him? Don't you love him now?"

Her eyes darted left, then right. "It's hard to love anyone when you're planning how you're going to feed your daughter and provide for her future."

I waited, my fists so tight they were growing numb, but I refused to speak until she gave me more than that pathetic answer.

Eventually she said, "Ali, I didn't know about Chase's family before, but I did look them up after what you said in the counselor's office. And his family situation is a problem. They're probably in a large amount of debt that would fall to you if you married him.

But . . . my reasoning for why you can't be with Chase was already in place before he showed up."

What?

I mean, *What?*

I pictured the wire transfer from the safe. "Did it start seven months ago?"

The car swerved, and I heard screaming before realizing it was coming from my open mouth.

"Why would you ask me that?" she demanded once the car was back in its lane. But she was at the edge of her seat, shoulders raised, gripping the steering wheel with white knuckles.

"I don't know!" I lied, my eyes glued to the white dotted line, praying to any god that she was fully back in control now.

It was silent for a moment as the tension heightened to an all-time high.

I gripped the roof handle and hoped to that same god that the look in her eyes wasn't her putting all the pieces together, that she hadn't noticed the scratches on the safe lock, that there wasn't just one thing that had happened seven months ago. . . .

But I knew her better than I thought. I saw when everything clicked into place, and in my head it sounded exactly like when her safe's tumblers had clicked into the unlock position. This time, though, my hands were sweaty with dread, not anticipation.

She sank back in her seat, disappointed. "How could you, Ali? My safe?"

"I had no choice," I whispered. "You never tell me anything. What was I supposed to do? It's . . . exactly . . . what . . . you would've done," I realized with horror. Fuck the apple and the tree—how had I let this happen?

She was shaking her head adamantly. "No, I'm the mother and you're the daughter—what you did was so disrespectful and just . . . I have no words, Ali! Did I raise you to be like this? I've completely failed as a parent!"

"You've barely raised me at all. And yes, you've failed, but it has nothing to do with the safe!"

I saw the hurt in her eyes, but there was so much anger pulsing inside me, it pushed out the regret.

"I don't know you at all," she whispered.

I already knew that, but somehow hearing it from her lips still broke me. "You really don't, Mǔqīn," I threw back at her. She flinched. "And instead of judging me, maybe you should take a good hard look at yourself first: the mother and wife who felt she needed a safe from her own family, who won't tell her husband or daughter where the money for this China trip came from, who gave up her previous family for a new one she doesn't seem to want either."

I'd struck her Achilles' heel with intention, and the regret wouldn't set in until hours later.

I didn't look at her the rest of the drive, and the car door slamming was the only sound as I left all this blue shit behind me.

Look out, Mǔqīn: I'm going to uncover your secrets on this trip. Every. Last. One.

THE PARK

AS SEEN FROM AFAR

THREE MONTHS EARLIER

At the center of the park, shrouded by shrubbery—the most popular rendezvous point due to the surrounding tree cover—a man with a scar extending from his upper lip to his nose met another man with missing teeth and a long, lucky mole hair.

The man with missing teeth took one last look at the now-familiar face staring up at him, and he prayed that this was the best for everyone involved and not just him. Especially now that he'd remembered what it was like to have loved ones.

Papers were exchanged.

"They can never know," he had whispered, repeating the words he'd heard over the phone, following each instruction to a T to ensure his payment. The words floated along the wind, landing in a shadowed corner of the park, tucked away in secret.

"Agreed."

That word summed it all up, and with those two syllables, the world shifted ever so slightly.

CHAPTER 23

FAT SOUP

Um, so it turned out I was totally okay spinning in the air for kung fu moves, but plane rides? Puke city.

I hated when my mother was right. Or maybe I was puking because my last conversation with her had completely sickened me and I couldn't get either her words or mine out of my head.

When all was upchucked and done, I expected to feel better, but this was not like taking a huge dump—I felt just as gross as before.

I popped a Dramamine and passed the F out. For the rest of the flights, plural.

A story of Ali on motion-sickness drugs in three parts: (1) a much-less-cute version of Sleepy Kitty in which I banged my head on everything around me (sorry, noggin); (2) drooling, open-mouthed sleeping with vivid dreams of sparring (sorry, neighbor); (3) ravenous, dehydrated monster (sorry, flight attendants). I'd always reacted strongly (and weirdly) to drugs; I guess I tended to take everything to the extreme, huh?

Twenty-five hours later, I arrived at the Shanghai airport. I just barely managed to drag myself from the pull of the Dramamine to get my luggage, and baggage claim and customs were somehow more stressful than the plane. Just so many bodies, all squished together, pushing and shoving—I mean, maybe it was so crowded in China that you had to learn not to need a personal bubble, but it took me by surprise. Who knew I could get culture shock when it was supposedly my culture? Except . . . it wasn't really, was it? I wasn't Chinese enough to belong here, just like Yun had complained to me previously, and I wasn't American enough for Indiana.

I almost walked right past the young man holding the sign that said ALI CHU in English (and I couldn't help feeling slightly offended—I knew my Chinese name, and they didn't have to make me stand out so much, did they?), but somehow he knew to wave at me and ask if I was Ali.

I did my best to smile at him, and even though I didn't want to, I felt a little baller following him out to a sleek black car that screamed, *Someone important rides in here.*

As I fought the last dregs of Dramamine in my system, I forced my eyes open to take in the ubiquitous neon, the glitzy malls boasting Western luxury brands, and the towering skyscrapers hiding tiny historical gems in between: Buddhist temples with smoking incense, a lush green cobblestone park. Was this what *the* park was like? Was it tucked away between brand-new buildings, forgotten and left to accumulate litter? Or was it far off the beaten path, a distant memory to most and no longer of note to the few who passed it?

I wanted Chase to see what I was seeing.

We sped past run-down shanties with crumbling roofs—and for a moment I couldn't imagine how people resided in those cluttered, cramped "homes." I thought of the houses in my town that everyone knew to steer clear of—that guy who kept a toilet in his yard among tires and old bookshelves, and that woman who kept as much furniture on her porch as indoors (and yes, she used it—she was often seen reclining in her porch La-Z-Boy), and while that was eccentricity at its best, this was just plain poverty, and until this moment I hadn't realized just how privileged I'd been.

Not three blocks later we entered a glittering neighborhood. The sleek glass structures signaled that this was the happening place, and I was surprised to see several white people in suits and pencil dresses milling about. Business district, perhaps? I heard Yun in my head from months ago: *My dad's bank job. It was a great opportunity for him but hard for me.*

We pulled up to a gated entrance, and I gawked at the spewing fountain and community center boasting, in big block Chinese characters, a swimming pool and fitness center. Maybe I'd chance a late-night swim in my underwear later.

As the chauffeur helped me unload my luggage from the trunk,

Yun and his dad ran over. There was a round of awkward hugs and over-the-top gushing from Mr. Kao about how great I looked and blah, blah, blah. I handed Mr. Kao the gift bag of American goodies from my mother: Indiana honey, sausage, crackers, hot sauce, and salsa (all from Shady Pines, of course). And yes, he followed with an ungodly number of thank-yous for a mediocre gift. I mean, the thought was nice, yes, but ten thank-yous and you-shouldn't-haves? That would be more for, like, a new saber or spear or rope dart. Or maybe I was just too biased about Indiana, like my bógōng had pointed out.

After reiterating that I should call him Uncle Kao, he waved Yun and me into the building as he discussed tomorrow's schedule with the chauffeur.

Yun nudged my foot with his. "Boop boop."

"Don't you mean, 'Cow've you been?'" I elbowed his side (gently), feeling so much less awkward than last time. "Are you ready to get into some udder nonsense together?"

"You know it!" He grabbed my bag, then led me into his lavish building, where the key cards controlled the elevator.

"Should we wait for him?" I asked, my hand stuck out to hold the elevator door open, but Yun shook his head.

And the second the doors shut, he said, "You remember not to say anything to my dad, right?"

I nodded. I wondered if his mom already knew or wasn't around or lived elsewhere or . . .

His shoulders moved an inch away from his ears. "Sorry, I just had to make sure. I know you know, but I just—"

"I get it." I put a hand on his arm. "And again, I'm sorry about everything last time. It's not an excuse, but I'm an awkward turtle, through and through, and in case it wasn't obvious . . . I got you."

And he finally relaxed, his shoulders moving the rest of the way down. "Thank you." The air thinned, the tension waning. He smiled. "I'm excited you're here. You get my American side. Together, we can be the wàiguóréns adventuring around, wreaking udder havoc."

I laughed. "Like eating our weight in food and yelling about how awesome America is?"

He tsked. "So stereotypical of you. But yes, that is how the Asia Asians see us Asian Americans: gross accents, weird dressers, and frugal. I believe there's a saying that goes, 'Shuōhuà yángqì, chuānzhuó tǔqì, huāqián xiǎoqì.'"

"They really say that? Damn." I glanced down at my blue jeans and hoodie. Maybe that was how the chauffeur had zeroed in on me at the airport. "What's wrong with the way we dress?"

"Eh, people just don't like what's different." He paused, and the heaviness of what else his words referred to hung between us.

"That was an udder mood changer."

He smirked. "Really, Chu?"

I shrugged. "It was right there."

I followed him into an immaculate apartment that was more model home than lived-in. Three bedrooms, view of the skyscrapers—man, with Shanghai pricing, this must be at least a few million dollars. In each bedroom I passed, stacks of perfectly folded shirts crowned the bed. I was about to make a joke to Yun when we walked by the kitchen and a woman waved hello.

"Kao Āyí hǎo," I immediately said, then thanked her in Mandarin for letting me stay with them.

"Oh!" She flushed the same color as the red bean soup she was stirring. "I'm the maid," she told me in Mandarin. "But welcome. Let me know if there's anything I can do for you."

Then, on the other side of the hallway, I saw the offering table. In the center sat a portrait of a pretty, smiling Chinese woman with Yun's eyes and nose. And with that, the cerulean blue in the apartment (except for Yun's secret) vanished in a trail of incense smoke.

"I'm sorry about your mother," I said quietly.

Yun just nodded and showed me to the guest room.

After I napped off the rest of the Dramamine, I cleaned up in the most luxurious rain shower I'd ever experienced. Feeling more like myself again, I journeyed with Yun and his dad down the street to Din Tai Fung for dinner.

"So, Ali, what colleges are you applying to?" Yun's dad—er, Uncle Kao—asked me as he poured us jasmine tea. I wasn't sure if I'd ever get used to calling strangers "Auntie" and "Uncle," at least not in English (in Mandarin I'd gotten used to it before I knew what the words meant).

"Well, my Common App is basically filled out, so my bases are covered," I said for maximal conflict avoidance in case whatever I was saying made its way back to my mǔqīn, which, given the dragon-fruit vine of tiny Asian communities, it likely would.

Mr. Kao pursed his lips to the side, which made the scar on

his philtrum stand out more. "Any top contenders?"

What was this, a job interview? I didn't miss this part of having Chinese family friends. "At this point I'm thinking I'll just cast a wide net and see who wants me," I joked (not very well) to try to lighten the extremely weird mood.

Uncle Kao's jaw tensed. "College is serious, Ali. It can determine your whole future."

Was he on my mother's payroll too?

I glanced over at Yun and was relieved to find him staring at me with eyes wide and unblinking, mouth pressed into a thin line. God, it was so hard not to laugh the moment our gazes met. I was glad I had someone here who got me at least somewhat.

The first of our food arrived, saving me. When Yun served himself, then passed the plate to me, his father frowned. Then, when I did the same, serving myself before passing the plate to Uncle Kao, he forced a chuckle. "At least you're similar—weren't you taught to serve your elders first?"

Yun huffed. "I don't know, Dad, weren't you the one who was supposed to teach me?"

"It's America's fault, not mine," Uncle Kao scoffed.

I tried to become invisible by focusing on the food.

When we'd first walked into Din Tai Fung, I had wondered if we were going to a generic chain, because according to the signs, they had locations around the world, including Los Angeles and Seattle. But it turns out, they had branched overseas because . . . the dumplings? Oh my God. UCLA and Washington just shot to the top of my college list, baby—anything for more of those soupy bites of heaven. I wondered if I should voice that aloud; I was sure Uncle Kao and *U.S. News*–rankings Mǔqīn Chu would be ecstatic at my reasoning.

I might have moaned. Yes, out loud. The waiter smiled like he was used to it, Yun nodded in solidarity with his mouth full, and Yun's father looked horrified. Sorry, Uncle Kao, for not following your lead and blasphemously spilling the "fat soup" on my plate *on purpose* to save calories. I dabbed my finger in the drop that had escaped and sucked it dry for emphasis.

Mr. Kao (I just couldn't do the "Uncle" anymore) cleared his throat and side-eyed my fat-soup love (he was lucky I hadn't licked my plate). "So what's on the docket for you kids tomorrow?" he asked in a distracted tone.

Confused, I said, "My mom told me she planned my whole trip out with you and the driver?" *Though I don't intend to stick to her itinerary.*

"Of course, of course. Pardon my forgetfulness—work has been very busy. It was so kind of her to figure all that out with me in advance."

Or did she have ulterior motives? But I nodded in response. "Thanks for letting me stay with you and all that."

He waved my thanks away and I rode out the rest of dinner with head nods and the occasional "uh-huh," all while devoting my attention to the spicy wontons, string beans, and stir-fried rice noodles, which had earned my attentiveness by being so damn tasty. If Mr. Kao's subsequent questions about my family lineage had been more delicious, maybe I would've been more responsive. Besides, I knew about as much as he did.

At least when I fell asleep that night in a foreign bed in a foreign country, my stomach was happy and sated. Maybe the only part of Chinese culture that really belonged to me was the food. Better than nothing.

Zhu Yingtai
Hangzhou, China

Shanbo gaped at the shape of my breasts, my robe just tight enough for my curves to be visible beneath the fabric. His mouth was wide open in surprise and his eyes as round as coins. Meanwhile I was gaping at the cloth coiled on the ground, encircling my gargantuan unbound feet like a giant snake that had just bitten me.

A long list of thoughts ran through my mind: I apologize for deceiving you. Women deserve to be educated. I wish our world were different.

But instead I said, "I love you."

He was still staring, his eyes wandering from my hair to my features to my breasts down to my feet and the cloth, then running the entire circuit again.

"Forget I said that." The words came out partly from fear that he didn't feel the same way, especially given that he was still

openmouthed, gawking, but they were also born of wisdom. He was betrothed to another, the matchmaker having spoken, another family involved. And when I had left, my mother had been narrowing down my choices as well.

"I love you too," he said finally. The words floated along the breeze and into my ears like musical notes, and I had to fight to keep from running to him—not before I was completely clear on what was churning through his beautiful mind.

"You love Shunan? Or me, Yingtai?" I asked before realizing, "Well, actually, I am the same person. Just . . . the outer packaging might be different from what you originally thought."

He ran his lower teeth over his top lip, and I knew he was gathering the courage to show me a part of him I hadn't known before. "I don't care what you are on the outside—I love you either way."

"You mean, as a man or a woman?"

He nodded.

I walked over to him, my cloth long forgotten on the ground, and I took his hand in mine. "I embrace that, and I love you for it." He raised his eyes to meet mine, at long last. "And I'm sorry I had to deceive you," I continued. "It was the only way for me to receive an education."

"Another issue I have with society," he said quietly.

"We're the only ones."

I grabbed his hands again, and we swung in a circle. He leaned toward me slightly, and I knew he was too shy to make the first move, but luckily for him, he'd fallen in love with me,

a non-sān-cóng-sì-dé woman who fought for more. So I pulled gently on his arms and he gladly fell against my lips.

He tasted like freedom.

In that moment, I was truly Zhu Yingtai for the first time, and I already knew I could never go back.

CHAPTER 24

UDDER NONSENSE

The maid packed Yun and me an enormous lunch for our day out. We waited until we were piling into the back seat, giant cooler in tow, to tell the chauffeur, Mr. Lin, that instead of journeying to Suzhou as planned by my mother, we were trekking to Hangzhou and the park. (I made Yun wait to make our itinerary known because I was worried Mr. Lin would tell Mr. Kao, who would tell my mom before I could make the trip, but Yun was right that I didn't have to worry—his father was already gone by the time we woke. Who worked on Sundays?)

Mr. Lin nodded in response to my request and peeled out, leaving me to wonder whether the park was so well known he'd heard of it, or if it was in his job description to know everything in a certain radius. Or perhaps my directions were somehow that good (thanks, Google Maps).

After riding in silence for a bit, Yun and I tore into the cooler of food even though it was ten in the morning and I'd just had some congee. I blamed it on the jet lag, but really, it was simply too hard to ignore the smell of fresh veggies and seasoned meat. And besides, wasn't most food better hot? Maybe that was another part of Chinese culture I connected with—I even preferred hot water to cold, despite Kyle telling me "only weirdos drink that, and I don't hang out with weirdos." Here everyone was a "weirdo" and the maid got my hot water without my specifying.

When our stomachs were way past full, I asked Yun, "Is this, like, your normal life?"

"Nothing feels *normal* about my life, least of all me."

I swallowed the slice of beef rib I'd been savoring as my last bite. "'Normal' is a terrible word," I said. "It really should have a negative connotation. You know, my . . . Chase and I have a running joke about how being as dry as toast is the worst." Hmm, that didn't sound quite so funny explained, did it? Guess inside jokes were meant only for those inside them.

Yun raised an eyebrow. "Your chase? Is that some new American term I'm too uncool to know?"

"Oh. No. Chase is a person. I just . . . well, I guess he's my boyfriend. Was? I don't know. We're going through some stuff."

"A white boy? Is that your preference or an Indiana supply problem?"

I laughed. "I don't really have a preference, but despite the super-white name, he's Chinese. In some ways more so than me, since he grew up in a Chinese community. And my mom *still* disapproves."

He clapped me on the shoulder. "Well, look on the bright side. I'm the president, and I officially welcome you to the Asians Club, where hiding shit from your parents is the only requirement for entry."

"Do you sell tickets for leaving?" Somehow it was easier talking about all this when we weren't directly addressing it.

"Psh. You think I'd still be here if I had access to free wishes?"

Even though it made me uncomfortable, I shoved my head through the metaphor curtain momentarily. "Hey, I'm really sorry, by the way. I mean, my stuff isn't nearly as . . . you know . . . as yours, and . . . yeah, it sucks." Egregious sympathy attempt, but much better than I'd anticipated.

He nodded, then leaned forward and folded his hands in his lap. "So tell me about your man."

My man. I repeated the phrase three times in my head just because I had to before I could move on to form words. "Chase is . . . not what I thought I wanted, but it turns out he's who I needed? He just . . . sees me." None of those words did him justice—how did you describe a feeling, the way someone made you more yourself? "I really miss him," I admitted in a small voice.

Yun shot me a sympathetic smile.

To change the subject, I asked the first question that popped into my mind. "Any luck for you?" Immediately I wished I could suck my words back in, especially after he lowered his eyes. "Sorry, I shouldn't've brought it up—"

"I'm too scared to even try," he blurted out. "I don't speak the language—well, not like they do—and I don't think it's all that open here, not that I've seen anyway, but again, I've barely tried. So half the time I hate myself for being a coward, and the rest of the time I'm afraid my father will find out even though I'm not doing anything."

"I'm so sorry," I said quietly, wishing I could've spoken louder.

"My mother died recently—well, I guess not that recently, it's been two years, but it *feels* recent—and my father and I don't know how to communicate anymore. Not that we ever really knew, but we've been tiptoeing around each other ever since . . . that day. She had a brain aneurysm that erupted. Came out of nowhere." He paused to take a breath, then just stopped, like he couldn't say any more.

We sat in silence for a bit before he changed focus from her death to her life. "My father was so in love with her. Always talking about how she was too good for him, too good for this world. He was born with a cleft lip—I'm sure you've noticed the scar under his nose from the repair—and back then, he claimed, it would've doomed him to being single forever, but he 'convinced' my mother to fall in love with him, which he claimed was his greatest achievement in life."

"I'm so sorry the cleft lip affected what he thought of himself. That's heartbreaking."

"Yeah, definitely." He paused. "I think when he said that about my mom, though, he was trying to point out how she only saw inner beauty, and how he loved her for it."

I nodded. "Sounds like they were really happy. Did you guys move here after her passing?"

Yun shook his head. "We were already here. It's been six years since we moved from Minneapolis."

"Minneapolis? Wow, you've moved around a lot. When did you leave Boston?"

His eyebrows furrowed. "I never lived in Boston."

"You had to have. How else did we have childhood gatherings together?" There was no way we'd met in Indiana—I'd remember that—and the only place I'd lived before that was Boston. I racked my brain again, trying to place child Yun at one of the Asian parties from when I was young, but even after seeing his old yearbook photos I was coming up blank. Had he really not been there?

"Wait," he said slowly, also confused. "You didn't live in Minneapolis?"

I shook my head. "Did you ever even visit Boston?" I asked. That would narrow it down, since I knew we had never traveled to Minnesota.

"No, not until earlier this year, when we were visiting colleges."

After an extra beat during which the revelation sank in further, I asked, "Why did they lie to us?"

"How did they think we wouldn't figure that out?"

Well, it did take us a while, I wanted to point out, but I didn't have the chance, because the chauffeur was pulling over at a crowded, hopping, rè'nào park entrance.

"Are you sure this is it, Mr. Lin?" I called out in Mandarin. But then I saw the sign at the entrance: HÚDIÉ HUĀYUÁN. And then, sure enough, beyond, just barely visible, were the papers.

"Yes, I'm sure," Mr. Lin responded in Mandarin. "It's not my first time here."

I barely heard what he was saying because *I was here*. My breath was ragged, my hands shaky.

Yun's voice broke through the haze. "You okay?"

"I don't know," I answered honestly. I wished Chase could be here with me, but an understanding friend was already more than I'd expected. So I placed a hand on Yun's. "I don't know why I'm nervous. It's just a park, right?"

Mr. Lin peeked at me from the front seat. When our eyes met, he asked, "So are you going in?"

I nodded, and I moved swiftly out of the car without giving myself time to hesitate. (Proverbial) balls in.

The local accents made me feel out of place, and more so, even though I looked like everyone around me, I was so used to Indiana it confused me. Yet at the same time, this place was so distinctly Chinese, with its jagged rock outcroppings, giant lily pads, and angled bridges, that I felt tethered to every part of it, down to the colorful "lucky" carp swimming in the clear ponds.

As my feet padded along the cobblestones, I couldn't help wondering who had trodden here through the years.

The entire space was cluttered with people. So many bodies. More than normal compared to the parks I was accustomed to. Was it because China was overpopulated? Were parks more meaningful here than in the States?

When I looked closer, something felt off. Everyone milling

about was middle-aged or older, and instead of enjoying the scenery, they were focused on the pieces of paper hanging from so many strings they appeared to be puppets, and the branches above, their puppeteers.

Some paused at the surrounding stone wall, leaning down, hands behind their backs, to glean information from the flyers tacked to the side. Others went so far as to take notes and photos.

The park was littered yet not. The areas that didn't hold papers were pristine and manicured, while seemingly designated spots were packed with scraps. Weirder still was that the only pockets crammed with bodies were the latter, even though common sense would have predicted the opposite.

What was this place with its peculiarly organized mess?

I glanced at Yun, and the furrow in his brow plus the intensity of his scrutinizing gaze told me this wasn't the norm here, and I scanned faster, trying to piece everything together.

My examination went first to the pages everyone seemed so interested in. Among a sea of simplified characters were photographs, sometimes at the top of the paper, others at the bottom, some completely random. I looked at one, two, another, and another. All fairly young adults—maybe between eighteen and thirty?—both genders, all East Asian. A few older photos could be found here and there, but not many.

I reached up and took down the closest one, determined to find the commonalities so I could learn the creepy secrets dwelling here.

Below a photo of a young man, in clean block text, his life

was stripped down to five traits: *Height: 175 cm. Weight: 68 kg. Animal: Pig. Job:* Something at the bank (I didn't recognize two of the characters). *Salary: 300,000 yuan.*

Sheet in hand, I turned to the wall beside me. Here the papers resembled the others but were grouped in pairs—always exactly two pages and two photos, one male, one female.

None of it was making any sense.

But then . . .

In the corner of my eye, something registered. It was instinctive, a flicker so strong that even though my glance was fleeting, my subconscious already knew.

It was that feeling you get when you catch a glimpse of a mirror.

Because the photo was me.

CHAPTER 25

TORNADO

My head whipped toward the paper so fast I strained my neck. But I barely noticed. Because it was me and Yun, in two photos on two sheets of paper, separate but side by side amid a sea of Mandarin words. The photo of Yun was the same one I'd found in my mother's safe a week ago.

The kindling was lit, crackling. Pieces of the messy puzzle of my life were inching toward each other like magnets, orienting themselves but not quite in place yet.

My eyes homed in on my name written beneath my photo, which preceded a demeaning list of facts: my height, weight, age, Zodiac animal.

The fire was going full roar now, the flames licking at all edges of my brain.

Then I recognized my mother's name crammed between characters I didn't know. And my bógōng's name listed beside an international phone number.

Suddenly the babbling canals, giant lily pads, and 凹凹凸凸 (āo āo tū tū: concave and convex) rock formations took on a cerulean tint, feeling more alien than paradise. I grabbed Yun's hand for support, just barely managing to point a finger at our papers.

He ripped them off the wall and handed me mine.

So many characters. "What's it say?" I begged, my mind too slow for the urgency that was consuming me.

But he didn't have to tell me. Because I had recognized enough characters to put it together with the other clues I'd gathered thus far.

Everything in my bones had told me to come here, that the answers were among the cobblestones, and even though it had turned out to be true, I wished I'd been wrong. Because knowing *this* was worse than being in the dark. Because not only was my mother a stranger, she was someone I should've been shrinking away from in horror, someone I needed protection from.

We were standing in a matchmaking park, and I was looking at the "success stories" wall. Apparently once a match had been made, the original flyers were posted here together—maybe to show others what a winning profile looked like? As proof this process worked?

I tried to tell Yun, but all I could manage was, "My mother . . . and your father . . ."

Before I could finish, the woman beside me squinted at my photo, then at me, and when she realized we were one and the same, she yelped.

"You can't be here!" she barked in Mandarin, pushing me toward the nearest exit.

"Why the hell not?" I sidestepped her aggressive hands and fought the urge to push *her* off the grounds.

"It's just—the problem is—you just can't," she stumbled.

"It's because the matches are completed without consent from the kids, behind their backs, just like ours," Yun said quietly. The fear in the woman's eyes confirmed his deduction. "She doesn't want us to let their secret out," he finished with a cringe.

His gaze met mine. And I boiled over. Started yelling in Mandarin at everyone around me. "Don't you think it's ridiculous that you all come here to matchmake in a park dedicated to two famous lovers who couldn't be together *because* of matchmaking? They died for it! They are turning in their graves because of this blasted place. *Turning!*"

"How can they turn if they're cremated?" someone called out.

"That's not the point! To honor them, shouldn't we do *away* with forced marriages?"

A small crowd formed around Yun and me, and they stared at us with blank eyes.

"Zhu Yingtai and Liang Shanbo's love was pure," an elderly woman to my right said, "which is exactly why we matchmake here—so some of their love and good fortune will rub off on our children, grandchildren, and their matches."

This was too beautiful a place for something so horrendous. The dichotomy made me bend over with nausea. "That's revolting. How can you sleep at night? You're taking away your children's freedom." I straightened, then turned in a circle and eyed each of them. "You have to take down all of these. These"—I swallowed some bile—"ads."

A middle-aged woman who had been reading my flyer over my shoulder pointed to a paragraph halfway down the page. "Aren't you Ali Chu? Your family was the first to put up matchmaking ads in this public park generations ago. They started all this."

I couldn't move. Couldn't breathe.

"Yes, it was such a fabulous idea, and so innovative for the time," she continued, oblivious to the storm raging inside me. "The idea spread through the grapevine, friends telling friends, and then most of the locals joined in. It's amazing what can grow when people come together, right?"

Yun, who'd been frozen since the revelation, flew into a rage, tearing down every piece of paper he could get his hands on. Since I couldn't form any words or thoughts, I joined him, tornadoing through the park and destroying everything in our path. I imagined each human advertisement to be one of my ancestors as I ripped, shredded, yelled, and stomped the remnants into the cursed earth.

CHAPTER 26

THROWING THE TEAPOT

We didn't make much progress before the crowd's uproar forced us to flee the serene hellhole. We sprinted across the street and collapsed at a table in a once-fancy hotel ballroom with yellowing tablecloths and dusty, faded tapestries. From our bird's-eye view on the second floor, we watched the parkgoers resume their matchmaking. It made me want to keel over and empty the contents of my stomach.

I stared at the street as Yun signaled to the waiter for just tea—also without words.

Eventually Yun spoke first. "How could they do this to us?

How could he not know me at all? I actually thought there was a chance he already knew."

I didn't have an answer for him, so we sat in silence as we sipped our oolong. Even though the steaming cup of familiarity brought some comfort, it was like trying to heal a broken bone with a Band-Aid.

"Maybe my father *does* know about me, and that's why he did this," Yun said, his voice muffled because his face was now buried in his folded arms.

I shook my head. "You don't know that. Maybe he was shaken up by your mother's death, or, I don't know, maybe—"

Yun's head popped up. "Don't defend him! How would you feel if I told you right now that your mother was just looking out for you and wanted the best for you?"

"I'd want to throw this teapot across the room."

We sank back into silence.

Ten minutes later Yun said, "I'm going to throw the fucking teapot."

On the car ride back to Shanghai, I could feel the steam coming off Yun, a kettle on the lit burner. Mr. Lin peeked back at us periodically. Traitors, every last one of them. How many times had Mr. Lin driven Yun's dad to the park?

In the elevator I reached over and squeezed Yun's hand once, and though his eyes met mine for a moment, it was all he could give.

He burst into the apartment, and since his father was in the living room, I quickly ducked around the corner to the guest room.

"How could you?"

I heard some shuffling, then a muffled response. I may have inched into the hallway a couple steps.

"I went to the park, Dad!" Silence. Another barely audible response. "Stop lying to me!"

I inched a few steps farther, as far as I could go without being seen.

In a strained voice Mr. Kao, whose back was to me, said, "Your mother and I did this together."

"That's not possible. Her death was sudden."

"We met through the park, son. Our parents, your grandparents, matched us up."

Boom-boom goes the fucking dynamite.

"My parents were worried about my ability to find a partner because of my . . . deformity," Mr. Kao continued. "And your mother's parents were having a hard time finding her a suitor because she was so petite—such tiny hips. Her potential in-laws were worried she wouldn't be able to bear children."

Yun started and stopped a few times before saying, "But you were in love."

"Yes, exactly. That's why we talked about going that route for you, too—we'd been planning it since before you were born. Now that she's not here, I'm sure this is what she would want—for you to be taken care of."

"By *you*! Not the park and some stranger!" I flinched, even though he was exactly right and I didn't want to be his beard. "Instead of being there for me, you spend your time either at work or making decisions for me behind my back."

"Exactly—*for* you, Yun! Everything is for you!" Sounded familiar.

"We had enough money years ago, Dad. You're just avoiding me."

Mr. Kao exploded as if his pin had just been removed. "Have you ever thought that maybe I see her when I look at you? Who's going to take care of me?" He broke down sobbing. "I had a tù chún! No one thought I could be loved, but your mother—"

"Oh shut up about your cleft lip already. It was only a thing because you allowed it to be." More shuffling.

"I just wanted you to meet Ali. And you two seem to be getting along. At first I returned to the park just to remember her and feel her presence, but then I saw Ali's ad, and I knew it was your mother telling me this was your soul mate. She was looking out for you, Yun, providing for you from the afterlife, pointing out the one Chinese-American ad in the whole park that was destined for you. Then when I learned that, generations ago, her family had been the first to matchmake there . . . it was even more of a sign. That's why I flew her out here this week. So you could get to know her and fall in love. Ali's mom and I have been trying to arrange it since our Indiana trip, because I couldn't take off more time to go there again."

His father seemed to be rambling in a spill-all way because he was uncomfortable, and with every new snippet of information, another puzzle piece slid into place. I wanted him to continue so I could fill in the entire picture, but then . . .

"Dad, I . . ." Yun took a shaky breath, and I sent him every good vibe I could, hoping he could somehow feel that I was there for him. "I . . . am . . ." And then the next part rushed out, replacing the intended word. "Not the marrying kind."

On impulse I peeked my head around the corner, trying to tell Yun that if this was his moment, I was here, and if not, I was still here. When Yun's and my gazes met, he said, his eyes still on me, "I'm gay, Dad. A hundred percent gay."

I gathered up every ounce of support in my cells and shoved it onto my face in the shape of a sympathetic smile. Yun's eyes left mine and returned to his father.

"Gay? No . . . you can't be."

And my heart sank into oblivion. I wanted to rush out and hug Yun, maybe shield him, but I rooted my feet in place—no moving unless he wanted me to.

Yun's voice was as small as his hunched body looked. "Is that all you have to say?"

"I wish your mother were here."

Yun's face changed from hurt to disgusted. "You and me both." He walked past me, telling me to pack my bags, then retreated to his room. By the time I'd shoved my few items into my duffel, Yun was already in the living room with a rolly suitcase.

"You keep a bag packed?" his father asked.

Yun's tone was surprisingly even. "I had no idea when you would figure out I was gay, and I wasn't sure if you'd let me stay here."

Oh, my heart. If I flung myself over Yun, could I protect him from this?

As Yun rolled his way out the door, his father said, "Wait," but it was so soft I wasn't sure if Yun didn't hear or if it wasn't enough.

In the elevator, Yun's spine straightened. "Let's get out of here."

"And go where?"

"Anywhere." He pulled out a shiny black credit card from his pocket. "My dad's treat. He won't miss the money, trust me."

And as soon as he said that, I heard my mǔqīn in my head: *He didn't come from a good family with money. . . . It's hard to love anyone when you're planning how you're going to feed your daughter and provide for her future.*

Then my great-uncle's voice: *Live.*

I reached into my pocket and closed my fist around Gerald, Bernadette, Randolf, and Klondike. "I'm in."

> From: AliAliOxenFree@gmail.com
> To: Chase.You@gmail.com
> Time: 10:27 p.m. CST
> Subject: I'm sorry
>
> I'm coming back early and have so much to tell you. Would you want to meet me and Yun, our family friend, at the airport and explore Chicago a bit? I'll forward the flight info to you. If you don't or can't, I totally get it—no explanation needed. Regardless, I can't wait to see you. I really missed you.

CHAPTER 27

MOTLEY

Yun and I slept through most of the flights (only two legs this time, woo-hoo!) because of our double need for Dramamine. *See? You're perfect for each other,* my mother said in my head. Except if we were perfect, he wouldn't need the Dramamine and would instead be holding my hair back as I puked, right?

When we landed in Chicago, I felt more rested than I had in a long time, despite the emotional drain I'd just gone through. Thanks, Dramamine.

As soon as Yun and I weaved our way out of the secure zone of the terminal, there he was, all five foot seven of him, just as dreamy and delicious as I'd remembered. I whispered to Yun that I needed

Also . . . there's another email coming your way that I should've already sent but couldn't. For the record, though, I wrote it a while ago. A couple days after. Progress?

💜 Ali/ 阿里 /Living Proof That Mountains Can Be Moved

From: Chase.You@gmail.com
To: AliAliOxenFree@gmail.com
Time: 10:30 a.m. EST
Subject: Re: I'm sorry

I'm sorry too.

I'll be there. (Always.) I CAN'T WAIT 💜 💜 💜

Always,

Your Pink Teddy Bear

a couple moments alone with my . . . Chase, then took off.

With my backpack pounding against my lower back, I ran to him, dodging other travelers and jumping over the extended feet of those sitting on benches, and finally, finally, I smashed into him.

Well, I had imagined it going a little more smoothly; I hadn't realized just how fast I'd been running.

Our chests banged together and knocked the wind out of me for a second, but the moment I recovered, I wrapped my arms around him.

"I missed you," I said, which wasn't enough but was somehow better than trying and failing to articulate everything.

"Shit, Chu—what've you done to me?" At first, I thought he meant just now when I'd charged at him full speed, but then he said, "These past few days have been brutal. You have no idea—or, well, maybe you do."

"It's not a competition, but you're the one who has no idea."

He laughed. "Everything's a competition with you."

Time slowed as he held me, and I savored the warmth and his enveloping scent.

"I'm sorry about everything," I whispered against him.

"I'm sorry too. You don't have to say any more."

I pulled back slightly. "No, I do. I want to." His eyes widened in surprise, and my chest may have puffed out with pride at how far I'd come.

"Your email was more than enough," he said. "In fact, I felt bad not saying more in mine, but I wanted to tell you this in person." He took a breath. "I . . . I think I may have taken out some of my family's shit on you. I couldn't see it at the time, but I was really struggling with my feelings and had no idea what I needed, but that's no excuse to blame you. And there was *no* excuse for the things I said just because I was upset. I'm truly sorry about that, Ali."

He gently placed a palm on my forearm. "You were right. My parents have been destroyed by their shame for so long that I let it consume me, too. Even though I wasn't ready to hear it in that moment, we *have* been caring about the wrong things. I heard you, and . . . I've been spending my free periods searching for Yang." No hesitation before he said his brother's name. "I want to find him so we can help."

I squeezed his wrist to physically show my support. He took my fingers and grazed them against the cool metal of his watch, which I had never looked at closely before.

My eyes met his. "Is that—"

"From Yang, yes," Chase filled in. "I was going to sell it and everything else I had, to pay back the families, but my parents moved us away before I could." He dropped his arm. "Every time I look at it, I feel such guilt and anger and . . . maybe even love?" A strangled noise came from his throat. "Why did he spend all the money on us? We didn't need that stuff. We'd rather have him." He grasped the watch with his opposite hand. "I can't seem to take it off, no matter how much I want to."

I broke his hands apart gently. "You don't have to feel guilty for wearing it."

He sighed. "I also have some other unresolved . . . stuff . . . mixed in. Like, maybe I'm still bitter about how my parents treated him versus me. Okay, definitely I'm bitter about it. And it's all wrapped together in one gigantic, messed-up . . ." He wriggled his fingers around an imaginary ball to finish his sentence. "Like, in some ways I feel like the clusterfuck happened because of how my parents coddled him. And, I don't know . . ."

"It's okay if a tiny part of you feels like he and your parents got what was coming because of how they hurt you," I said quietly.

Chase shook his head. "No, I don't want to feel like that. It's too terrible."

"No, it's human."

He gave me a tight-lipped, upside-down smile, and I watched as he struggled with his emotions.

I continued, "You can love Yang but also be mad and bitter and jealous and whatever else you're feeling. It's impossible to tease apart when it's woven together so tightly." He nodded slowly. "It's okay to just be a mess for a bit."

He gave me another sad smile, this time a horizontal line. "I guess if I'm this muddled, then my parents will need a lot more time, huh? I realized earlier this week that because of our different upbringings, I can never fully get what this is like for them."

I nodded. "They have a different lens from us. But you're trying—that's the most important part."

He shrugged.

"So are they talking to you?"

Chase sighed. "No. But . . . they've stopped slamming doors in my face when I bring it up?"

"That's progress." I pulled him to me. "I'm really proud of you."

"Thank you, for everything," he whispered in my ear, sending chills down my spine.

"You're welcome, Retreat."

"Hmm?" he whispered lazily, half present.

"Retreat, the opposite of 'chase.'"

He burst out laughing, I joined in, and the world felt right again.

"Ahem."

We turned to see Yun polishing off a pretzel and wiping his salty lips with a napkin.

"Did I time it perfectly?" he asked excitedly. "You just told him, and ta-da, here comes the fiancé?"

Chase's arms tensed around me.

I didn't know where to start. "Uh, it's not exactly how it sounds—" I began, but Yun cut me off.

"Well, what were you guys talking about if not that?"

"We were making up." Or trying to.

"Psh. Not from where I stood."

Chase placed a muscly arm across my waist and dipped me backward. Despite the quickness of the movement, his lips met mine softly, and even though I despised the cliché move, I melted into him.

To make up for the sexism, though, as soon as we stood, I dipped him backward and planted one on his surprised lips.

Yun clapped twice. "That's more like it. And dude, put some of that testosterone away. Ali's like my sister; you can stop staking your claim like some chest-beating caveman." He then winked at me as if to say, *But it's kind of hot, isn't it?*

I shook my head in response; I liked the teddy-bear side of my Chase better.

I noticed Yun didn't explain why there *really* wasn't a need for chest-beating. I tried to give him an *I've got your back* smile to remind him he never had to tell anyone he didn't want to.

Chase's eyes ping-ponged from me to Yun and back. "Is anyone going to explain the fiancé thing to me?"

Yun and I shared a look, which made Chase straighten his spine, and I said, "I'll tell you on our way out of here."

Turns out the story was shorter than it felt, because by the time we'd made our way to Chase's parents' car, he was up to speed.

Just like Yun and me, he was speechless. It was completely quiet as we piled in the minivan and drove off.

Then, eventually, all he could say was "I can't seem to wrap my head around it."

"Join the club," Yun muttered.

"So that's why she didn't want us to be together," Chase said slowly, and I could almost see the pieces clicking together in his head like they had for me. "But what about after she saw us? Why was she so hell-bent on pairing you with someone she barely knew?"

"Maybe because he's rich?" I guessed. "She's convinced she's miserable because my father doesn't make enough money."

Yun leaned forward from his spot in the back seat. "Wait, that's why you think your mom chose me?" He shook his head.

"Man, this just keeps getting better and better." He tapped the side of Chase's seat. "So do your parents actually love you and spend time with you instead of using work as an excuse?"

Chase grunted.

Yun settled in. "We might as well get to know each other since we're all weirdly tied together—you know, you dating my fiancée and all. Spill it."

As the familiar rumble of Chase's voice enveloped me, I closed my eyes and breathed in the scent of freedom. I must've dozed off, because when I opened them, Lake Michigan was staring back at me, glistening in the sunlight as if waving and winking.

Um, what was this magical place, and why couldn't we live in Chicago?

I felt like a little kid as I pressed a palm to the glass and leaned closer to get a better look. Maybe wherever we stopped, we'd just start running for the water. It'd probably be hella cold, but gah, I wanted to cannonball in there.

"Beautiful view, isn't it?" Chase said softly to me. "And I'm not talking about the lake."

Yun piped up from the back seat. "Um, am I going to be third-wheeling it this whole time? Because if so, then we need to find me someone, 'kay?" I laughed, mostly from embarrassment. "Actually, that's a great idea. We really should work on finding me someone." He glanced over at Chase nervously. "A . . . boy."

"I'm happy to be your wingman," Chase said without missing a beat.

Yun sighed contentedly. "I can't tell you how good it feels to be surrounded by English, non-neon buildings, and, most important . . . people who accept me. Thanks, guys. Feels like I'm home."

I felt at home too, but it was because of the man—*my* man—in the seat beside me. As if he could read my mind, Chase placed a warm hand on my knee, and I grasped his fingers and squeezed. Then I stored this moment in my mind's safe, promising myself I would visit it often so it wouldn't grow old and withered like my mother's photos.

"We're here!" Chase announced as we walked out of the parking garage and into the afternoon sunlight.

"Where's here?" I asked, looking around.

Chase led us across the street to . . . a park with a bunch of giant metal pants. Not kidding.

"Of all the places you could've taken us in Chicago, you drove us here?" I asked. Not that I wasn't grateful, but . . . pants?

Chase put a fist on his hip. "Who suddenly became pretentious being engaged to a rich guy for three days? Well . . . three days that you knew about it."

I shielded my eyes from the sun and took a step back so I could appreciate the entire visual. Upon closer examination, they weren't pants, but reddish, nine-foot-tall sculptures had no heads or arms. And they looked . . . deep in thought? Mid-step, pondering life, all sorts of together but not, just like most people in the world, walking in parallel but with eyes that never strayed from their own path.

"It's ridiculously weird and I love it," I finally said.

He grinned. "Way better than the Bean, don't you think?"

"The Bean is dry toast," Yun said. I'd forgotten he was there again.

Chase's eyes flicked to Yun, and though I hadn't thought anything of it at the time, I was now kicking myself for having told Yun one of Chase's and my inside jokes.

"Did you have to bring him along?" Chase whispered to me as Yun tried to climb up one of the sculptures.

"Give him a chance." My eyes followed Yun as he found an outcropping to push himself up on. "He's having an even harder time than I am."

Chase wrapped his arms around me from behind. "Who's the pink teddy bear with ruffles now?"

"If I'm a teddy bear, it's one dressed like a ninja. With an eye patch."

"Copy that, Pirate Ninja. And just so you know, kung fu isn't the same without you. Hell, nothing's been the same without you."

"My pink teddy bear." I poked his side. "So Beardy, Mole Hair, Baldy, and Grand-Shīfu can't hold a candle to me?"

"Wait. Oh my God," he said, thinking out loud. "Grand-Shīfu? That . . . is the best thing I've ever heard. I've been calling them Beardo, Mole Hair, Tiny, and Not Chuck Norris."

I burst out laughing. I was completely touched to my core, maybe even a little overwhelmed, and so naturally it came out of me in the form of laughter (not the worst option, really, for how things could come out of me).

"Are you laughing at your own cleverness, Chu?"

I shook my head. "I'm laughing because Yu are the first one to get my really weird sense of humor."

"I like weird."

I gestured to myself. "Obviously."

He nudged me. "Weird is so much better than being—"

"Dry as toast," we said at the same time.

His hands grasped my waist and spun me to face him. I immediately took a step back into a horse stance and held up my fists. It only took him a second to register, and as soon as I saw that flicker in his eye, I attacked.

Just like that first time, he met me blow for blow, and as my arms and legs arced in the breeze, my entire heart, head, and soul filled with a fullness that can only be described as happiness. Though we were technically sparring, it felt like a flirtatious dance, and each time our skin touched, a spark zapped down my forearm, my leg, my spine.

Block—punch—sweep—elbow. Everything, even our breath, was in sync.

His hand circled, landed on my wrist, and pulled gently— much softer than the form and sparring in general called for. The momentum stopped when our faces were inches apart. Even though I knew it was coming, it still took my breath away. *He* took my breath away.

We stared at each other for a moment, his face aglow in the sunlight, and I breathed him in. Citrus and cedar. Holy hell, that was delicious.

Yeah, maybe it sucked that we had to sneak around, and maybe

Plainhart, Indiana, needed some PC CPR, and maybe it sucked that Chase and I were both a little lost . . . but being lost with someone else somehow had the power to make you feel less adrift. Before, I'd only had that kind of mooring with kung fu, but with a person . . . it was a whole new kind of bond, one I hoped to cling to. I'd never wanted it to be about a guy or because of a guy, but this wasn't infatuation or lust or hormones. It was about being able to see yourself mirrored in another, with the return reflection making you clearer, more focused. With Chase, I was 100 percent Ali.

When I kissed him, he tasted like freedom.

We eventually broke apart when Yun gave up trying to hitch a ride on the towering non-pants.

"That's how I picture Baldy in real life," Chase whispered, gesturing subtly to Yun's defeated expression. "Perpetually grumpy on account of the whole no-hair thing. But he's my favorite. He channels all that frustration into his Bajiquan."

I scoffed. "Mole Hair could kick Baldy's ass anytime. Don't you know mole hairs are lucky?"

"You can't see it, but Baldy has a rash behind his ear—those are the luckiest of all."

I didn't stop laughing for a full minute.

Since Chase's face and mine were no longer plastered together, Yun deemed it safe and jogged over. "Are you guys hungry?"

Chase pointed across the street toward Yolk, whose sign was complete with a fried egg in place of the *o*. "Our next stop, if it sounds good to both of you." Then, quieter so just I could hear, he said, "I figured you'd need to jiā fàn."

I waved some imaginary pom-poms.

As we waited for our table to be cleared off, I watched Yun drink in the scene in front of him as if he'd just realized he'd been parched for years. The two young men sitting before us were holding hands over scrambled eggs and so lost in their own world they were oblivious to the staring teen beside them. My gaze followed Yun's, then bounced over to the Black family in the neighboring booth, then settled on the half Hispanic, half Asian family trying to keep track of their two little ones running wild.

When Yun and I glanced back at each other, his eyes were as shiny as Lake Michigan, as glassy as mine felt.

Yes, there were places better than what he and I were used to.

We shared a meaningful nod as we followed the host to our booth.

Over plates of cinnamon French toast (Chase), a California omelet (Yun), and chorizo eggs Benedict (me, *yum*), I realized that because of Dramamine, it had been a long time since I'd eaten a proper meal. I added a side of corned-beef hash and fruit. The server looked at me with disgust, and some childish part of me wanted to open my mouth and show her my chewed-up food. But then I noticed Chase's left arm casually draped over my chair as he sipped his orange juice, clearly not caring how or what I ate. Well, that skinny-ass server could suck it. I added on a side of cheesy grits, too.

After a few more bites, I was less woozy and more present.

"He really said that?" Chase was saying. "Jesus."

Yun started laughing and I butted in with, "Are you talking about embarrassing things your parents have said? I win this one—my mom used to talk to me in Chinese in public and it would be like *Chinese Chinese Chinese* 'tampon' *Chinese*."

Both of them turned to stare at me.

Chase cleared his throat. "Yun was, uh, filling me in on how things played out with his dad right before you guys left."

"Why were you laughing, then?" I asked Yun.

"Because all of this is just too fucking ridiculous! Isn't it? I mean, God. I'd played in my head a million different ways I could come out to my dad, but screaming it at him after finding out he'd arranged my marriage to a stranger . . . all while my fiancée listened in . . . It's just . . ." Yun shrugged.

He started laughing first; then I joined in, and then Chase.

We were motley, I tell you. Motley.

After our late lunch of breakfast food, we moseyed our way to the Art Institute. The stone lions guarding the entrance shot a pang through me, but since they didn't have curly hair and weren't holding balls under their paws, it passed quickly. These were clearly American lions, not Chinese.

Chase led the way up the stairs. Upon entering the impressionism wing, I came face-to-face with a Renoir of two sisters on a terrace, called—I looked at the plaque—oh. *Two Sisters (On the Terrace)*. The paint swirls created a dreamlike quality, but their eyes . . . they looked real, like they contained souls. The girls, especially the younger one, stared out at me, wondering what I was doing on their terrace. Mesmerized, I stared back, willing myself into their dreamworld.

By the time I turned away (and Chase was gazing at me instead of the painting—totally missing out, if you ask me), Yun was across the museum chatting with a Black boy with long hair and toned shoulders.

I nudged Chase in the ribs. "He's cute!"

Chase pouted and I startled him by responding with a deep chuckle at the same time the boy threw his head back in laughter. "Oh, Yun, you are just so witty and I'm so into your weird mix of bluntness and adorable awkwardness." As the boy put a hand on Yun's arm, I said, my voice still deep, "As long as you're not engaged to some random person, let's have some fun."

Chase caught on and imitated Yun's effervescent voice as the real Yun took a step closer to the boy. "Well, seeing as she doesn't have a penis, even though she's the coolest, most badass person I've ever met, I can't marry her." Chase paused, then said in his own voice, "Well, I'm assuming you don't have a penis." He paused again. "Totally okay if you do, though."

"Totally more than okay that you feel that way." We shared a smile. "And for the record, I like my vagina, but I'm no longer as defensive about it as I used to be. My mother always wanting me to be something I wasn't pissed me off and made me, I don't know, hold my ground? But I've never felt like the kind of girl society wants me to be either."

Chase was staring at me so intently I had an urge to reach up and check my nose for boogers or reach down and cover my genitals.

"Yun is the second luckiest," he said, "being engaged to you, even if it was a sham. And I'm the luckiest for, well, obvious reasons, and I'll leave it at that so I don't send you gagging in the corner."

I smiled so wide my teeth were visible. "I'm the luckiest."

Chase pretended to fall over and faint. "As I live and breathe," he said dramatically. "Did that block of cheese really just come out of your mouth?"

"I'm all gouda for you, baby."

He collapsed in my arms, a hand draped over his forehead, and it took all my strength to keep us both upright. When I started laughing—huge, gulping heaves—we toppled to the floor in front of the Renoir.

"I don't know those two monkeys," I heard Yun yell from across the gallery.

I almost yelled back, *I'm your fiancée!* but I held back, not wanting to spoil his moment with the Cute Boy.

Chase responded with some monkey noises, then pretended to pick some fleas out of my hair.

"Actually, that's a good idea," I said to him as we clumsily stood. "I haven't showered in a while—see if you can get some of my dandruff while you're at it."

"You guys are gross!" came from the other side of the hall.

"We're relationship goals and you know it!" I shouted back. I shook my head at the couple staring at me, then gestured to Yun with my thumb. "Fiancés, am I right?"

"I'm actually a monkey," Chase said, raising his hand.

I high-fived his upstretched palm. "Me too!"

The five or six people in our vicinity were all staring now, and I was glad Chase hadn't specified "on the Chinese zodiac." Instead of feeling different, I felt like we had our own language (which we had too), and it was just a reminder how much we understood each other.

"I'm a monkey too," a voice called out, and I turned to see a petite East Asian girl making her way toward us, a huge smile on her face. She pointed to the Monkey King enamel pin clipped to her backpack, gave us an air high five, then split to look at a Van Gogh. When she left, the others dispersed as well, and I stared after the only other female monkey I'd seen in years, and even though she had already moved on, I high-fived the air in her direction.

A few hours later, Chase, Yun, and I made our way to the Hancock Building (sans Cute Boy, who exchanged numbers with Yun but had to be home for dinner). After waiting in line for twenty minutes (during which Yun gushed about how Cute Boy went to the Art Institute for inspiration on his music), we were finally allowed in the elevator to ride up to the top . . . so we could wait in line again for the restaurant.

But after thirty seconds, Chase tugged on Yun's and my sleeves, and we slipped out of line and around the corner to stand very awkwardly in the middle of a busy aisle. All around us, people were enjoying lavishly plated food (and not enjoying the hovering teens).

"We're here for the view, not the food," Chase whispered. "The observation deck was pretty pricey, so I thought we could catch a glimpse this way."

Floor-to-ceiling windows lined the entire wall, and up here on the ninety-fifth floor, the view stretched to the water and beyond. I couldn't move. I'd been surrounded by farmland for so long that until this week I'd forgotten what cities looked like. And I'd never been this high up in any building, anywhere, before. The tallest structure in my hometown was the three-floor health center that housed every doctor, dentist, and chiropractor in a twenty-mile radius.

I stared out at the skyscrapers, the cars tinier than Matchbox toys, the lake that expanded to what felt like infinity. There was so much in this world I hadn't seen yet; I'd barely lived. In this week alone, I'd glimpsed brand-new places I'd only read about, and that had opened my eyes to how much was still in front of me and how wrong my mother was.

I was exactly where I was supposed to be.

"You're my person," I told Chase, not because I was clinging to him in place of my mother, but because I chose him.

He put an arm around me and whispered, "Right back at ya."

"You guys can't stand there," a waiter hissed at us as he whooshed by with a tray on his arm.

I took one last look around before we got in line to wait for the elevator down.

Earlier, it had felt absurd to wait so long to get up here, but it made sense now.

"We don't need them," I said to Yun, my eyes glued on the wall beside us as if I could see through it to the view. "It doesn't mean we shouldn't still try, but . . . maybe it's okay if we don't agree with them."

"Yup," said both my boys.

Zhu Yingtai
Hangzhou, China

Finding true love should be shared smiles, coy glances, and spilled secrets in the moonlight, but for me it entailed plotting my escape and cutting ties with everyone I'd ever known.

Each time I thought of never seeing my beloved fùqīn again, I changed my mind. But how could I return home and marry someone I could never love? Even if he was perfectly kind—which, based on my mother's list of requirements and the options she had been considering when I left, he likely was not—my heart belonged to another.

The leaves swirled around me and Shanbo, swept up from the enormous piles littering the ground.

I knotted my hands in front of me. "How many more days can these trees hide us? How long will the chair pushed against our door at night hold the others out? And the school year is ending soon; we cannot keep doing this."

"I respect whatever you want to do," Shanbo said from beside me on the park bench.

"I want to be with you and be free. I want to be myself."

He squeezed my mess of tangled fingers. "How do we do that?"

"I don't know yet."

As we sat in the park—our park—I felt an impending doom. How long could I keep running from the inevitable before the universe yawned in boredom and swallowed me whole?

CHAPTER 28

GETTING SERIOUS

The jet lag started catching up to Yun and me, so, courtesy of Uncle Kao, we checked into the Radisson Blu Aqua Hotel downtown (mostly because I loved the wavy outcroppings on the building). We congregated in one room to order Gino's East deep-dish pizza, but at some point Yun would split off to a second room.

When we opened the box to what was definitely not pizza—more like a mountain; the filling was at least an inch and a half thick—we simultaneously gulped and drooled.

"Uh, do you think this plastic knife is enough?" Yun asked.

"I think we need a handsaw and a shovel," I said, only half joking.

After we dished it out (with difficulty) and dug in with a

combination of forks, knives, and hands, Yun clicked through the pay-per-view selection.

"Oh my God, there's an entire sausage patty in here!" I exclaimed, my mouth full. "I think we're going to get serious," I said to Chase, winking.

He laughed way more than my comment deserved, but I guess that was what the "inside" part of the joke did.

Yun hovered over a movie title, then looked to us for approval. I nodded absentmindedly; I didn't recognize most of the options, and besides, I was busy.

I froze mid-bite, some tomato sauce sliding down my chin, when Yun's credit card was declined.

"Shit," Yun whispered before a silence descended.

I'd known we couldn't go on gallivanting like this for long, but I had expected at least another day or two.

"Think if we bring half of this monstrosity back to Gino's, we'll get a partial refund?" I asked, trying to lighten the mood.

Just like our Cokes, it fell flat.

"Yun, I'm sure you could stay with us in"—I swallowed— "Indiana." Bitterness coated my mouth like a bubble of acid reflux. *My mother would just looove that.*

Yun said nothing, just changed the channel. After a minute of silent chewing, he snatched up the key to the other room and swept out.

I glanced around our sleek turquoise-and-black room, which suddenly felt huge with one less body. "Think he'll be okay?"

Chase shrugged. "He's your fiancé." Then, with warmth, he

added, "He seems tough. But we'll check on him in the morning and see what he needs."

I nodded, the mix of cheese and cornmeal suddenly tasting like cardboard. When I put my plate and leftovers on the desk, Chase mirrored me, and the second our food was out of the way, I lunged for him, heaving us onto the king-size bed. Apparently, I had sauce on my face, because I smeared a red trail across his cheek, which I wiped off.

Just like in the movies, I couldn't help laughing to myself.

We paused for a moment with me on top, straddling his torso with my thighs, and we shared a look that communicated more than words could say.

Chase's and my lips met: familiar, loving, and safe—none of the urgency of kisses past. Our bodies melted into each other like molasses creeping in to fill nooks and crannies.

I slipped beneath his shirt to explore his muscles with my fingertips. My nerve endings sizzled, sending shocks of pleasure from my lips, my chest, my legs—every bit of me that contacted him—up to my brain.

His hands glided under my sweater and caressed my lower back, then higher. He ran his part-silky, part-callused palms up and down my back, to my shoulders, beneath my bra strap. Each time they traversed my shoulder blades in the vicinity of my armpits, I wondered if he'd notice or care that I didn't shave.

I gave him my consent with a nod, and he unclasped my bra with ease. For a moment I wondered how many times he'd done this before, but then I realized I didn't care—they were in the past, not me, and if anyone could understand that difference, it was this unshaven girl with two thumbs and a vagina. All my past experience revolved around practicing, not meeting Prince Charming.

I pulled his shirt over his head and sucked in a breath at the lines carved into his pecs and abs. And as for the two lines that led from his hips to his waistband . . . I traced them up, then down until my fingers met the softness of his boxers.

I grabbed the hem of my sweater and yanked it over my head, my bra getting caught in the fabric and coming off with it. He inhaled sharply just as I had, and while his eyes did explore my curves, his gaze kept returning to my face.

We didn't go any further, not because he wasn't the one or because either of us wasn't ready (which would have been totally okay too), but because we didn't need to, not at this time. But we did take full advantage of that hotel room, and we didn't come up for air for some time.

CHAPTER 29

SEXY NINJA CONFUCIUS

I woke to swollen lips, the sun streaming in through the crack in the curtains, and a (quite muscly) arm slung over me. After nodding off spoon to spoon last night, I'd wormed out of Chase's grasp the second his breathing had shifted, needing some space to sleep comfortably. But waking with our limbs touching and bodies adjacent as if he'd been drawn to me in his sleep . . . well, that was something I could definitely get used to.

"Morning, beautiful," Chase mumbled, pulling me closer and burying his lips in my hair.

I sighed, snuggled closer, then drifted back to sleep. Dozing with Chase, all my defenses down, I'd never felt more vulnerable. Or safe.

I dreamed of running in the cornfields, sparring with Chase, eating a biàndāng in the parking lot, but some construction worker kept interrupting everything with a jackhammer.

Oh. Someone was banging on the hotel door.

"Guys, I need to talk to you!" Yun's voice called out from the other side.

Chase kissed me on the back of the head, then went to pull his shirt on. "Is it just me, or is the third wheel in need of a little greasing?" He pointed to the refrigerator, where our Gino's East box had been crammed in (with difficulty). "Some breakfast grease for you too?"

I nodded, then went to open the door. Yun burst in just as Chase was dishing out three slices (if they could even be called slices . . . three heaps?).

"My dad doesn't get to do this or make me feel bad for telling him the truth," Yun said breathlessly, looking from Chase to me. "We've been tiptoeing around each other since my mother died, and, fuck, it needs to stop. I have a thousand things to say to him, and the worst outcome would be what he's already done—be ashamed just because I'm gay." He collapsed on the bed. "How is it fair that some of us have to fight for who we are?"

"I'm sorry. It's not fair. It's really not." I reached over and put a hand on his. "Maybe because you're fighting now, this won't be a thing one day." Even as I said it, I knew it wasn't so black-

and-white. "But that doesn't take away from the fact that it's awful for you."

Chase sat by Yun's head. "You're really brave, dude. I admire you."

Yun didn't move. Then eventually he said, "I'm not that brave when my biggest reason for standing up for myself is that I have no other family left."

"That still takes guts," I said.

"And it's so much more complicated than that," Chase added. "Sometimes it's just easier to focus on the fear or anger or whatever emotion is strongest and bubbles to the top."

My gaze fell on my sexy ninja Confucius.

Yun gagged. "Stop it, you two, at least while I'm sandwiched between you."

I swatted his arm.

Yun sat up. "Um, I know I joke about you guys a lot, but really, what you have is inspiring. If only that damn park could see that, right?" He forced a sad chuckle. "But if I had to be engaged to any girl, I'm glad it was you, Ali, for so many reasons." After a moment he cleared his throat. "I'm going to use the last of my cash and my frequent-flyer miles to hop a plane back and face this shit storm head on."

I tried to find something insightful to say like Chase-fucius, but all I managed was, "You got this."

Yun turned to me. "What are you going to do?'

A smile curled on my lips, more sinister than intended. Or

maybe not. Maybe it was exactly as sinister as I wanted. "I have some ideas. Don't worry about me."

Yun patted my shoulder twice. "I'm more worried for your mother."

We embraced slightly awkwardly but with so much emotion. I pulled an imaginary engagement ring off my finger and threw it at him. All three of us laughed, and then our motley trio became two.

CHAPTER 30

(NOT) SET IN STONE

On the ride home, on Lake Shore Drive, Chase and I passed a giant rectangular sign telling every passing rider, YOU ARE BEAUTIFUL. Chase pointed to it as we zipped by, then winked at me.

I used to hate that word and how it implied the importance of physical attributes, of arbitrary lines, shading, and curves, but with Chase that word didn't refer to my untamed eyebrows or unplump lips, but to my brashness, my views, and the traits that were attached to *who* I was.

Thanks, Chicago. You're beautiful too.

I knew we were closer to home when the billboards shifted to HELL IS REAL, JESUS IS ALIVE BEYOND REASONABLE DOUBT, and advertisements for fireworks, which were illegal in Illinois but not Indiana.

After passing the smokestacks and suffering through the distinct sulfur smell of Gary, we turned off the highway. At the start of our trek, Chase had told me he had a surprise planned. I sat in silence, taking in my surroundings and letting the anticipation envelop me. Better than Christmas morning (and not just because the Chus didn't celebrate other than unwrapped bargain-bin school supplies).

The Indiana Dunes curved and sloped, pyramids of sand that illustrated the beauty, expanse, and wonder of nature—and maybe even a little danger. Were there dune avalanches? I pictured the wind carrying one too many grains of sand, and the second that camel-breaking particle touched the tip, the entire bluff would crash down like a wave, engulfing all the beachgoers, discarded plastic bottles, and seaweed in one enormous elephant bite.

As soon as the car stopped, I flung the door open, jumped out of my shoes and socks, and booked it to the waterfront.

I just kept running until my feet were submerged, and after bending down to quickly roll my pants up as far as they would go, I waded in, inhaling the unique freshwater-lake smell that was a mix of crispness, elements, and life. The chill was intense, but it only made me feel more alive.

I heard splashing behind me, and before I could turn around I was in the air, Chase's arms wrapped snugly around my waist.

We didn't talk. We didn't need to.

As I waved to the languid windmills and nodded hello to the cows and horses, I slowly steeled myself. By the time Chase dropped me off at home, I was ready. For *anything*.

I was greeted at the front door by my great-uncle.

In Mandarin I said to him, "I know what you did." No shock registered on his face. In fact he seemed to be expecting this, maybe even relieved it was finally out in the open. I reached into my pocket and thrust the crumpled flyer toward him, the one I'd dragged across the world for proof. "You're the contact on the ad. *My* ad."

I barreled on. "How could you look at me, talk to me, and not tell me what you'd done? Not only did you know my fate, you were the one who helped arrange it! Did you feel any guilt posting these, meeting with Mr. Kao to orchestrate all this to strip your great-niece of her freedom to choose her own husband? How could you of all people do that to someone else?"

He gazed at me with those sorrowful eyes that had seen too much, and for a second I felt bad.

"Please tell me you did it to get out," I whispered.

He nodded over and over. "Of course. Your mother guessed I needed money—from that letter, the one I regret writing to my father—and she contacted me and offered payment in exchange for finding you a proper suitor through the park. I said I would do it if she helped me come to America, and . . . yes, I'm ashamed that getting out was my only goal at first, and I was desperate enough to match you at any cost, to anyone. But then . . ."

His eyes softened. "Ali, I came here to meet you. To have a

family again. As your mother sent photos and told me stories, and I pitched you over and over to those other parents, I got to know you. How could I not love the little girl whose favorite movie star was Jackie Chan and whose favorite pastime was teaching her stuffed animals kung fu?"

My mǔqīn had seen that?

"It's why your mother agreed to send you to take classes," he continued. "Because you loved it so much. She tried to push dance at first because it was cheaper, but when she saw you didn't like it, she scraped together the money for the more expensive kung fu."

Why hadn't she just told me? Why was I hearing this from Bógōng and not her?

"She always saw your spirit, Ali, and before I'd even met you, I saw it too."

What happened to the girl who didn't leave her father's side for two days after he was denied tenure? I heard Bógōng say in my head from beside me on the bench.

My mother had noticed. She'd been watching all along.

How could she know me so deeply in some ways and not at all in others? Unwelcome tears streamed down my face, and I wiped them roughly, my emotions tangling to fuel the one I knew best: anger.

My great-uncle took a step closer to me. "I am so glad I got to meet you, because you are everything I thought you were and more." His face grew serious. "I'm sorry about what I did. I truly believed you and Yun *could* get along—I worked hard to find someone you matched with on paper—and I knew that if you didn't like him, you were strong enough to fight. I hoped that, unlike me, you had choices. But in case you needed help, I tried to remind you of your freedom, that you can live." He paused. "I hope you can try to understand. At the very least, please accept my sincere apology."

I stared at him, my heart already melting but my exterior not quite catching up yet.

"Is that just your face or are you still angry with me?" he asked, a little glint in his eye.

I laughed, not able to help it.

Humor is one of the greatest weapons the world has to offer.

I cut my own laugh off. "It's not that simple."

"If it were simple—"

"Then more people would do it," we said at the same time.

We stood there in the hallway, my expression softening.

"Ali, you certainly are not made of stone—but you are as strong as it and as resilient as a turtle." He smiled and revealed his missing teeth. The gaps still tugged at my heart, but I also saw the character they gave him, announcing his bravery to the world.

As we stood there saying so much in the wordless space between us, my father stumbled into the hallway—clearly on his way elsewhere and hoping to avoid people—but he jumped when he saw me. "Ali! Why are you home early? How did you get here?" Then his eyes took in the expressions on Bógōng's face and mine, and after ping-ponging back and forth between us for a minute, he asked, "What's going on?" The jealousy in his voice both pained and frustrated me.

"You should ask him what he went through," I said to my dad. "You're the closest family he has left."

My father was completely stunned, reminding me he was unaware of how much I knew, that the cerulean blue wasn't limited to me.

Spotting the flyer, he snatched the paper from my hands and read with wide, hurt eyes. "What the hell?" he finally said. His eyes searched my face, then landed on my bógōng. "How could you do this?" he yelled in Mandarin, startling me. I hadn't seen him get worked up about anything in years, and on my behalf? Unfathomable.

"It was Mǔqīn," I said calmly, even though I felt anything but.

My father gaped at me. "How could she?" he eventually whispered.

"Maybe because she blames her unhappiness on love? She sacrificed too much, then assigned anger to the wrong parts of your relationship." I paused. "Why do you need me to tell you this?"

"I don't." His voice was barely audible.

"How could you let this happen?" I asked, comparing the beaten-down man in front of me to the one from the photo. "You fell in love despite so much and fought for each other, only to let it die."

"We both sacrificed so much. Too much."

"That's not it and you know it."

My father's shoulders hunched, and though a part of me felt bad for causing his pain, I knew he had to be completely broken before he would make any progress.

I plucked my ad from his hands. "I have to take care of this. Where is she?" I looked behind him and my sympathetic-faced bógōng. "I know you can hear me right now, Mǔqīn!" I called out. If she was home, she wasn't far away, and the fact that she hadn't surfaced meant she knew what was coming—Yun's dad had probably called.

Remembering the flyer, my father regained some life and followed me as I marched into the kitchen.

"You are unbelievable," I said as soon as I saw her, my voice more clarion than I would've predicted. Maybe the Lake Michigan air had cleared my head.

My mother continued cleaning the already immaculate countertop without acknowledging me.

"How could you do this to me?" I yelled just as my dad said, a hand over his chest, "How could you?"

"I did it *for* you, Ali," my mother said calmly.

We faced off, except it was one-sided because she just kept up the incessant scrubbing, eyes glued to some imaginary stain.

"This"—I slammed the paper onto the table—"was not *for* me."

She paused, but only for a second.

"You think you're so clever," I said, "doing this horrible sneaky thing on the other side of the world. But I still figured it out. Didn't you think about that when you sent me to China?"

She threw her towel down. "Shanghai is two hours away! I didn't think you'd be able to find your way there or that Yun's father would let you!"

"How could you do this without consulting me?" my father said, his voice and stance gaining more confidence.

"Stay out of this!" she hissed, intimidating him into a corner, which, since the kitchen was so small, was only a few steps away. "I wouldn't have gone down this path if it hadn't been for your selfish choices!" she yelled. "You moved us here where there were no other Chinese families around, creating an environment where our daughter's number-one requirement on her dream-boyfriend list is *not Chinese*. What choice did I have?"

"You created that environment, not me," my father fired back just as I said, "You read my diary?" It was the least of my concerns in this shit storm, but there were so many balls flying toward my head, my instinct to take a swing at all of them was kicking in.

She whipped her head toward me. "I did this to take care of you. You should be thanking me! I'm saving you from all the mistakes I made and can't correct now. Trust me, when you're older, married, and living in comfort with more money than you know what to do with, you'll be so grateful."

"You lied to me!" I yelled. "Made decisions for me! You took away my freedom, Mǔqīn!"

I dèngyiyǎn-ed *her* for the first time.

She slapped the counter. "Ali, I did this so you wouldn't wake up one day full of wrinkles, wondering where your hopes and dreams disappeared to! Why are you making me feel like the villain when all my actions and thoughts revolve around your future?"

"You've never cared about me," I whispered, my voice trembling so much I thought I might shatter into a thousand pieces.

"Said like someone who was privileged enough to be born and raised in America. What parent would go to the trouble of ensuring

272

their child was matched with someone worthy, sometimes at their own sacrifice to complete the marriage contract? Only one who truly loved their child."

I wasn't sure if I wanted to cry, scream, lie down, or all three.

Her head drooped forward, her past weighing her down. "I regret not listening to my parents, Ali; it's one of the biggest regrets of my life." She took a breath. "My parents tried to set me up with someone, a match made through the park." It was my turn to suck in some air. She continued, "I refused, choosing your father, and it was the wrong choice." She glared directly at him as if daring him to butt in. "I followed up with the suitor they chose, and he's incredibly successful, living a grand life with his large family in a mansion in California—California! Where you never need a winter jacket! Where there are Chinese people everywhere!"

I readied myself to deliver a blow, but my father piped up. "How. Dare. You." A wet trail dotted his cheek. "You never even told me about your family's disapproval or your arranged marriage until we were already married and in America. *Then* you told me you were glad to cut ties from such an archaic family with despicable traditions. And then you go and do the same to our daughter without consulting me? What happened to you?"

My mother turned her face away. "You don't get to call her your daughter, since you're never here and you chose your work over our well-being. I'm the only one looking out for her."

"No one's looking out for me," I interjected, "and I'm not going to pine for it anymore." I smiled, genuinely, with teeth and pride. "I ended my engagement—which was a sham from the start—and

I'm going to change the park into something good, Mǔqīn."

Her hands gripped the countertop, her knuckles turning white. I gave her a chance to say more, to make me understand, but she shut down instead, folding herself into a nearby chair.

"Jin Fei," my father said, and it made me realize I hadn't heard him say my mother's name in much too long. "I always told you your secrets would be your downfall."

"Maybe I wouldn't've had so many if you were a better husband!" she shot at him.

His head snapped back in shock. "Me? *You* doomed us from the start, attaching too many expectations to your sacrifices—ones you didn't even feel the need to loop me in on until later. How could I ever live up to them?"

"How dare you blame me! I may have had expectations, but the man I loved exceeded them! That man died when you were denied tenure. Instead of letting me be part of your sadness, you disappeared. Then you cut me out of family decisions. You—"

"I was ashamed!" my father yelled, throwing his hands in the air. "I couldn't look at you because I had let us down. I couldn't even look at myself."

My mother's eyes were as wide as mooncakes as the cerulean blue bled out of the room. "Why didn't you tell me?" she said finally, quietly.

If I hadn't been so stunned, I might have laughed at the irony of Mǎmá Pot's question.

My father crumpled, physically and emotionally. Then, switching to Mandarin, he said, "Don't you remember that day you told me you wished you had never gone to Ali Shān, had never met me in that park at sunset? How you had been such a fool to think it had been proof of our aligned fates? How could I say anything to you after that?"

My mother didn't react, but her face told me it was true—she had said those words at one point and meant them. But... perhaps she didn't mean them quite as much anymore. I thought back to the Ali Shān paintings I'd found—all of them at sunset, I now realized—and even though my parents had plummeted to a place where they could no longer see each other, a bud of hope bloomed in my chest, a cherry blossom born from the very same calligraphy strokes inked by my mother years ago.

I left. This was no longer my conversation. I had said what I'd needed to, and they were finally fighting again.

"Ali, wait!" my father called after me, but I kept going. There was so much they needed to work through first, and it didn't involve me, not really. I focused on the path before me: college, Chase, and wherever the wind might take me. And *nothing* was set in stone, especially not my fate.

As I passed Bógōng on the couch reading a dog-eared book, I nodded to him. He gave me a *you'll be fine* wink in return.

THE PARK

AS SEEN FROM AFAR

The butterfly garden was purchased by Zhu Yingtai's father, a failed attempt to appease his soul for what had happened. Even though he was least at fault, he felt as if their deaths were on his hands. He blamed society and only wished his daughter had come to him first—had he not shown her that he put her above all else and was willing to bend the norms for her happiness?

Zhu Yingtai's father would pad along the cobblestones, reminiscing about her laugh, her spirit, the way she used to say bào bào to him and reach her chubby toddler arms up. He would close his eyes and sway in the breeze, imagining her grabbing his hands and dancing to music only they could hear.

The garden began as a place to remember her, to honor love, and to warn about the perils of fighting an emotion so powerful it needed to be respected.

Alas, along the way, after Zhu Yingtai's father was long gone, the intent was twisted and warped until it only resembled its former self in shadow.

But shadows could take on a life of their own, couldn't they? Maybe with a little pixie dust, a lot of dreams, and one strong-willed, badass teen?

CHAPTER 31

OPERATION MURDER

I went straight from my house to the library, texting Chase on my way out the door. As I put my plan into motion at the computer by the children's section (even rubbing my palms together for good measure), I laughed to myself that here, unlike the empty high school computer lab, Chase and I would have to hold it together and not scar the nearby babbling kids with our PDA.

Okay. I had to just F-ing do it. The selfie gene had somehow never manifested in me, but because of the asinine way the park worked, I didn't really have a choice—our final product had to resemble the other ads enough to blend in. I took about ten photos of me grimacing before Chase arrived, belly-laughed (which I

didn't appreciate), and then told enough jokes about Baldy, Mole Hair, and Grand-Shīfu to turn my scowl upside down.

Taking a usable photo of Chase was annoyingly simple.

Then came the even harder part. Writing—and in Mandarin—about my feelings. Chase wrote beautiful, eloquent sentences that made my insides melt, and all I could come up with was: *Everyone deserves a choice, so just stop it, goddamn it.*

In the end we kept both, wanting to capture two different perspectives, and after piecing everything together into something flyer-shaped, we emailed Yun.

Operation Murder the Park was in motion.

Zhu Yingtai
Hangzhou, China

We took off: disappeared into the darkness of night and became different people. We became who we really were, and with new names to match our "new" identities.

But I did not leave without a kick to society's teeth, because Yingtai, Shunan, all versions of me couldn't live a happy life otherwise. On my last day, I marched into the classroom, chest out, and showed every beating heart in that school that the best student was, in fact, a woman. If I had been menstruating, I would have also bled all over their precious floor for emphasis, but alas, it was not my cycle.

As everyone gaped at me, I slapped the journal I had been keeping onto my instructor's desk, then left without a backward glance, my spine straight and chest still thrust out.

Unfortunately, news of the woman who proved females worthy of education has not reached me, and I do not know if I made a difference. But other tales have reached us. Stories rooted in truth but dusted with magic—too much magic, in my opinion, for the

most magical of tales do not need embellishment to sparkle.

I've heard from neighboring farmers about legendary Zhu Yingtai and Liang Shanbo, who found true love and tragedy. When they couldn't be together, frail Shanbo died of heartbreak and Yingtai threw herself in his grave to join him instead of marrying another. Then both turned into butterflies to be together in ... butterfly heaven? I'm not quite sure of the intention of that ending, but it certainly sounds mystical, doesn't it?

I often poke fun at Shanbo for being the weak one to have keeled over from heartbreak, to which he always responds, That simply means I am romantic, which is certainly true, as evidenced by the flowers he leaves by my bedside every morning.

I miss my fùqīn, and I did what I could to learn news of him before he passed. So many times I had to stop myself from traveling back just to tell him I was more than alive—I was happy. But Shanbo and I had journeyed far to create our new lives, and returning was not an option, not for simple farmers like us who worked for every penny we had, and especially not after I bore children. I hoped my father could somehow feel in his bones that I was well, surrounded by loved ones and so many books, which Shanbo tracked down to quench my thirst for knowledge, books that I used to educate my children, and that one day, with luck, they will use with their children.

And I've remained loyal to my father in my own minuscule way: Shanbo took on my surname so that our children would still be Zhus. I go by Huang, but I am still a Zhu on the inside. And every time someone calls us "the Zhu family," my heart flutters like butterfly wings.

CHAPTER 32

ALI-FUCIUS

"I do care about you." That, coming out of my mother's mouth after two weeks of silence, caught my attention.

I turned away from my desk to face her as she stood in my doorway, looking even smaller than she already was at five foot one.

She paused, looked down the hall, then shrugged.

That's it? What about how you treated me? What about your lies, your absence, your unachievable (penile) expectations?

The brief surge of hope that had seeped in vanished.

But then she came over and perched on the far side of my bed, which made me sit up and fold my hands in my lap awkwardly,

as if my giving the appearance of a guāi kid behaving would keep her talking.

"What did you say to him?" she asked me. "To Bǎbá. That day. I heard you two talking, but I couldn't hear the words. He's . . . different." I could tell from her eyes that in this case, different meant better.

"I just said what he needed to hear."

"Oh."

Would it have killed her to say thank you? Or anything else other than that sad little "oh"?

I thought she might ask me to elaborate—and I was ready to tell her—but instead she said, "Why do you talk to Bógōng and not me?"

Now it was my turn to give her a sad little "oh." Followed by "Um . . ." And that was all I could find.

She continued, "The most I ever get out of you is . . . when you call me 'Mǔqīn' . . . which makes me . . ." She shuddered, and guilt flooded through me, mixing with the ever-present anger in a confusing oil-and-water blend.

When I still didn't say anything, she sighed, then said, "Ali, I don't *like* keeping secrets from you. I didn't have another option. When I was young, I didn't know any better, and I rebelled for what I thought, wrongly, were the right reasons. Then I was cursed with a daughter"—my fists clenched—"who was even more headstrong than me, who I knew would take all the wrong steps I had and more. The secrets were necessary for me to help you."

I scoffed. "How could you be so sure what I'd do when you barely know me at all?"

She was silent, but her eyes locked on mine. I couldn't read what was going through her mind. Finally she said, "I know you better than you think. But I *am* guilty of not showing you all of me." She paused again for what felt like a year, and I had to fight the urge to lie down on the floor in exasperation (or maybe desperation?). "I wanted you to have a strong female role model in your life . . . but that wasn't me. So I tried to be her, which meant I had to distance myself so you wouldn't see through my act."

I stopped breathing. I was scared that if I moved even a millimeter, she would close up again.

"It's hard for me here." She shook her head. "Not just hard. Impossible." Her eyes flicked to the wall. "I hate meeting with . . . your counselor. His name is hard for me to pronounce. But I do it anyway, for you, to make sure you are getting all the opportunities you deserve. I always worry you are being treated differently because you're not white." Her gaze lowered to her hands. "I hate driving—it scares me, and I still don't know the area well. Going outside and having to speak to people in a different language—have you ever thought about how hard that is? To have to talk to someone in a language you didn't grow up with? Everyone says things so fast and with different accents, and they sometimes stare at me like I'm a foreign object that belongs in a museum, or worse, a zoo." She was speaking so fast her sentences were jumbling together. "And yet I do all this for you, then pull myself together before I walk into this house so you can have someone worthy to look up to, even if she isn't truly me."

She gulped a breath. My ears were buzzing, my palms sweaty, and my throat dry. Part of me wanted to comfort her, thank her, and compliment her English, while the other part needed more time to reconcile this new side of her with the mǔqīn I'd always known.

Cautiously I said, "Just because you were trying to do the best for me doesn't mean it was the right choice. Or that you get full immunity."

She didn't agree, but she didn't disagree, either. I hoped to any god that she was turning my words over in her head.

Except she wasn't. Because her next words were: "Things would be so different if you were a boy."

And there it was. I boiled over. "Do you have any idea how much it hurts every time you say that?" Genuine shock registered on her face, which confused me enough to ask, "Why did you want me to be a boy so bad?"

"Because the world is better to them. Everything is easier. I see so much of me in you, and all I can picture is the heartache that will follow you through life. I prayed and prayed while you were in my womb that you would be a boy."

Her explanation was not at all what I'd thought it would be. Just like with kung fu and so many other things. Why hadn't I asked her sooner to clarify?

Slowly I said, "And just because I wasn't, you thought it was okay to make me feel terrible all the time?"

My mother was quiet for so long I carefully debated throwing several items in the room: my windowsill bamboo (I liked it too much), the textbook on the floor (too heavy, could pull a muscle), my lamp (too functional to break).

Finally she said, "I didn't know it made you feel like you did something wrong. I was trying to tell you how sorry I was that I couldn't protect you more."

Um, super-screwed-up way to communicate that. But still, I felt some of the anger sliding off in small waves. "Well, it didn't come across. I . . . I need you to stop saying that, okay?"

She nodded, the briefest dip of her head, but I saw it.

Then, very hesitantly, she admitted, "Perhaps I was taking out some of my own stuff on you."

"Not just with the boy thing, either."

She flapped a hand up and down in exasperation. "Ali, I still stand by my actions. I truly believed Yun could be your soul mate. Was it so bad to make sure you weren't missing an opportunity? I pushed the China trip harder because I wanted you away from Chase, yes, but I also needed to make sure you explored all your choices—and, yes, it was a choice," she added when she saw me raise my eyebrows. "I wanted to see if you could fall for Yun of your *own* accord. I did once believe in love, after all."

"But to do all that without telling me? To forbid me from seeing Chase? Can you see how wrong that was? In your efforts to supposedly help me, you hurt me." The more I showed her Ali, the better I felt.

"I didn't want you to suffer like me, so wrapped up in feelings—ones that can fade so easily—that you can't see your future. I was trying to fix for you what had gone so wrong in my life." Her last sentence was barely audible.

"Your relationship with Bǎbá 'went wrong'"—I made air quotes—"not because he wasn't the right person, but because you both blamed love for your situation when it was what could've gotten you through it, together. It's still there—you need to work to find it." She turned away, and from her rigid exterior, I could tell that my words were bouncing right off. I started to call her *Mǔqīn* to get her attention but stopped myself. "Mǎmá, you once thought he was worth sacrificing your family and so much more. How could—"

"I sacrificed everything!" my mother shouted, stunning me. "What did he sacrifice?"

"It's not a contest," I said softly. "You can't view your relationship that way." Ali-fucius. "You're resenting Bǎbá for what your family did to you when it's not his fault."

"If he were more successful, maybe they would have approved," she said, staring down at her folded hands. Then her voice gained confidence. "But they were right to be worried." She looked up at me, fire in her eyes. "Look at where we are, how we live. Don't tell me this is your dream life. Ever since we arrived, my entire life has been consumed by money. Do you want to one day have to give your daughter's dog away because you can't afford it?" My heart skipped a beat. I forced myself to push Cupid away for the moment so I could focus. "Ali, are you really so naive that you think Chase's family debts won't burden your future?"

"That's just ridiculous. First, I'm seventeen. And second, do you think I'd be with someone who wouldn't shield me from that?"

"Family is family. It's not as simple as that. You cannot escape your blood."

"You escaped yours," I said.

"And it haunts me every day, telling me how I messed up my own life and how you're going to ruin yours."

"Whether or not Chase is right for me has nothing to do with how much money he has, or where or who he came from. Close your eyes for a second and try, just try to remember what it felt like when you met Bǎbá. Fell in love. Try to imagine the Ali Shān clouds above you. Breathe in that mountain air."

I was shocked when she closed her eyes, and even more shocked when they scrunched in pain as if she were trying to wade through the carnage to what once was. But she opened them quickly, and they were blank again.

She would need time. But at least she was trying. It was a step, albeit a small one.

After a beat she said, "A long time ago, people used to point to a pregnant friend's stomach and say, if we have different-gender babies, they'll get married. And that was it—a pact. As you can imagine, most of those matches led to misery. Later, when one of our family members lost a daughter to suicide because of her ill-suited marriage, the grieving mother started a tradition at the local park that was already dedicated to the Butterfly Lovers. It became a place to matchmake based on personality traits, when the children were older. It was a step forward, and our ancestors were touted as visionaries. That park is the pride and joy of our family."

I let her finish before responding, "Maybe it was a step forward then, but it doesn't mean it's okay now." She didn't speak, so I pressed, "Do you really condone taking away people's freedom to choose their own partners? Are you really siding with your parents? With Zhu Yingtai's and Liang Shanbo's families?"

"Zhu Yingtai," my mother said, her voice far away, the name holding more weight than I understood. "I grew up hearing about her, but the version we told in my family ended with her and Shanbo running off to the countryside and raising a family."

I sputtered a bit before eloquently saying, "Huh?"

My mother shrugged. "It's probably made up, but when I was a child, oh, I believed it with my whole heart. And growing up with that version . . ." Her eyes grew dreamy in a way I hadn't seen since I was little. "It was why I wanted to marry for love. I looked up to Yingtai so much."

"How could you fall so far from who you once were?" Even as I said it, I—ex-Allie—already knew the answer.

Tears clouded her eyes. "I don't know."

It was the most honest thing she'd ever said to me.

"We should fight, Mămá. Be more like Yingtai. You and me. It's no coincidence that we share a surname with her. Oh, wait. I guess you don't—"

"I do," she said, her voice so quiet I wasn't sure I heard correctly. "Chu is my maiden name *and* my married name."

I said nothing, embarrassed I knew so little, even if it wasn't my fault.

"And . . ." Her voice was hesitant, digging up a thousand pains that had been long buried for survival. "That's actually another reason why my family didn't approve of your father: we had the same last name, and since a long, long time ago everyone in the same village shared a surname, they believed we were distantly related, and thus . . . it was not allowed."

"They thought it was incest? But there are, like, millions of Chus out there. It'd be like saying a Smith can't marry another Smith."

"That thinking has gone away, or at least it was nonexistent among my friends, but for my parents' generation, it was more common. Not law or anything, but enough for them to disapprove."

"I'm so sorry, Mămá."

She gave me a sad smile. "Traditions can sometimes feel like a noose, can't they?"

After an incredibly long pause that felt like a lifetime, she asked, "What do you have planned for the park?"

THE PARK

AS SEEN FROM AFAR

THREE MONTHS LATER

It's amazing what can grow when people come together, right?

Turns out, that middle-aged woman from the park on that fateful day was completely, 100 percent correct. Of course, she wasn't expecting what followed. It really was quite astounding what a younger generation plus the internet could accomplish in a few months once they learned that a repressive tradition was happening in the park they had previously written off as "the one the old folks frequent." Or perhaps the recent and rapid changes in Hangzhou's most popular húdié huāyuán weren't so surprising given the youth's passion and their leaders: a badass, her softie ninja boyfriend, and a lovable sweetheart. Once the trio's story hit social media, it spread faster than juicy gossip down the Asian dragon-fruit vine.

Because of the possibly-but-really-more-than-likely *true* version of Yingtai and Shanbo's story, as the badass was convinced, Operation Murder the Park had been altered to Operation Refuge. The hope? To create a haven for all, where the downtrodden, the discriminated-against, and the outcasts could find much-needed support.

The resulting wave was large enough to bring long-lost family members—ones who had once so believed in matchmaking that they'd disowned their daughter—from Taiwan to the Indiana shore. Not physically, but with a letter first, then a phone call. Nothing was directly addressed, and no one spoke of the giant elephant that had plopped its plump rear between them for almost two decades, but with an overnighted box of authentic Taiwanese pineapple cakes and a returned surprise of Shady Pines sausage, honey, and crackers, a sweet-and-salty bridge formed between two islands that had been secretly pining to be reunited for far too long.

Yingtai would've been proud. The motley trio certainly was, as was a hard-to-please mǎmá (not mǔqīn). And since the park was, now, after a century-long dearth, frequented by butterflies, the true believers (including the badass who had never believed in much before) were convinced they were Liang Zhu, cheering and celebrating.

SEVERAL MONTHS LATER

Outgoing text to Chase

Are Yu ready for tomorrow?

Chase

Who dis?

Me

A ninja teddy bear with an eye patch, duh.

Chase

Right, right, sorry. I don't recognize you when you es-Chu pants.

Me

I'm a bear, I always es-Chu pants.

After a minute,

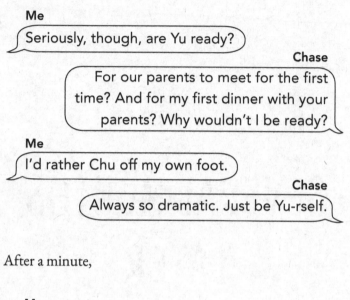

Me

Seriously, though, are Yu ready?

Chase

For our parents to meet for the first time? And for my first dinner with your parents? Why wouldn't I be ready?

Me

I'd rather Chu off my own foot.

Chase

Always so dramatic. Just be Yu-rself.

After a minute,

Me

I love Yu.

Chase

Right back at Chu, my love.

I straightened the chopsticks—something I can unequivocally say I had *never* done before.

"Stop fussing, Ali, it's fine," my mother said with a swat of the hand. "Come help me finish these wontons."

I was dressed in a plain green sweater and jeans—but my nice jeans, the pair faded only three shades and with just one tiny hole on the back right pocket. So, you know, practically mint condition.

My mother eyed me up and down but refrained from saying

anything, and for once our lack of communication was a step forward.

"Ali," my mother said, and our eyes met over the kitchen table. But only for a second, because she dropped her gaze to her hands, then deliberately poked a hole through the wonton skin with her fingernail. I gasped as the instinctual urge to hide the broken skin came over me; I could already hear the reprimands about wasting money.

My mother calmly dipped her index finger in the bowl of water, then pressed it against the tear, kneading, kneading, trying to merge the two sides. "Messiness and mistakes happen." She paused. "It doesn't matter whether or not I meant to poke the hole—I see that now. The hole at the end is what matters." Her mouth pursed to the side as if she wanted to say more, but a nod was all that followed.

We weren't exactly communicating, but we weren't avoiding each other either (which was also how my mother interacted with her parents on their new monthly phone calls). I could get on board with metaphors. That was all I could handle right now too.

Bógōng rushed around the kitchen, dusting this countertop, dusting that dish with salt, until my mother said in Mandarin, "Aiyah, sit down before you give yourself or one of us a heart attack."

Their nervousness was making me sweat.

"Why don't you work on your origami how-to book?" she suggested to him, pulling out the empty seat beside us. "Aren't you teaching a class with Ali at the library in a few days?" When Bógōng padded over happily, a slight bounce in his step, she turned to me. "Shui An and Xin Jie, right?" she asked again.

"Yes," I confirmed. "And their last name is Yu."

My father bustled in, dressed in his Monday best (because he taught on Mondays—Sundays were for lounging around in his tighty-whities).

My mother looked at him and nodded, and he returned a smile.

"Great folding, niū niū!" he said, coming over and putting both hands on my shoulders. "Such a star." He gestured to the partially folded wonton in my palm. "Leave one all messed up, though, okay? It'll serve as my demonstration piece when I give Chase the fatherly warning."

Part of me felt he hadn't earned the right, another was grateful, and the last bit wanted to barf.

My mother cleared her throat. "I don't want to be a downer, Ali, but . . . are you going to explore in college? Maybe you can see each other but also date other people."

"Oh, so you went from wanting me engaged to wanting me to sow my wild oats?" I had the urge to flick wonton water at her.

She let out a short exhale that may have been a laugh, but because I hadn't heard her laugh since childhood, I couldn't be sure.

"Okay, that's fair," she said. "But just . . . I don't know. Don't limit yourself. Especially if you're not at the same school—long distance is never easy."

I grunted.

My great-uncle put down the half-folded square paper in front of him, poked my cheek with a salty finger, then said in Mandarin, "Regardless of what happens with Chase, don't lose your sunny demeanor, okay?" He chuckled. "That sounded sarcastic, but I mean it—don't change too much." He paused, pointed at me, and then slowly, in accented English, he said, "Special. Very special."

I suddenly had some wonton filling in my eye.

The doorbell rang (thank God), sending my mother into a tornado of worrying, cooking, and wiping the counter for the thousandth time as my father and Bógōng tried to tell her to relax.

I jogged to the front, passing the paintings of Ali Shān lining our hallway, and, as always, I took a second to appreciate them despite the waiting visitors.

I flung the door open, and seeing that his parents weren't with him, I yelled out, "It's just Chase!" in the hopes of alleviating my mother's tizzy. "We'll be there in a sec," I added, hoping for a private moment first.

He thrust his phone at me, his screen zoomed in on some text. For a second I thought it was something about the park, but then I saw the maroon-and-white logo on top.

"You got in?" I screeched.

"Full ride!"

Chase and I jumped up and down, the phone sandwiched between our joined hands (and a few origami turtles spilling out of my pockets because now that I knew how to make them, they were everywhere). I had been accepted early action to the University of Chicago, and Chase had applied early decision in their second round.

As I daydreamed about eating our way through Chicago and

joining the kung fu team together, Chase said, "My parents told me something earlier today when I saw the acceptance."

"You've known about it longer than one minute and didn't tell me?!"

He laughed. "I came over as soon as I could. My parents and I were . . . talking. They told me they were proud of me. And . . ." He paused.

"Oh my God, tell me!"

He chuckled. "They finally admitted, out loud, that they stopped speaking to me after everything happened because they were ashamed of themselves. They felt they had let Yang and me down. Can you believe that?"

"Yes," I said sincerely, thinking of my own father. "I'm so glad you guys are finally talking." I grinned. "Ha! Look at me, so mature, the queen of communication."

Chase's eyes softened. "I don't know where I'd be without you," he said. "If it weren't for you, Ali-fucius, I wouldn't have been working on my relationship with my parents the past few months, and we wouldn't be where we are now: almost past our shame, on the road to healing ourselves, and so close to finding Yang."

The private investigator hired by the Yu family had recently tracked down an address, and in a few days Chase and his parents were driving out to Cheyenne, Wyoming, hoping to find the lion's head to Chase's butt.

I cupped the side of his face with my palm. "*You* made all that happen."

He leaned into my hand before pulling away to run his fingers through my newly cropped hair. "I love this—it's so you."

My mother had almost pooped herself when I'd come home the day before sporting the bob, but I had dèngyiyǎn-ed her, she'd clenched her jaw, and eventually it had passed, unspoken. Then my dad barely noticed, my great uncle smiled his approval, and within an hour it felt like something that was such a part of me it wasn't worth acknowledging.

My mother came up from behind and Chase flinched automatically.

"Congratulations," she said as kindly as she could, pointing to his phone.

Are you sure you want to limit yourself? her eyes said.

Mine said a version of *Back the fuck off.*

She smiled, genuinely this time, a weird, closed-lip monstrosity. "Truly, I am proud of you both. Getting into a top university— you've worked hard."

I smiled back, also a weird, closed-lip eyesore (apple, tree, and all that). "Thank you," I whispered, hoping she knew it was for everything: the praise, her effort, the college tuition.

"Qǐng jìn, qǐng jìn," she said suddenly, welcoming Chase in and making me briefly wonder whether she had wanted me to have a Chinese boyfriend so she could communicate with him in her native tongue.

Chase immediately went to the kitchen and asked what he could do to help. As he impressed my family with his wonton-folding skills, I sent a little thank-you up to the universe, to whatever gods might be out there, to the flying spaghetti monster.

I simultaneously felt like I must've done something good to deserve this and also that it was owed to me. What a bizarre, wonderful position to be in.

By the time Chase's parents arrived, the (tiny) table was set with steaming dishes: spicy chili-oil wontons, steamed fish, zhàjiàng noodles, and scallion pancakes (of course). We had pulled up folding chairs and even a recliner to get everyone around the little circular wooden table, and it all felt so cozy and homely and familial.

"I'm so sorry for the, uh . . ." My mother gestured weakly to the chairs.

Mrs. Yu, who was nothing like the ghost from the last time I saw her in the middle of the night, shook her head. "Not at all. Everything is lovely—your home, the food—and your daughter is so . . . spirited."

Should I not have batted her hand away when she'd tried to examine my face when she'd first walked in the door? Even though she probably meant the word "spirited" as criticism, I took it as a compliment, which clearly Chase did too, given the way he was looking at me, all heart eyes and gooeyness.

"Seems like they certainly found a match in each other, hmm?" my mother said, a faint tilt to her lips. "Not sure anyone else would be so fond of such *spiritedness*."

"Or my son's competitiveness," Chase's mother laughed, and everyone sat down to eat. I spent an extra moment taking in Mrs. Yu's relaxed shoulders and the emphasized crow's feet resulting from her wide smile—all brand-new.

"Fate has a way of working things out," Bógōng added from

beside me, so quiet I was the only one who could hear. "A wayward kind of fate in your case."

I beamed at him.

When we were all seated, my father raised a glass. "Huānyíng!"

We toasted, welcoming the Yu family into our home.

"Ali, what a beautiful necklace," Chase's mother said, pointing to the jade pendant lying on top of my sweater for all to see.

"It was my mǎmá's," my mother said, a sheen appearing on the whites of her eyes. "Handed down generation after generation."

When my mother had given me the necklace on my fifth birthday, she'd said, *This is a part of me, and I hope it will be the same for you.* In light of this new information about its history, those words now took on another meaning. They also told me my mother had been hopeful for a family reunion longer than I'd realized. I enclosed the heirloom in my fist, a much more welcome legacy than the matchmaking park.

We dove in, grabbing whatever food we could reach (no passing dishes around in a civilized manner—we were a free-for-all kind of family). Chase and his parents joined in the frenzy like old pros.

"Ah, cōng yóubǐng, my favorite!" Chase's father exclaimed, dishing himself three. "They look and smell of my childhood in Tainan."

As the parents reminisced about Taiwan and all the sights, sounds, and food they missed, I saw my mother light up in a way I hadn't seen before. She never spoke about any place here the way she spoke about the Taiwan rail system or that hole-in-the-wall breakfast place with "the best yóutiáo and soy milk on the planet."

I vowed to find a way to visit Taiwan to grab hold of one more piece of my parents. I'd already tracked down a handful more than I'd possessed a year ago, and with luck, maybe one day I could put together a clear picture.

Chase nudged me under the table, and we played footsie like the gross couple we were growing into. I hoped to myself it would never change.

Before Mrs. Yu left that night, she patted my back three times in an awkward hug, at which both Chase and his father widened their eyes.

"Thank you," she whispered in my ear, her eyes shiny. "I know it's because of you I might see my other son soon."

When she let go, Chase swept me off my feet and planted a tender kiss on my lips. His mother smiled, my bógōng whooped, and my father and mother exchanged a longing glance that wasn't quite love but was full of hope.

🐢 🐢 🐢

There was just a link in the email—no hello, no "what up," no "smell ya later." I clicked with hesitation, but as I scanned the forum that popped up, tears clouded my vision. I blinked, then clumsily swiped at my eyes as I continued to read so fast my brain had to work overtime to fill in the gaps.

Below the photo of the park—now filled with flyers of Yun, me, Chase, and others I didn't recognize—were the stories. A high school senior who had decided to pursue his film passion. One couple who'd gained the courage and support they needed to end their arranged marriages to wed their true loves. A young woman coming out to her parents about being a lesbian.

After absorbing a few more tear-inducing journeys into my heart, I clicked the little green phone beside Yun's name.

"Hey, bud," I said, ticking my chin up toward the laptop camera when we connected.

He grinned. "The park is now not only a source of inspiration—it's a sanctuary."

My heart fluttered like butterfly wings. "Everyone deserves to belong somewhere."

An awkward pause followed, then he cleared his throat. "I'm coming to the States early. My father is, uh, a little worried about me. I, um, came out quite publicly and . . . there've been threats. Not a ton, but I mean, one is too many, right?"

"Yun, I'm so sorry. We shouldn't have done this. Shit, why didn't we think this through more?"

He looked down at the corner of his screen. "I don't regret anything. It's not easy to come out . . . well, anywhere, in any way, but we still have to, right?" He lifted his eyes and chest. "I'm proud, Ali, and I'm not hiding anymore."

I put a hand over my heart and gave him a singular nod that said more than I could. "You're amazing," I told him, even though it wasn't enough. When he looked away humbly, I asked, "So are you coming to stay with family? Do you have family here? You can come to Indiana, you know."

"Actually . . . my dad is coming with me; he's transferring to the New York branch."

"Yeah?" My voice rose in pitch with hope.

"Yeah. We're . . . okay. Not great . . . not yet, but, um, it's not the worst?"

I nodded. "I'm glad it's getting better."

"New York and Indiana aren't all that far away," he said with a wink.

"Much closer than Shanghai and Indiana, ex-fiancé." I held a fist up. "Safe travels, all right?"

"See ya on the other side, Chu." He brought his fist toward the screen and we air-bumped from across the world.

"On three—one, two, three!"

On my count, everyone pushed their glowing lanterns into the air, and the cold Indiana wind carried them up, up, and into the clouds.

"Happy New Year!" I yelled as Chase lit the firecrackers, the popping indeed scaring the hypothetical monsters and evil spirits away. I glowed like one of the lanterns, thinking about how I'd just said "New Year" and not "Chinese New Year." To me, this was my New Year, and everybody else could just deal.

"Thanks for helping me organize this," I said to Mr. Laurelson, who gave me a nod and a wink. We hadn't really talked about what he'd done, but I knew he felt bad because he'd let my last five arguments with Racist Robinson go without paperwork. And when Chase and I had mentioned our idea for this event to him, he'd scraped together enough money to get the good lanterns, the ones we could write our New Year's wishes on.

Wendy patted me on the back with a "Happy New Year, Ali!" and her nephew danced around us in a circle. Brenda had given me a hug at the start of the celebration, but she now had her hands full keeping Ava and especially Kyle in good spirits.

There were ten of us out here braving the cold to bring in the Year of the Tiger. We did not suddenly all get along—there were fucking *lanterns*, giant ones, involved, and who wouldn't want a piece of that?—but . . . it was a good step. It was still all kinds of screwed up that I had to ease these turtle eggs into another culture with something familiar and "not scary," but whatevs. I was here to see the sky light up.

The lanterns glimmered and winked in the enchanted air. Like flashing fireflies. Ones that were no longer flashing out of instinct, but because they wanted to be seen.

Just like I had told Yun, maybe one day this would become the norm, and perhaps our efforts would mean that someday there'd be more acceptance and appreciation rather than judgment. This was one step in the right direction in a thousand-mile journey.

Chase grabbed my hands and started dancing with me to the pops of the firecrackers. A few kids had brought sparklers, which felt like an appropriate melding of traditions. As Chase and I dissolved into flirty sparring, my laughter drew the attention of my former friends, who stared at me like I'd just sprouted a bushel of mole hair.

That's right—Allie was completely gone.

I took an extra moment greeting Beardy, Mole Hair, Baldy, and Grand-Shīfu, as I usually did now. I didn't believe in a higher being, but I sort of got the appeal, because I liked to tell my council of grandmasters my hopes and dreams and troubles.

As I stepped into the practice hall, I inhaled, then exhaled an obnoxious "Ahhhhh." As usual, everyone else thought I was disgusting for enjoying the stench of stale sweat.

You wish you contributed as much as me to that mustiness, I thought, because, well, not all things change.

I didn't see him come in, but I felt a rush of wind from my left and immediately dropped into ready position, my legs in mǎbù and my arms protecting my torso. I let out a whoop as we fell into it—rough, just the way I like it.

"Hey, stranger," Chase panted between ducks.

"Hey yourself." *Elbow—wrist grab—yank.*

I snuck a kiss in before bringing him down with a foot (gently) to the back of his knee. It was becoming my special move.

Marcin entered, and we quickly straightened and saluted.

As I pushed myself to the limit with every stretch, push-up, and sit-up, I reveled in how this was no longer an escape but a celebration and a safe space. Just as the park had become a safe space for so many in need.

Beads of sweat collected in my hairline and trickled down, splashing onto the carpet.

Everything was going to be okay.

AUTHOR'S NOTE

Dearest Reader,

Thank you for taking this journey with Ali and me.

The Zhu Yingtai and Liang Shanbo legend, better known as "The Butterfly Lovers" or "Liang Zhu," is one of China's Four Great Folktales. I have changed most details in this retelling, only maintaining Yingtai dressing as a man to attend school, their falling in love, and the butterflies. Everything else—the time period, their interactions, and their backstories—has been altered. The alternate account of Liang Zhu's fate that was passed down in Ali's mother's family is also my addition to the legend.

A version of the park from this novel exists in Hangzhou, China, with the same purpose, with similar papers put up by parkgoers, and also dedicated to the famous lovers. In *Our Wayward Fate*, I have taken many liberties with the park, creating my own fictional rendition to best serve the narrative. The change most of note is the secretive nature of the park and its arrangements.

Last but not least, to anyone who feels like an outcast, is struggling with their identity, or has a hard time communicating, please know there are people in the world who care, who understand, and who want to help.

I write for you.

You are not alone.

Jiā fàn!

Gloria Chao

ACKNOWLEDGMENTS

To my readers: so many hugs to you. I appreciate you, I see you, and I write for you. Hearing from you all is the best part of this amazing job, and I have no words to tell you what your messages have meant to me. They inspire me and get me through the harder writing days. Thank you!

To my village: you are the bee's knees and the firefly's light and the butterfly's wings. Thank you for believing in me and for your support. More specifically . . .

Kathleen Rushall: you are simply the best. Thank you for being so invested and always going above and beyond. I can't imagine a better champion for my work.

Jen Ung: I am consistently blown away by how much you get my characters and writing, and how you always know how to elevate everything to the next level. I am so grateful to work with you.

Simon Pulse team: I couldn't have asked for a better home, and I am so appreciative of each and every one of you. Special thanks to Mara Anastas, Liesa Abrams, Chriscynethia Floyd, Nicole Russo, Lauren Hoffman, Caitlin Sweeny, Alissa Nigro, Christian Vega, Anna Jarzab, Amy Beaudoin, Sarah Woodruff, Michelle Leo, Chelsea Morgan, Tom Daly, Karen Sherman, Valerie Shea, Stacey Sakal, Christina Pecorale, and Emily Hutton.

Sarah Creech: I am in awe of your talent. Thank you for finding the most beautiful ways to capture the heart of my stories.

Kim Yau: I am so lucky to have you in my corner! Thank you for all you've done and continue to do!

Many thanks to the talented writers who read early versions of this novel, helped me brainstorm, and had writing dates with me: Susan Blumberg-Kason, Rachel Lynn Solomon, Lizzie Cooke, Kelly deVos, Samira Ahmed, Maddy Colis.

Thank you, David Arnold, for encouraging me to write this book over french fries all that time ago.

A heartfelt thank you to the librarians, teachers, booksellers, bloggers, readers, and indie bookstores who have supported me and my books. Hugs to you all!

Thank you to everyone who submitted names in the *American Panda* preorder campaign! The winning names, Randolf and Klondike, were submitted by Katharine Traasdahl and Danielle Lynn.

Thank you to family and friends (you know who you are!) for supporting me and my career.

Thank you, Mom and Dad, for your support. I love you both so much. Also, thank you for answering endless questions for this book, especially about the Mandarin. (I'm pretty sure we've had more conversations about the phrase tīnghuà than anyone else, ever.) Thank you, Mom, for giving me the article that inspired this book.

Anthony, what words are left? There were never enough for me to express my love, my gratitude, everything, and now that I've already attempted it once, there are even fewer words for round two. All I can say is your love makes me invincible.